CJ_2010

S0-BYK-401

She started to cry then, as if her heart were breaking. He held her even closer, realizing that, now that she had put her past behind her, she was struggling to accept the future, whatever it might turn out to be.

He led her from the gallery to his bedroom between the gallery and his tiny kitchen, picked her up, gently laid her down the bed and pulled a soft down comforter up around her shoulders. Wide eyed, she stared at him in a room lit only by moonlight.

Ace saw the confusion in her face and spoke softly. "It's all right, Leese. You are here and that's all that matters. I love you, and I know you love me or you would not be here."

He leaned over and kissed her and she felt her body begin to relax. She knew then that she was safe, was cared for and was loved by this wonderful man.

Then he knelt on the floor beside the bed.

"Leese," he said, "I knew you would come to me—because I love you."

ALL I'LL EVER NEED

MILDRED RILEY

Genesis Press, Inc.

INDIGO LOVE STORIES

An imprint of Genesis Press, Inc.
Publishing Company

Genesis Press, Inc.
P.O. Box 101
Columbus, MS 39703

All rights reserved. Except for use in any review, the reproduction or utilization of this work in whole or in part in any form by any electronic, mechanical, or other means, not known or hereafter invented, including xerography, photocopying, and recording, or in any information storage or retrieval system, is forbidden without written permission of the publisher, Genesis Press, Inc. For information write Genesis Press, Inc., P.O. Box 101, Columbus, MS 39703.

All characters in this book have no existence outside the imagination of the author and have no relation whatsoever to anyone bearing the same name or names. They are not even distantly inspired by any individual known or unknown to the author and all incidents are pure invention.

Copyright © 2009 by Mildred Riley

ISBN: 13 DIGIT : 978-1-58571-335-6
ISBN: 10 DIGIT : 1-58571-335-x
Manufactured in the United States of America

First Edition

Visit us at www.genesis-press.com
or call at 1-888-Indigo-1-4-0

DEDICATION

To Leticia Peoples—mentor and friend.

ACKNOWLEDGMENT

Many thanks to my family and friends, whose love and support have always been there for me.

PROLOGUE

During their three-year marriage, they had been down this same road too many times to count. Each time the confrontation had ended with Elyse Marshall deferring to her husband's wishes. It had been the same with her mother. Theirs was not a typically warm mother-daughter relationship. Many times during her adolescent years she had endured scoldings, harangues, advice, dire warnings, so many that she learned to turn off her ears, answer "Yes, Mother," and distance herself from the source.

There was the time she was reprimanded for allowing James Rhodes, a junior classmate in high school, to walk home with her. As they sat on the front steps, talking about school, Elyse heard the front door open. She turned, saw the anger on her mother's face.

"Get in this house right this minute, young lady!"

With a wave of her hand to the startled James, she obeyed her mother, whose face flushed as she yanked her daughter over the threshold and into the house.

"What's wrong with you, bringing that boy to our home? Don't you know who he is?"

"He's in my high school class . . . moved here . . ."

"I know all about him! He's the kid whose father just went to prison for beating his wife so badly she's in a coma! What's wrong with you, child? Don't you have the sense God gave you? I'm not raising you to mess around with trash like that!"

Her mother had continued to push her towards perfection. "Remember you've got to measure up to the high standards of this family!"

The words echoed even now in Elyse's mind. Even her MBA from Harvard and her thriving book and gift shop received scant approval from her mother. Elyse's marriage to Barry was marginally accepted.

"He just works in a drugstore," Elyse heard her mother tell a friend over the phone. The fact that Barry had a degree in pharmacy and was a registered pharmacist did not impress the woman.

Another bitter memory rose up in her mind. She was fifteen, a sophomore in high school. She had been so happy, excited because her new jeans fit perfectly. But when she went into the kitchen to breakfast, her mother took one look at her.

"Oh, no," her mother had said. "You are *not* wearing those overalls to school!"

"Why not?" Elyse had protested. "Everyone's wearing them, and they are not overalls, they're jeans!"

"I don't care what you call them, you're not leaving this house dressed like a farmhand! I won't have it. Now you go right back upstairs and put on that plaid wool skirt I bought you from Filene's!"

The remembered scene made Elyse's face flush all over again as she relived running up the stairs to her room, desperately flinging hot tears from her eyes. Her broken sobs made her gasp for breath.

She nearly collided with her father coming out of the bathroom, a white towel draped around his neck.

"Hey, hey, Leese, what's wrong?" He swiped at his damp chin with a corner of the towel. "Why are you crying? Tell me what's wrong."

"Mom. She says I have to change . . . can't wear my new jeans to school," she sobbed into her father's chest as he held her close.

"And, and," her voice elevated to a thin pitch, "I bought them with my own money, too! She says I have to wear a plaid skirt. And, Dad, everyone is wearing *jeans*! I don't want to look different! Mom never lets me do anything I want to do! Why, Dad?"

Jerome Joyce took a folded handkerchief from his trouser pocket and tried to wipe the tears from his daughter's eyes. He led her to her room and together they sat on her bed. "Listen, hon." He still had his arm around her shaking shoulders. "Your mother loves you . . . wants only the best for you, you know that."

"But, Dad, I never do *anything* right for her. Never!"

"Today you can," he told her. "Go ahead and change. It won't hurt you to please your mother. Put on the skirt and I'll drive you to school. The bus has come and gone, but I'll get you there before the first bell."

Jerome Joyce knew the time had come when he had to explain certain facts to Elyse . . . about her mother's bleak childhood.

He was a CPA, with an office on Blue Hill Avenue in Mattapan Square. It was only a few miles from their home, and his daughter's high school was halfway between the two locations.

A large man, well over six feet, with a tendency toward a roundness in his build, he tried to keep his weight in check by taking walks at noon around the square. His straight nose flared slightly at the tip, indicating his African-American heritage. He had smooth skin, walnut-brown coloring and dark brown eyes beneath well-shaped eyebrows. On meeting him, people often remarked that he resembled Colin Powell, the soldier-statesman, a comment that he would accept with a modest smile.

Frances Joyce had married Jerome shortly after his return from Vietnam. With the GI Bill, he'd earned a degree in accounting and passed the difficult examination to become a certified public accountant. As a CPA he was able to open his own office. Over the years his business had done so well, he added to his staff. It was not long before the young family bought a house in Milton, one of Boston's most affluent areas.

Frances had just graduated from nursing school and worked as a private duty nurse at many of the city's major hospitals. When she married Jerome she knew she was doing the right thing. She visualized a life much different from the grim life that had been ahead for her at Orchard Park.

For his part, Jerome was fascinated by the feisty, attractive young nurse. He had met her at the social that St. Barnabas Episcopal Church held weekly for the youthful parishioners. Although petite, Frances Joyce was strong and healthy. Later, her husband would remark to his friends, "Frances may be small, but believe me, she's as strong as an ox. Should see how she can carry our daughter on one hip, and with groceries loaded in the baby's stroller, haul everything into the house in one trip!"

This day it was Jerome's hope that somehow during the short drive to the school he could help Elyse understand her mother. As soon as Elyse was settled in the car, her seatbelt secured, her book bag in her lap, he started out of the driveway of their home.

Jerome took a quick glance at his daughter as he waited for the morning traffic to allow him access into the street. He saw her twist and clench the damp tissue in her hands. He handed her a fresh one from the console. He wondered what she was thinking.

Her anger towards her mother likely still bubbled up in her mind. At fifteen she just knew she could make up her own mind. Since it was her life, she thought she could do what she wanted. He knew her rebellious nature was a vital part of her growth and development. He had to accept that reality.

He cleared his throat, got his daughter's attention. She looked over at him.

"I want you to know, Leese," he said, "your mother is a wonderful woman who loves you with her whole heart. Would give her life for you. She wants only the best for you. And you have to understand something. Your mother, well, she didn't have a mother. I believe from what she's told me her mother died when she was three.

She barely remembers her. Vaguely recalls being lifted up to see her dead mother's body in a casket."

He glanced over at his daughter, saw a softening of her face. He continued to talk.

"After her mother's death, it wasn't long before her father, left with four children, married a widow with three little girls. Frances told me that from the time she had a stepmother and three stepsisters, her life was pure torment. Like the fabled Cinderella's. Her stepmother always told her, she said, 'You're not goin' 'mount to anything. Earn you livin' on your back.' Meaning as a streetwalker. Frances told me that she vowed to make a liar out of the mean, dreadful woman."

There was silence in the car. They were almost at the school. Jerome realized that Elyse had been stunned by his words. He knew she was not comfortable with what he had just revealed to her, but he sensed that she was receptive and that was what he wanted.

"So, if Mom isn't always hugging and kissing you, it's not because she doesn't love you. It's because she never had a mother to demonstrate affection in *her* life. But, dear daughter of mine, hear me when I tell you that I fell in love with the most wonderful, strong woman who brought into *my* life the essence, the love, that makes me whole, brings me peace and fulfillment. And my fondest hope is that someday you will find a love like that."

Her father pulled into the school parking lot. He placed the car in park and leaned over to kiss her goodbye.

"Bye, Dad," she said as she threw her book bag over her shoulder. She ran up the stairs into the building, thinking about what her father had told her. She felt quite ambivalent about her situation. *Who am I, anyway?* she thought. *Do I always have to please her? When can I do what I want?*

So, for the past fifteen, sixteen years, she had followed her own path from high school to college graduate school at Harvard. But today that memory forced her to wonder why *she* had fallen in love with a man whose impoverished, loveless childhood had been so like her mother's. In Barry's case it was the lack of the father he never knew. He had been raised by a single mother who tried to meet her only child's needs.

But Elyse loved him. There had been other young men, one she came close to marrying until Barry Marshall came into her life with such an air of self-confidence and strength that she found herself drawn to him. And then later, when he began calling her his queen, "Queen Leesy," it made her feel as if she were the most important woman in the world. She fell hopelessly in love with him. He never left her side without saying, "Love ya." She knew that was true, but why did he stall when he knew that her happiness would not be complete until they started a family?

She decided to broach the subject one more time.

Standing in front of his dresser as he adjusted his tie (they were due at the realtor's office in twenty minutes), Barry heard the angst in his wife's voice as she expressed her concern.

"Barry . . ."

"Yes, hon, what's up?"

"Barry, you do know that my biological clock is ticking, slowing down, possibly . . .".

"Oh, babe, of course I know. But not to worry. We're going to do just fine! We'll start *that* project just as soon as our house is built. I promised you happy days when we got married and I intend to live up to that promise. I want our child as much as you do. Family means a lot to me."

He shrugged into his sports jacket and turned from the mirror to face her.

"I intend to give you nothing but the best. A beautiful home and a wonderful family of our own." He flashed his warm smile at her.

She sighed deeply when he pulled her close and kissed her. She knew his background made him reluctant to start a family, but she longed for a baby, knew she would not feel complete until . . . She moved away from her husband to put on her makeup.

"My mother did all she could," he had explained to her early on when they first started dating, "but she could never scrabble enough money together to buy us a house. All my life that's been my goal, to own a home. Sadly, Mom's gone now, and I can't give her . . ."

"I understand," Elyse had said, but she didn't, not really. *That was then, this is now*, she thought. *Now he's my husband.*

She turned back from her vanity table and watched her husband, who was slipping his feet into a pair of dark brown boat shoes. He looked up at her. "Are you almost ready? Promised the real estate agent we'd be at her office at ten."

"Yes, I'm ready, but, please, Barry, think seriously about *my* ticking clock. It will be another year before we can move into our new home and then if I *do* become pregnant, another nine months . . ."

"Oh, Leesy," he interrupted her, "we *are* going to have it all! Trust me. I haven't let you down thus far, have I?"

"And I'm holding you to your word, husband mine. And don't you forget it!"

She tried to keep her tone of voice light and cheerful because she was deeply in love with this man. He was her future. She knew that he loved her. She linked her arm in his and they walked to the car. His car, really. His beloved 1996 Volvo, the first purchase he had made as a registered pharmacist. Although not new, with tuition bills still to pay, it was all he could afford for now.

They found a cool, serene atmosphere when they walked into the realtor's office. Carla Gentry was a middle-aged woman of color whose frosty white hair framed her warm, unlined face, and whose firm yet soft handshake put Elyse at ease.

"Please come in, both of you. It's great to see you, and I have all the documents ready for you to sign."

"We're very excited. Right, Elyse?"

"Can hardly wait," Elyse said. "It's an exciting start for our future," she told the real estate agent who placed a large folder on the center of her desk as she sat down.

"You know that I wish you both all the luck in the world, and if ever I can be of assistance to you, please just let me know."

"We most certainly will," Barry said.

"Thank you very much," Elyse added, hoping the agent realized that she was an equal partner in this negotiation. She had made up her mind. This purchase of land for a house was not going to be the only change coming into their lives. One of the reasons she loved Barry was his singular determination. He chose a path to follow, always the right one so far except for the baby . . . why wasn't he more agreeable to that idea? It could not be money. Her book and gift shop was doing well, and he had a great job as a pharmacist. Well, okay, he'd wanted to be a doctor, but hadn't had the money. That's why he'd joined the National Guard. The promised stipend would help.

She always knew, too, that her husband saw the anxiety she was experiencing whenever they made love, knowing how much she wished to become pregnant. He did not discount her determination.

"You wouldn't pull a fast one on me and forget your diaphragm, would you, Leesy?" he asked her one evening as they were preparing for bed.

"Of course not! What kind of a woman do you think I am?" she bristled. "I want to have our child. And more than that, I want you to want it, too. It's extremely important to me that we're in this marriage together."

"Honey, of course we are, and I intend to be the best father in the world."

Elyse did not answer him, remembering something her mother had said about "two strong-willed people butting heads and making trouble." But there had to be a compromise. She was not willing to give up on their marriage.

The change came sooner than either of them had expected.

Barry Marshall knew that he could no longer delay telling his wife about the dreadful news that would so drastically alter their lives. Jay Collins, his best friend and lawyer, had put it quite simply.

"Man! This is going to mess up your future big time. You know that?"

"Of course I know it, but I never thought it would come to this. I mean, I joined mainly for the benefits, school tuition and such. Knew I could be called to active duty, but overseas in a war? Iraq?"

"You never gave up on the idea of med school?"

"No, it was always my dream. Thought pharmacology would be satisfying, but it has only made me want a career in medicine even more. The tuition from the Guard would help me do that."

Barry and Jay were almost like brothers. In fact, people often thought they were. Both were tall, with slim, muscular bodies, perhaps because they had participated in track and field in high school and college.

Barry had run the 440 relays, and Jay had won honors in the high jump. Both had reddish-brown skin tones and each had dark brown hair, close cropped.

Although much alike in physical appearance, their personal lives were very different. Jay was the last of six brothers, and as he told Barry many times, "Bro, I had to fight my way out of everything! My brothers wouldn't give me an inch!"

"That's why you're such a good lawyer."

On the other hand, Barry had no siblings. He had been raised by a single mother.

When they said their goodbyes that day at Jay's office, Jay had promised to help Elyse in any way, should she need him.

It was a tense moment. Jay clasped his arms around his friend. His voice was choked with emotion. He could barely get his next words past his lips.

"Take care, man. Be safe, and come home soon."

"Will do, God willing," Barry said, his own voice husky with restrained tension.

As he left Jay's office building that afternoon, he thought of the one burdensome detail in his past that he had not shared with his lawyer-friend. If he should not return from Iraq, what would happen to the girl? Where was she, anyway?

As he walked to his car in the parking lot adjacent to the office building, he remembered walking out of the hospital after his daughter's birth. He had just signed the papers that the social worker of the adoption agency had given him, *relinquishing all rights and responsibilities to said child.* What else could he have done? At the time he had only been eighteen, a college freshman, and had neither the money nor the inclination to support a wife and child. Both he and the girl (what was her name . . . Tiomara something) had agreed to put the child up for adoption. Who knew that the consequences of *one* sexual experience would be a child, another human being? He hoped Elyse would never find out about this child.

And only last week, again, Elyse had broached the subject of starting a family.

"I'm cutting it close, you know, Barry. My biological clock is ticking. On my next birthday I'll be thirty-one."

"Oh, honey, don't worry, we've got plenty of time," had been his reply, hoping he was right. "We've got the land to build our dream house on, and we're right on track for our future."

He had tried to sound convincing, but now the news he would share with her tonight would blow everything to hell. He had gambled on their future and he had lost.

Elyse loved to cook. She was good at it, and Barry was appreciative of her culinary skills. He had told her so many times.

"Girl, you sure know how to work those pots and pans. Julia Child better watch out. Here comes Leesy!"

She had left The Kwanzaa Book and Gift Shop at five that day. Emerald Stokes, her partner-friend, would close the store at nine that evening. It would be Elyse's responsibility to open the next morning at ten. They had agreed as co-owners to alternate days of openings and closings. So far the system had worked well for each of them.

Because she had the time and because it was an unusually warm day, she had decided to prepare a lobster salad for dinner. She shopped at a local fish market on her way home to buy fresh lobster meat, then ran into a nearby fresh fruit and vegetable store to get a head of lettuce and some tomatoes. From the deli counter of the store she plucked a fresh loaf of the French bread her husband loved.

She hummed to herself as she worked in her small but adequate kitchen. She was happy with her life. That happiness could only be increased when she and Barry had a child. He was a wonderful husband. He loved her, and she loved him. He was truly the other half that made her whole. So far, life was good and she was grateful. Maybe tonight her dream of a child . . . who knew?

She heard the key turn in the door lock. Barry was home. She called out, "You're right on time. Garlic bread's about to go into the oven."

She put the prepared bread into the microwave oven and set the timer, then turned to greet her husband.

It was his drawn and downcast face, his eyes dark with despair, that alerted her. Something was terribly wrong. She gasped, her hands flying to her mouth. She had never seen him look so awful.

"Barry! What is it? What's wrong?"

She moved toward him. He stopped her forward momentum with an extended hand, as if he could not bear to have her come close.

Stunned and horrified by her husband's obvious distress, Elyse backed away from him as if he had become a stranger.

Straining, reluctant to release the words, he struggled to speak.

"My, my . . . my unit's been called up."

"Called up? Called up?"

"To Iraq. Medical unit needed."

The words dropped from his trembling lips. Then they rushed into each other's arms. Their eyes flooded with mingling tears that streamed down their stricken faces as they clung together. The microwave timer rang, indicating that the bread was ready to be removed. It signaled the end of everything else as well.

It was a night neither would ever forget.

Trembling, shaken, bewildered, by her husband's news, Elyse clung to Barry as he tried to reassure her. He held her close, his voice husky with emotion.

"Leese, honey, it's . . . it's going to be all right. Remember . . . I'll be stationed at the base hospital . . . won't be close to enemy fire. And my deployment is only for eighteen months. I'll be home before you know it."

"Barry, I can't make it without you," she sobbed into his chest. "I know I can't. Oh, Barry . . ."

"Yes, you can. I know you can. You're a strong woman . . ."

"Not without you," she whispered, clinging to him as if she were drowning in despair.

Somehow they made their way into their bedroom, the evening meal forgotten.

"When . . . when . . . do you have to leave?" she asked him.

"In a month."

"That soon?"

"Just enough time to get my paperwork in order, important stuff, legal documents, you know. But every person in the military has to do that, Leese."

"I can't stand it! It's awful!"

"I signed up, honey, and I *have* to go. But I promise I'll be back. I'll be safe, not in harm's way. Trust me."

He threw his jacket on the bench at the foot of their bed, loosened his tie and took off his shirt. He lay down next to his wife, whose tear-stained face nearly broke his heart. What could he say? How could he comfort her? The life he had envisioned with the love of his life was spinning out of his control.

Elyse's sobs had turned into breathless hiccups and Barry went to the kitchen for a glass of water for her. When he returned, she was undressed and in bed, the staccato breaths racking her whole body.

"Here, hon, drink this."

"Thanks."

With a trembling hand she accepted the drink, sipping the water slowly as the spasms continued to shake her.

"Better?" he said as she finished.

"Yes, I . . . I think so."

CHAPTER 1

Elyse's morning shower revived her somewhat. She had suffered through another one of the sleepless nights that had tormented her since her husband had been deployed in Iraq for over a year now as a member of the National Guard's Fifth Medical Unit.

"Elyse, honey, don't worry," he had tried to reassure her, "I'll be safe. Well behind any military action, no enemy fire. As a pharmacist, I'll be safe. Be home before you know it."

But oh, how she missed him. After three years of marriage, living alone without Barry was taking its toll on her. As she toweled her body she could see how much weight she had lost. Her ribs were more starkly outlined than ever before, and her cheeks seemed to have deeper hollows. Even her skin coloring had changed from its naturally soft brown blush to a sallow, washed-out appearance. Barry Marshall had always said that it was her delicate, rosy-brown smooth skin that had attracted him to Elyse in the first place.

"When I saw you walk into the dining room at college, I said to myself, 'Bro, you've got to meet *that* one and quick, too!' "

Later he told her that it was not only her stunning looks but the way she walked. "Tall and self-assured, like an African queen," he'd said.

As she applied her favorite lotion to her skin, she wondered what Barry would say if he could see her now. Probably fuss at her for letting herself get into such a sorry state. Thank God for the e-mail he'd sent her last week with the welcome news that in two more months he would be home. She marked off the days on her kitchen calendar each morning.

She draped the damp towel over the shower rod, then went into her bedroom closet to decide what to wear. Still thinking of her husband, she selected her blue velour pantsuit because Barry always had said he loved her in blue.

As she dressed she prayed silently, *God, keep my husband safe and bring him home to me.*

She went into the kitchen, made a quick breakfast for herself of coffee, dry toast and orange juice. After she finished eating, she rinsed out her coffee mug and juice glass and turned them over to dry on the kitchen counter. She picked up a black marker from the "catch-all" tray on the counter and marked an X on the date. It was Monday, August eighth, the anniversary of the atom bomb on Hiroshima and Nagasaki. She shivered as she remembered.

She was glad that her store, her pride and joy, was doing so well that she didn't have to worry about it. Thank God for Emerald Stokes, her friend and partner, who always kept things in order. Elyse's concerns were few, especially when it came to the day-to-day routine of running the store. Ever since she was a small child she had dreamed of owning her own business, and with her inheritance from her paternal grandmother, Margaret Joyce, she had opened The Kwanzaa Book and Gift Shop. In her dreams she imagined owning stores in other major cities if her enterprise in Boston proved successful. It didn't hurt a bit, either, that her MBA degree was from the Harvard Business School. If only Barry would get home safely.

Before leaving her condominium townhouse, she checked her e-mail. There was the usual overabundance of silly, inane jokes and messages that she had neither the time nor the inclination to bother reading. There was nothing from her husband. *Well*, she thought, *no news is good news.* At least she hoped so.

She thought of how glad she was that Barry and she had already decided to live in a small town south of Boston. The plot of land they had acquired was located on the Atlantic Coast. The area provided summer get-aways for the Irish families from South Boston. Many folks called it the Irish Riviera. It would take her only forty minutes to reach her store. She was glad of that.

When she arrived at the store Emerald Stokes was already at her desk in the back room. The smell of freshly brewed coffee greeted her, along with Emerald's cheery voice.

"Just in time!" She waved her hand in a welcoming gesture. "The blueberry muffins are to die for. And don't you dare tell me, with your skinny self, that you can't eat at least one!"

"Well, maybe one. Only had juice, coffee and dry toast this morning," Elyse admitted.

3

"See that!" Emerald scrambled out of her chair, went to the rear of the small office, popped a muffin into the microwave and returned two minutes later with a steaming cup of coffee and a fragrant warm muffin on a paper plate.

"There you go. Have at it, kiddo!"

She placed the items on Elyse's desk and returned to her own desk.

Emerald's short stature contrasted with Elyse's tall, slender figure, but with her feisty attitude she could hold her own with anyone. Her *I may be short, but oh my, don't mess with me* approach was apparent in her dealings with people.

Elyse always jokingly told folks, "Whenever Emerald starts a phrase with *'Now let me tell you one thing,'* the listener had better be aware because the girl means business."

However, she was honest, fair and hardworking, qualities that a budding entrepreneur appreciated. Elyse knew how much she needed Emerald's support. She was more than a business partner. She was a valued friend and confidant.

Silently, Elyse munched on her muffin. Her sad face was not lost on her companion.

"No news from Barry this morning, right?"

"Right. No news."

Elyse picked up her coffee dup, took a tentative sip of the hot brew and sighed deeply. Emerald became more aware of her friend's pain and responded briskly.

"Girl, pull yourself together. The only thing your husband wants is to find you safe and healthy when he gets back home. Sittin' around worryin', getting thin as a rail isn't goin' to cut it! And besides, you've got this business to run!"

"I know you're right, Em. I've got plenty to do, check inventory, and I have a new list of books to order . . ."

"Well, there you go. Some of that I can do for you."

"That *would* help me a lot because I really want to check into that shipment of African stuff from Benin. I'd like to get an ad together. Christmas is only a month away and," she tapped her fingers on the desk, "I still would like to fit in one day for the book fair."

"You mean the one in Atlanta?"

"Yes, that's the one."

"It's usually the first weekend in December, if I remember. Have you made reservations?"

"I have, and I plan to visit my brother and his wife while I'm there."

"Sounds like a good idea to me. A change of scenery might do you good, Elyse."

"Maybe," Elyse agreed.

"Just let me know what you would like to have me do. Why not make a list? That way we can check off each task as completed."

"Good idea, Em. Don't know what I'd do without you."

"Don't worry. I aim to stick around."

"Good, because I sure would be lost without you, sister-girl."

She took one last sip of her coffee, pushed aside the half-eaten muffin and rose to her feet.

Emerald noticed the abandoned muffin but decided not to badger Elyse about her weight loss. She already had plans for a nutritious lunch. She planned to do everything possible to help Elyse. Not only did she care a great deal about her partner, she had a sizeable investment in The Kwanzaa Book and Gift Shop.

Emerald was proud of the shop, too. It was her idea to have a pair of rocking chairs plus a colorful rag rug in the corner of the store near the display of children's books. Mothers, and fathers, too, were delighted to sit and read to their children. An easel with unlined art paper and a box of crayons were available for children who wished to display budding artistic talents. Emerald selected and framed exceptional ones and presented them to extremely delighted parents.

"Good for business, don't you know," she told Elyse.

"I know, more than one way . . ."

"To skin a cat," Emerald added with a knowing grin.

CHAPTER 2

Elyse went into a small neat and tidy room at the rear of the store that she used as her office.

She looked at her husband's picture on her desk, a small photo of him that she had taken when they went on vacation in Barbados.

He was wearing an open-necked jersey, white with short sleeves that matched his white tennis shorts, and holding his tennis racket. The wide grin on his handsome brown face let the viewer know this man was ready for a good, hard game. His forehead was broad, his hair blocking eyes so dark that they seemed to see everything. His tall, well-proportioned body was that of a strong athlete. Barry had met, fallen in love with and married Elyse Joyce within three months of meeting her.

"Couldn't help myself," he'd said many times to Elyse. "When I saw you, tall, stately and regal as a queen, there was never a doubt in my mind that I'd found the love of my life! Don't you ever forget, my dearest one, life without you would have no meaning, and I mean that!"

Elyse heard her husband's voice in her mind echoing the phrase that meant so much to her, that comforted her in his absence. Their plans, now delayed, had been to build a house and start a family. So far, all they had was the land. Her hope for a baby had not materialized, despite their frantic coupling that fateful night.

She placed her pocketbook in the lower right-hand drawer of her desk, booted up her computer and opened her e-mail. Just maybe she'd find a message from her husband. Just maybe.

Quickly scanning the list of messages, she found none from Barry. She deleted most of the mail as it consisted of inanities. As she did so she thought of the thousands of miles that separated her from the man she loved and how much it meant to her to receive his messages, if only a few words . . . a tenuous lifeline at best, but it was all she had.

Sighing deeply, she turned her attention to the advertisement she had been working on for the upcoming holiday season. Her small office was her sanctuary. It was here that she worked, explored and searched for creative ways to improve her shop.

This year she thought she might offer to present the week-long festival of Kwanzaa at her store. That should bring in new customers, especially those parents anxious to impart African culture to their offspring.

She decided the advertisement should appeal to their cultural pride. She would frame the ad in the popular colors of Kente cloth, sure to catch the reader's eye.

She took out a large sheet of white paper and began to work. After a few minutes she turned to her computer and began to design her advertisement. She worked diligently for over an hour, pleased with her efforts. She could hear her husband's voice, almost as if he were standing over her shoulder.

"Hey, hey, knew what I was doing when I married you! You're one smart sister!"

She could feel the warmth of his arms around her, but she shuddered with the knowledge that the man she loved, missed with almost unbearable pain, was thousands of miles away.

It seemed to her that she could smell Barry's aftershave lotion, the warm spicy fragrance that she loved. A friend of hers, Margaret Anderson, who'd been widowed a few months ago, told her that very often she noticed the scent of her husband's aftershave around her, although she'd thrown away all of his shaving toiletries.

"I think it's in your memory somehow, and some stimulus brings it back. I really believe it means how close we were, how much we loved each other," Margaret had admitted, adding in a sad voice, "It's like a reminder our love will always be there."

As Elyse sat at her desk she began to massage the back of her neck, and as she did so the memory of their last night together rose up in her mind. It had been months ago, a night of pure magic, and she remembered it vividly.

Just the week before Barry had gone over all the final paperwork.

"My will, the paperwork for the property we bought, my birth certificate, our marriage license, all of my military papers are in this packet," he told her, pointing to a large brown envelope. "Everything you would need. But I promise I will be back, not to worry."

But she did worry despite Barry's reassurances.

Their last night together had been bittersweet, with each of them trying to be brave and optimistic.

"Hold me," she whispered in their darkened bedroom. "Put your mark on my flesh so I'll always be yours. Love only me, Barry. Promise me that," she murmured in his ear.

His response came quickly as he kissed her. With his lips still on her mouth, he breathed the words she needed to hear.

"Only you, my dearest Elyse, only you do I love, and always will."

He kissed away the tears that squeezed beneath her closed eyelids, murmured softly, "I'll be back. I promise you, I'll be back and we'll start all over again. First the house, then our family. It will be our new life, you'll see."

"I hope so," she whimpered.

"Trust me, we're going to have it all sooner than you think when this temporary setback is over. You'll see," he repeated as if to reassure even himself.

When morning came, neither of them wanted to say goodbye, so each acted as if it were an ordinary workday. The only difference was the military uniform Barry wore and the duffel bag that waited at the front door of their condo.

He cupped her face in his hands as he bent to kiss her. Tears flooded her eyes so much that she could barely see him, only nodded as he whispered, "I'll always love you, my sweet Elyse, and I'll be back." And then he was gone.

She fell face down on the sofa in the living room, sobbed and screamed aloud in the empty apartment, "No! No! No! Don't leave me! Please, don't leave me-e-e."

She cried until her throat was parched, her breath punctuated by dry hiccups. She got up, a sofa pillow clutched to her abdomen, went into the kitchen for a glass of water. She was in such severe pain she could hardly fill the glass. Her hands shook and her body quivered from the deep loss and despair that overcame her. She thought she was going to die.

She heard the clanging noises from the street that meant it was Tuesday, rubbish pickup day. Had Barry put out the rubbish cans last night? She rubbed her eyes and checked outside the front door. Empty space. Well, she wasn't going to die just yet. She had to quickly put out the trash before the truck came.

CHAPTER 3

Elyse studied the computer screen. She had outlined the seven principles of Kwanzaa: unity, self-determination, responsibility, cooperative economics, purpose, creativity and faith. Each principle was blocked off individually and arranged in a circle around the central word *Kwanzaa* formed in large letters.

Satisfied with the wheel-like structure on the screen, she added the bright colors of the Kente cloth she had selected, then printed out her work, the store's address and store hours, also the upcoming festival.

"That really should do the trick," Emerald said over Elyse's shoulder.

She placed a tuna sandwich and a steaming bowl of chicken soup on Elyse's desk.

"I surely hope so," Elyse said, stretching her shoulders to straighten out the kinks.

"I really want to do well this Christmas season."

"You will. I know you will, and now looking at your flyer, I just had a thought . . ."

"About what?"

"We should place as many of these around the city as we can."

"Like?" Elyse questioned.

"The churches, beauty salons, barber shops, convenience stores . . . you know, any place our folks tend to gather. That way word of mouth will get around."

"Good idea, Emerald. Don't *know* what I'd do without you."

Emerald's answer was quick. "Not to worry, kiddo, I'll stick around. Always told you *that*."

"I'm thinking that I'd like to offer a raffle gift for customers who come to the store."

"You have something in mind, Elyse?"

"Yes, as a matter of fact I have. Remember I told you about the young brother who made up those fantastic vases?"

"The ones with the colorful fabrics decoupaged on ceramic vases and urns? Is that the one you mean?"

"Right. He's a young artist, has a store on Mass Avenue, and I believe he has a distinctive eye. The way he cuts out his designs, adheres them to the selected object then seals it over with polyurethane solution really makes his finished product unique. I bought a lovely vase from him with some gorgeous colors that I think would be attractive in any home."

"It would be great publicity for him if you were to display it in the front window or on a special table here in the store."

Elyse agreed with Emerald, adding, "If we put it in the front window, it might really draw customers into the shop. I'll bring it in tomorrow and together we can decide what to do, how much the raffle tickets should be, where and how to display the vase."

"How much did it cost?" Emerald wanted to know.

"I paid two hundred."

"Then we should figure out the cost of the raffle tickets so you can at least get that money back."

Emerald was pleased to see the sparkle in her friend's eyes and she reached over to give Elyse a warm hug. "We're goin' to do just fine, sister-girl. You wait and see!" Emerald insisted.

Elyse recognized the cheerful support that her colleague/friend was offering to her, and she realized just how much she relied on Emerald.

She drove home that evening, parked her own car, a Toyota, in her assigned parking space, gathered up her briefcase, purse and a small plant that she thought might put her in a holiday mood, although she doubted the little plant placed on her coffee table would be able to do so. She knew she was asking almost too much of the little red and green plant.

Sebastian, as usual, met her at the door. His deep growl-like purring welcomed her home. She was glad she had not forgotten to purchase his favorite treat, canned tuna. The sale item, five cans for a dollar, had caught her eye at the check-out counter so she'd bought ten cans. That should hold Sebastian for a while, she thought.

"Hi there, old man, and how was your day?" She bent down to scratch his head as he wound his lithe, glossy black furry body around her legs.

"Okay, I know you're glad to see me, and, yes, I have your treat."

She watched as the large cat leaped up to his favorite perch on the living room picture windowsill. She dropped her coat on the sofa and retrieved her briefcase and handbag to take into her bedroom.

She went to her desk, booted up her computer and searched her e-mail. She scrolled down the usual trivia; then she saw it.

Hi, babe! All is well. Hotter than a firecracker, but I'm okay. The baby wipes help. Send more. Be home soon. Sorry, after Xmas. Next year is our year! Love you. Take care of yourself. It was signed *B.*

Quickly, she hurried to print out the message, tore it from the machine and pressed the paper close to her chest. She reached for the phone.

"Yes?" Emerald's voice came reassuringly over the phone.

"I got it! I got it! He's coming home in a month! Oh, Emerald, kid, I'm so happy. One month! Did you hear what I said?"

"I certainly did. Great news, and I'm happy as I can be for you both!"

"Oh, Em, I can hardly believe it. My husband's coming home!"

"Believe it, honey, believe it."

"I just had to let you know. I'll see you in the morning. Don't know how I'll get to sleep tonight, I'm so keyed up!"

"My advice is to take a warm shower, have a glass of wine and go to bed."

"Okay, good night."

"Nite," Emerald said. "See you in the morning."

She fed Sebastian and then could not decide what she wanted to eat. Her stomach was roiling, from nerves, she expected. She opened a kitchen cabinet door and selected a can of clam chowder. With some milk and crackers, that should hold her. She knew that her stomach couldn't take much more.

While she was sitting at the kitchen table, Sebastian wandered in and looked up at her as if to say, *What's up?* He jumped into Barry's chair as if he sensed a change in Elyse.

She reached over to rub his head and he twitched his tail in response.

"Your master is coming home. Did you hear what I said?" She grinned at the animal.

The cat continued to purr. His sleek fur rippled with strong muscles as he leaped from the chair into Elyse's lap.

"You miss him, too, don't you?" she said.

Sebastian was Barry's four-year-old cat. Barry adopted the stray animal he found one morning shivering in the parking lot of the pharmacy. With good care and love the animal had thrived. Although not a cat lover, Elyse knew that an important bond existed between the pair, and she accepted the relationship.

Sebastian had accepted her as well, almost as if he understood the relationship between husband and wife.

Elyse had not grown up with a household pet. Her mother was a city girl, had lived in an apartment where pets were not allowed. Her father had spent his childhood on a farm. The dogs that had lived on the farm were not allowed in the house. They guarded the house during the daytime and spent their nights sleeping in the barn.

Elyse was happy that Sebastian had accepted her in his life. He had become a comfort to her. With Barry overseas, Sebastian was a constant in her life, dependable and steadfast.

That night when she finally got into her bed after following Emerald's suggestion of the warm shower and small glass of wine, she was grateful to slip beneath the cool, relaxing sheets. She pulled the down comforter up and tucked it under her chin. She couldn't help thinking of all the thousands of miles that separated her from her husband. Where was he sleeping tonight?

"Nite, Barry," she whispered into the darkness.

"Nite, babe." She could hear his voice in her head.

She reached over to grab her husband's pillow and held it close. She took several deep breaths, and comforted by the knowledge that her husband was returning soon, she slept.

"Didn't I tell you that you'd have good news?" Emerald's voice was cheerful and confident.

"You don't know how happy I am now that I know Barry's almost on his way home." Elyse beamed as she hung up her coat on the coat rack.

Emerald gave her a warm hug. "The best is yet to come, sweetie. You can count on that!"

The day sped by quickly. They made decisions about the raffle tickets for the vase to be displayed in the front window of the shop and finished the flyers. Emerald told Elyse that her cousin who owned a messenger service would be happy to distribute them.

They came to her condominium at eight that night. When the doorbell rang, Sebastian accompanied her although she tried to push him to one side with her toe. "No, Seb, you can't go out, not tonight." She opened the door. When she saw them, two military men accompanied by her pastor, Rev. Kingman, she felt her knees turn to jelly. She staggered back away from the door as one of the men reached for her to steady her. Her hands clasped over her mouth with stark fear. Her eyes wide with disbelief, she could only moan, "No-o, no-o, no-o! *Not* my husband!"

Major Hawkins, she learned his name later, helped her to sit down on her living room sofa. Somehow in the depth of the dark pain that enveloped her whole body, she realized that she could not escape the searing horror that had come into her life.

She reached out her arms in supplication to the only person she knew.

"Oh, Rev. Kingman, what am I going to do-o-o?"

Her face was wreathed in tears as she pleaded for some comfort.

"I'm truly sorry, my dear, that this had to come to you. I will try to help you in any way that I can." He stroked her shoulders as she sobbed against his chest.

"Your folks?" he inquired.

"Be home Sunday," she told him, her voice cracking with emotion. "They're . . . they're on vacation in Jamaica."

"I see." The minister turned to the military men who stood waiting respectfully, each man's cap tucked under his left arm.

"I'm going to call one of Mrs. Marshall's friends to come and stay with her. If you officers have additional information, you may call my office," he said as he gave each man one of his cards. He resumed his seat beside Elyse, put her head on his shoulder and continued to try to comfort her.

The major reached into his breast pocket, retrieved a card which he handed to the minister.

"Anything we can do for Mrs. Marshall, anything at all, we will be honored to do. Anything. Our staff will contact you, Rev. Kingman, as soon as more details are forthcoming." He bent to reach for the young widow's hand, touching it lightly, saying, "Please accept my deepest sympathy." Then the two men left.

Rev. Kingman walked Elyse to her bedroom and helped the distraught, weeping woman lie down. He covered her shaking body with a comforter from the foot of the bed.

"Em, Em, get Emerald," Elyse gasped as she continued to shake in her grief. She gave her pastor the telephone number, her voice quivering with emotion.

"Please come. Elyse needs you," she heard the man say.

⁂

A military escort led by Major Hawkins accompanied Barry Marshall's body form Dover Air Force Base to Logan Airport in Boston.

Elyse was staying at her parents' home, and the morning of the expected arrival, she approached her father.

"Dad?" He knew what she wanted from him and he held her close. Her eyes were brimming with tears, her voice weak from the burden of her deep sadness.

Her father kissed her on the forehead as her thin frame trembled in his arms. His heart ached for his daughter and he vowed inwardly to do all he could to ease the pain he knew she had to endure.

"Don't worry, hon, I'll be there when Barry comes home. I'll take care of everything."

He left the house a few minutes later to join one of his Masonic brothers, who was also the mortician responsible for the services.

"At least it's a sunny, mild day," Jerome Joyce remarked to John Louis, who grunted an agreement as he eased his bulky frame into the driver's seat of the funeral hearse.

"How's Elyse doin'?" he asked Jerome.

"As well as can be expected," her father told him. He took a look at his long-time friend, whose forehead was shining wet with perspiration. The brother never seemed to lose any weight. Jerome wondered how the man could maintain the stamina needed to keep up with his business.

"If we can just get her through these next few days . . . right now we've got her on quite a bit of medication. Doctor's orders, you know, and she's doing pretty well, but well, you know . . ." His voice trailed off.

"I *do* know. All you can do, Jerry, is be there for her."

"You know that she and Barry just bought land . . . planned to build, start a family. This is a really rough time right now."

John Louis seemed to know. He had been in the business for almost forty years, had seen all kinds of grieving families. He was not at all surprised when Jerome told him that he would like to view the body. "For Elyse's peace of mind," he said.

"We can do that, but I understand there will be no public viewing."

"Correct," Elyse's dad said. "There will be a photograph of him in full uniform on the memorial service announcement."

John Louis drove the hearse to a special area of the airport and pulled up alongside a large military transport plane.

He got out of the vehicle, exchanged documents with Major Hawkins. After the legal transfer was complete, the military group transferred the flag-draped coffin from the plane into the funeral car. The squad leader barked his commands. Barry Marshall had come home.

The organist had concluded the prelude and Elyse heard the sonorous voice of Father Malcolm Ambrose, the priest who had married them, intone the introit. She wanted to scream, "Stop it! Shut up!" but at that moment, as if sensing her thoughts, her father squeezed her hand, whispered in her ear, "Easy, easy, it's going to be all right. I'm right here."

She nodded wordlessly, the scream dying in her throat while tears washed down her face, blurring her vision. She saw only the stripes of the flag, and they seemed to be undulating, waving at her. She closed her eyes and listened as Father Ambrose's rich baritone voice flowed seamlessly in her husband's last rites.

Months later she told Emerald she remembered very little of that December day.

CHAPTER 4

Austin Brimmer eased his Toyota into his assigned parking space behind the mercantile building that housed his rented art studio and shop. His establishment was on the first floor overlooking Massachusetts Avenue near the Christian Scientist Mother Church. He was not too far from the Berkeley School of Music. He relished having young students pass by his store on their way to their classes. Their interest in music was akin to art, and he hoped to foster that relationship. It would be good for business.

It had snowed during the night, but the sidewalks were already cleared. He was pleased to see a slight rosiness on the eastern horizon. A clear, sunny winter day lay ahead. *What could be better?* he thought. *It should be a good sales day, with Christmas coming soon.* Maybe his new line of decoupaged ceramic ware would start to be a big sales item. The young woman from The Kwanzaa Book and Gift Shop had purchased one of the new vases just a few days before and had said she planned to exhibit it in her front display window.

She'd looked very sad when she first entered the store, but seemed to brighten when she spotted the large vase he had set on a table near the store's entrance. There were two smaller companion pieces arranged on either side.

He thought it was an attractive display with the vases resting on a black crushed velvet table runner.

Bold bright stripes of Kente cloth, brilliant blues, golds, azures, plus warm enticing hues of orange, red and yellow, had been artfully glued to the ceramic vessels. The glistening heavy lacquer enhanced their unique appearance.

Austin got out of the car, retrieved his briefcase from the passenger seat and set the car alarm. He pulled his coat collar up around his ears and hurried into the warmth of his store.

Inside, he shrugged off his overcoat, thought ruefully of the warm days he had experienced in Cameroon. He was a tall man, athletically built with olive brown skin. Upon meeting him, receiving a firm handshake from him, no one would believe that this tall, strong, young man who looked like a linebacker was an artist.

He possessed a broad forehead and wore his hair close-cropped. His emerald green eyes caused queries about his forebears. When asked, he'd give the questioner a shrug, a raised eyebrow and answer, "Your guess is as good as mine."

His nose was straight with slightly flaring nostrils, and the narrow dark moustache he had cultivated over his full lips had always attracted many women, none of whom had attracted Austin Brimmer or deterred him from his goal of becoming recognized in the African-American art world.

Armed with his degree from the Lancaster School of Art, he had first sought employment as a commercial artist, but the assignments preparing workups for newspaper advertisements were not fulfilling, not the type of art he really wanted to pursue. He'd decided to make a change. His decision had led him to the Peace Corps, to Cameroon, a republic of Central Africa with coastline on the Bight of Biafra. As an instructor in art and English, he fell in love immediately with the vibrant colors of the country and its people.

It was amazing to him to see how cheerful the people were, even though they lived in dire conditions. He found their music to be exciting with drums, brass cymbals, and woodwind-type instruments fashioned out of native woods. Even some crudely made stringed banjo instruments produced music that engendered excitement. All of the people responded, from the respected elders with gnarled fingers and stiff bones, to the youngest whose supple bodies reacted to the wildest rhythms with joy and vigor. Austin was entranced, felt strangely connected to all of it.

Then there was the language. He embraced the French and English that he heard, but the polyglot of sixty or more tribal dialects intrigued him.

His assignment was to teach English to freshman high school students. The village was approximately ten miles from a moderately sized city, Dualla, which Austin visited often, especially the marketplaces.

He learned to love the people, especially the children. They were bright, eager to learn, and just as eager to teach him, particularly how to play soccer.

Observing last night's snowfall, he smiled at the memory of trying to explain to them the mystery of snow falling from the sky. They could scarcely believe him, although many had seen some movies with scenes of snow.

"You mean it really falls from the sky?" one young lad of thirteen asked.

"Indeed it does. Much like your monsoon rains, only it is white and very, very cold. Sometimes the winds blow it around like they blow sand here, but that only makes it colder, something that we call a 'blizzard.'"

"I don't think I would like it," his student had said, shaking his head.

"You'd have to see it to believe it. But when the sun shines, it can be quite a beautiful sight."

He remembered the sadness he'd felt when his two-year stint was over. How he hated to leave the many friends he'd made. He had promised to return . . . one day. He had enjoyed teaching so much he began to wonder about his career choice. Although he relished teaching, his creative side was the part that nourished him, made him content.

He was satisfied that he was making progress with his store. So far he was able to meet all the necessary requirements for the operation of The African Art Store. He did the buying and selling and created some of the artwork, such as his ceramic vases and urns, and made sure that his financial records were in order.

Man, he thought, *it will be a great day when I can hire some help. Then maybe I can start to live a little.* So far he kept the store open five days a week, from one in the afternoon until eight at night.

He went directly to the basement to check the fired pieces in the kiln. He could hardly wait to see how they had turned out. Mornings were exciting for him because seeing his creations come to fruition validated his belief in his ability.

When the storeowner, Elyse Marshall, purchased one of his first vases, he thanked her.

"I'm so happy that you decided to buy this," he said to her as he wrapped several layers of tissue paper around it.

"I really fell in love with it as soon as I saw it," she told him. "It is so different, so unique. I plan to raffle it off at my bookstore and gift shop."

"Wonderful! And your bookstore . . ."

"I'm located on Blue Hill Avenue, on the square," Elyse said as she handed him her credit card.

While Austin completed the transaction, Elyse took one of her business cards out of her purse. After she had signed the credit slip, she gave him her card.

"The Kwanzaa Book and Gift Shop," he read aloud. "I'll have to pay you a visit."

"Please do. I'll be happy to have you come by and see how we present your fabulous vase," Elyse said, lifting her purchase into her arms.

"Oh no," Austin said. He took the bundle from her. "Let me take this to your car."

He had noticed her tentative smile, the aura of sadness around her. But she was lovely, tall, slender, with butter-soft rose-tan skin. He had also seen a slender gold band on the ring finger of her left hand. So, she was married. But what made such a lovely young woman so sad?

CHAPTER 5

Holly Francis shut her apartment door with a vigorous slam. As she clattered down the steel-coated stairs of the converted factory loft, she thought for the millionth time how much she hated her life . . . the crappy apartment, the lousy job as a nursing assistant at the Prime Care Nursing Home. She knew she was lucky to have the dingy place she called "home," but that didn't stop her from hating it.

She thought of how little time she really spent in the apartment. Mainly it was a place to sleep. She rarely invited anyone to visit her because her life didn't make that possible. In order to afford the one-bedroom apartment she had to work four twelve-hour days each week. The forty-eight-hour week was beginning to tell on her, but she had to support herself. There was no one else to help her. Her grandmother, Theodora, had died in the very nursing home where Holly was now employed.

Of course there was Branch. He picked her up every morning and drove her back home whenever her shift ended. He wanted very much for Holly to become Mrs. Branch Adkins. She had told him many times that marriage was not for her.

"If you don't stop asking me, Branch, I'll have to stop riding with you."

"Won't ask you again until next week," he joked.

"Promise?"

"I promise." He smiled at her, happy that she was with him in his car, enthralled by her soft brown skin that reddened whenever she became emotional. Her short, dark, silky brown hair curled in a shimmering nimbus around her delicate face. But she was physically strong, that he knew full well. He had seen her manage patients in a firm manner, particularly the difficult stubborn ones.

The two had met at Medical Technology Academy, known usually as MTA, one of the many educational schools that offered training in the medical field and promised an entry level job at the completion of the course.

Branch had graduated as an operating room technician. A tall man with a football player's strength and muscles, many of the surgeons he assisted were amazed by his deft handling of the various surgical instruments. Some were reluctant at first when Branch, gowned and gloved, appeared at their side in the operating room. It was often reported that Branch knew what instrument the surgeon needed even before he asked. Very often, if certain physicians had to perform surgeries at other facilities, they asked Branch Adkins if he could work with them. He was well-known and appreciated for his innate abilities.

He waited for Holly to fasten her seatbelt before he placed the car into drive. He understood her anxiety about cars. He knew he'd feel the same way if someone in his family had been killed by a drunk driver, especially one's mother.

He also understood the depth of Holly's grief over losing her mother five years ago. It changed her life drastically. Seventeen years old then, college was no longer a possibility, and a career choice from MTA was the best she could hope to achieve. Her mother's small life insurance policy made that possible. Then her grandmother died. Branch thought it sad that Holly never knew her father.

He'd asked her about him once. At her brief, curt reply, "Never knew the man," he'd raised his eyebrows and had sense enough not to pursue the subject. Still, he wished he could help ease the pain he knew she endured.

She was so unhappy with her life and he so desperately wanted to bring love, peace and tranquility into her future. But Branch Adkins knew that patience and persistence would be his allies.

"Looks like a brisk fall day," Branch observed as he drove down Warren Street towards Dudley Square and the nursing home where Holly worked.

She glanced out the car window at the blue sky and the cotton-white clouds that moved slowly, unhurriedly, across the blue dome.

She sighed, "Just another day to me. Another depressing day."

"Oh, Holly, it won't always be this way, I swear. Look on the bright side!"

"Okay, Branch, I'll try."

He pulled up behind another car that several other young women had just gotten out of. They were walking toward the building.

"Haitians, Dominicans, Mexicans. I don't understand a word they're saying," she said to Branch as they both listened to the mellifluous patois the women were speaking.

"One thing I know for sure," Holly said to Branch as she released her seatbelt. "This place would go out of business if these folks didn't work here."

"They fill a need, eh?"

"Sure do. No one wants to do this kind of work. Babysitting, feeding, diapering old people . . ."

"But somebody's got to do it. Right?" Branch said.

"You're right. We're all going to get old someday. Have to pray that there's someone around willing to give us a glass of water if we need it."

"Thank God, Holly, that you're that kind of person."

"Do the best I can. Thanks for the ride. See you tonight about eight. And you have a good day, hear? See you." She waved goodbye as she left the car.

He watched her run up the stairs of the brownstone building, now converted from a residence to a nursing home facility. Shaking his head, Branch drove away from the curb. She is one independent, self-sufficient young woman, he thought. But her depression worries me.

Prime Care Nursing Home was one of many franchises owned by a corporation whose main offices were located in Tennessee. The franchise owner had been able to obtain funds to rehab two brownstone homes into one large building.

From the outside it appeared to be a typical brown-stone, but inside were wide corridors with handrails along the walls. It was well lit to accommodate patients with failing eyesight. Doorways were wide and swung easily to admit wheelchairs and stretchers.

The lobby resembled one found in any moderately priced motel. Comfortable upholstered armchairs were clustered in groups. Several were placed near a gas burning fireplace; others formed an arrangement with a coffee table that invited residents to gather into conversational groups. Fresh flowers and attractive lamps resting on dark mahogany tables worked to create a homelike atmosphere.

Besides the lobby, the first floor contained offices, a medical suite, dining room and a kitchen, as well as elevators leading to the two upper floors.

The second floor contained fifteen rooms occupied by those patients needing total care around the clock. The third floor housed ambulatory individuals who could meet their own needs with minimal assistance from the staff.

As Holly hurried into the building she flashed her badge at the security guard.

"Mornin'."

"Mornin', Miss Holly," he responded from his high stool behind the lobby desk. "Make it a good one," he added.

"Goin' try to," Holly said over her shoulder as she moved toward the elevators. She punched the button for the lower level that would take her to the basement locker room. It had been set aside for the female employees. Even before she reached the door she could hear the hubbub of the employees who had arrived before she had.

The room was crowded with mainly young girls stripping off their exotic blouses, jeans and colorful skirts to change into their work uniforms. Some wore the blue and white uniforms of dietetic assistants, the employees who passed food trays and assisted those patients unable to feed themselves.

Other employees, mainly older, more matronly women, wore a gray and white uniform that identified them as housekeepers. The words *Prime Care* were embroidered on the left upper pocket of each uniform. In addition, each person wore an identification tag with their name and photograph.

"Hey, hey, Leola, how're you this mornin'?" Holly greeted a stocky brown-skinned twenty-something-year-old trying to confine heavy blonde-dyed dreadlocks into the required hairnets.

"Be fine, soon's I get this hair of mine in this damn net. Branch bring you in this mornin'?"

"Yeah, he did. Good ole Branch."

"Hey girl, don' knock the blessin'! Wish I had somebody like him."

Holly knew that, like most of the other female employees, Leola was a single mother supporting herself and two small children. Her two girls, Pearl and Diamond, Leola said, were her "precious jewels" and she had moved from Portsmouth, Virginia, and their worthless father to make a better life for them in Boston.

Holly agreed with Leola. "Yeah, I know I'm lucky. Branch is a good guy."

"All's I know is you'd better snatch him up 'fore some no-good hussy grabs 'im," Leola said, zipping up her uniform, grabbing her set of keys from her locker. After turning the key she waved goodbye to Holly, who was moving towards her own locker at the far end of the room.

"See you later, Lee. Have a good day," she said. That was when Holly saw the envelope. Her heart skipped a beat. A large business-sized envelope had been taped to the front of her locker. *Now what?* she wondered.

"Please report to my office at your earliest convenience," the note inside read. It had been signed by Jane Dagleish, R.N.

Holly's face flushed as she read the brief message, realizing she had been holding her breath. She exhaled slowly, wondering why *she* was being summoned by the nursing supervisor. Was it her work, complaints from a patient's family . . . what? She couldn't think of *anything* she'd done. Or was she being let go? There had been some talk of downsizing. Oh, God, she needed this job, as bad as it was.

She checked her appearance using the small mirror taped inside her locker. It would surely be a bad idea to look less than perfect for Ms. Dagleish, who was a stickler for the proper appearance of her nursing staff.

Holly's hair, a soft, silky brown, was about the only facet of her appearance that pleased her. Her mother's hair had been similar, but she had worn it either long, about shoulder-length, or in twin braids. Holly, however, wore hers in a short pixie-like cut that accented her large, dark brown eyes. She never thought it was true, but others told her that she resembled Halle Berry. "Almost look-alike," they would say.

Satisfied that she looked as presentable as possible, she adjusted her name tag on her left breast pocket, placed her handbag in her locker, locked it and put the key in her pocket.

She breathed a quick silent prayer, *God, help me*, as she approached the supervisor's office on the main floor.

"Good morning, Ms. Dagleish. You wish to see me?" Holly asked when the nurse told her to come in the office.

"Yes, Holly, how are you?"

"I'm fine, fine."

"Good. I have something I'd like to discuss with you." She went right to the point. "Are you up to the challenge of a new assignment?"

Jane Dagleish was a small woman, about forty years old. She was always dressed tastefully in elegant skirts and blouses, though she wore a white laboratory coat as a gesture to her medical career. The one thing Holly had noticed about the woman was her hands.

Her skin was pearlescent, almost transparent. Her fingers were slender and delicately tapered and her nails were polished a rose tint. The gold Claddagh ring she wore on the ring finger of her right hand accented her fingers.

Holly had decided that the woman's clear, pale white skin and coal black hair worn in a pageboy, along with her startling blue eyes, could be considered a testament to her Scotch-Irish heritage.

At this moment those eyes were focused on Holly as she sat in the chair in front of the supervisor's desk.

Her tone of voice was warm and friendly, which did little to ease the tension Holly felt. She smiled as she repeated her question. "So, are you willing, Holly, to try something new?"

Not knowing what to say, Holly hesitated. "I . . . I . . . think so . . . if you think . . ."

"Oh, my dear, I have no doubt that *you* can meet *this* challenge. I've been watching you and I believe that you have potential. A great deal of potential."

"But I'm used to where I'm working now. You know, used to the patients and the routine . . ."

"And you are doing an excellent job on that unit. And *that's* why I wanted to talk to you . . . to offer you the opportunity of a lifetime."

Holly's eyes widened in wonder. *What on earth was Ms. Dagleish talking about? 'The opportunity of a lifetime'?*

"Well, you see, Holly," the nurse began to explain, "the management of our facility has decided to go into a new direction by adding patients who need short-term rehabilitation services, especially those recovering from strokes, knee or hip replacements. This type of patient may not require as much hands-on care as most of our older residents, but instead need support, education and therapy to restore them to health. It's estimated that their stay here could be from a few weeks to perhaps a month or two. I'd like to assign you to this new unit."

"Me?" Holly's voice cracked in disbelief.

"Yes, you. I feel you are just the person. I believe that you can work effectively with the ancillary staff, physical therapists, speech therapists and the various other disciplines that will be part of this special unit. How about it, Holly? Willing to try?"

"If you think . . . I don't know," Holly said slowly. "But if it doesn't work out can I go back to my old unit?"

"Of course. But really, my dear, I wouldn't have made this proposal if I didn't feel confident about your abilities."

Jane Dagleish's eyes opened wide and her smile . . . it upset Holly. Rarely in staff meetings had she ever noticed a smile, the warmth, the widening of her eyes as if the two of them were in on some special secret. It made Holly more nervous than ever. She'd never seen her supervisor like this.

As Dagleish continued, her enthusiasm about the new project began to unsettle Holly's nerves even more. Her palms were sweaty and she could feel perspiration moistening under her armpits.

"There's more," the supervisor said, her smile broader than ever.

"More?" Holly asked, already overwhelmed by the news she'd just received.

"Yes, there is more. You will receive a salary increase, and the chance to advance." Automatically lowering her voice as if wanting to convey secrecy, she began to explain.

Holly's thoughts were on the patients that she had been caring for the past few months. There was old Mr.

Harkins, whose idea of a joke was to pretend he was sound asleep when she went to his bedside each morning. He'd open his eyes, stare around as if he didn't know where he was, and then in a voice of surprise say, "Oh, it's you. Who are you, young lady?"

"Mr. Harkins," she would say, "you know right well who I am. And good morning to you, too. Sleep well?"

"Well as could be expected with old man Grabel in the next bed snoring like a freight train all night."

"Well, how about the earplugs that I got for you?"

"Girl, I lost them things a long time ago."

Waiting for the other shoe to drop, Holly listened as the nurse continued. She had always admired her supervisor as a no-nonsense person who knew who she was, what she represented, and always exhibited fair and equitable treatment to all. She had earned loyalty and respect from her staff and colleagues.

Holly moistened her lips, her mouth dry with apprehension as she waited for Jane Dagleish to continue.

"You will be on duty Monday through Friday, and your hours will be from nine to five."

"No more nights or weekends?" Holly asked. "Ten hour shifts?"

"No more. Now, Holly," the woman leaned forward, "I'm sure you're wondering why I have selected you . . ."

"Yes, why did you pick me?"

Jane Dagleish settled back in her chair and gazed steadily at the shocked girl's face. She spoke slowly. "Because you are hungry. You want more out of life. I've watched you . . . how you treat our patients, even the most difficult, the most cantankerous residents that we have. I've noticed, too, the innovative ideas you've used to make life a little more pleasant for those facing the last days of their lives. And really, Holly," and this time she smiled, "you remind me of myself. Someone once gave me, a second-generation immigrant Scotch-Irish girl, a hand up. I'm only doing likewise for someone else. You. Never in God's green earth did I ever believe that I would accomplish all of this," she waved her hand at the citations and degrees framed on the wall behind her desk, "but once the door was opened for me I walked right through it. I expect you will do the same. Don't disappoint me."

At eight that night, when Branch picked Holly up to take her home, he hardly recognized the bubbly, excited girl that got into his car.

"Hi, Branch! How are you?" Holly's voice lilted with her unbounded excitement.

"Hey, girl, what's happenin'? What's got you so fired up?"

Holly fastened her seatbelt and began to share her news.

"You won't believe this," she began.

When she had recounted the startling news to Branch, he pulled the car into a nearby parking lot, turned off the ignition and faced Holly.

"Congratulations, my dear." He hugged her, happy that she was happy.

"Branch," Holly asked as he started to drive, "can we stop at The Kwanzaa Book Shop? I promised Mr. Harkins that I would pick up the latest copy of *Ebony* for him."

"Sure, no problem."

Emerald was about to begin her store-closing procedure when Holly ran into the store.

"I know it's late, but I'd like a copy of this month's *Ebony* magazine," she said breathlessly.

"Right here," Emerald said as she slid the magazine across the glass countertop.

"Thanks very much," Holly said and she was out the door.

Emerald felt a flicker of recognition cross her mind. I've seen that girl somewhere before. But where?

CHAPTER 6

Jay Collins dreaded the task that lay before him. The military funeral of his friend Barry Marshall had been difficult enough, but now he had to face the man's grieving widow again. This would surely bring more fresh pain into Elyse's life. But he had to carry out his friend's request.

He took a breath and exhaled deeply, replacing his cell phone in his pocket. Elyse had agreed to be in his office at three that afternoon. He had anticipated her questions.

"I thought all of Barry's affairs had been taken care of," she had said to him.

"Well," he had tried to explain, "there's a last bit of information that he wanted you to have. This was his wish, the delay, that is."

Elyse replaced her phone in its cradle, wondering why Jay Collins needed to talk with her.

As Barry's widow and executrix of his will, she was certain everything had been completed as dictated by her husband's will. The deed to the property they had secured before he went to Iraq had been changed into her name as the new property owner, and all debts that Barry had had already been paid. *What now?* she wondered.

That afternoon as she drove to the lawyer's office, she recalled the last time that she and Barry were together. On that memorable day Jay went over some legal documents, their wills, a copy of the deed to their land, and tried to reassure both of them about his availability to Elyse at any time. She blinked away her tears as she drove into the law office parking lot. She sat for a moment trying to steady herself. *This is so hard.*

After drawing a few deep breaths, she sighed, then checked her face in the rearview mirror. *Perhaps a fresh dab of lipstick would brighten my face a little,* she thought. She was still losing weight. Emerald was on her case about that, but even so, it wouldn't do to appear too haggard. It had been six months since Barry's death. She could not remember any details of the funeral except for the moment she was handed the flag with the presenter murmuring something about "a grateful nation" as her husband was laid to rest in the Cape Cod National Cemetery.

She could not remember how she had survived those harrowing frenetic days and nights after that visit from the military telling her the dreadful news that changed her life. She had endured the ordeal of the past six months only through the support of Emerald and, unexpectedly, Austin Brimmer.

It was Emerald who fed her body, encouraging her to eat.

"I know you like peas and rice, so, girl, I want you to try these," she'd say to Elyse, thrusting a steaming dish of the nourishing food in front of her. "Now, don't tell me you don't have an appetite! I don't care 'bout that! Just eat! An' you know I'm going to stay on your case 'til you do!"

With Austin it was different. Shortly after the Christmas holiday he had visited the store to find out how the raffle of his unusual decoupaged vase had turned out. Emerald had given him the news.

"Indeed, Austin, considering all that happened, we did fairly well with the raffle. You know Elyse's husband was killed overseas . . ."

"My God, no, I didn't know that. How awful! How . . . how is she doing?"

"I'd say as well as can be expected. We try to keep busy. The raffle went very well considering." She reached onto a shelf below the glass counter and handed him a slip of paper.

"Wow!" Austin said as he checked the slip. "You mean you sold over two thousand dollars in raffle tickets? That's amazing!"

"We did, and the winner of the raffle drawing was an elderly woman who donated the vase to a local art school."

"That's nice to know."

"We thought so, considering what was going on at the time."

"It must have been difficult. Please give Mrs. Marshall my deepest . . ."

"She's here, in her office. I think she would be pleased to see you."

"If you think . . ."

"I want to keep her on the side of the living," Emerald pointed out. "A fresh face will help, I think. Let me get her."

Austin tried to prepare himself. What did one say to a bereaved woman? *I'm sorry* did not seem at all adequate in such a situation.

Elyse came from her office at the rear of the store. Austin was not surprised to see how thin she had become. She approached him with a tentative smile. He reached for her hand. His voice was calm and he hoped reassuring and sincere.

"Mrs. Marshall, I'm *so* very sorry to hear of your loss. Is there anything, anything at all that I can do for you?"

He searched her face, saw the gleam of unshed tears in her eyes.

"Could you . . . would you . . . just, just hold me for a moment?" she asked in a quiet voice.

Wordlessly, astonished by her request, he pulled her close and held her. Her head rested on his chest. To him it felt as if he were calming a wounded bird. Her body trembled, and he could feel her boniness. He tightened his hold to steady her, murmured into her ear, "It's going to get better, I promise you. It *will* get better."

She stepped out of his embrace, breathed, "Thank you. I needed that . . . to feel a man's strong arms."

"Anytime, just let me know," he said with a warm smile. "These arms are available anytime you need them."

From that moment she began to heal. Austin provided encouragement.

"You've got to keep on keeping on," he'd say. Quite often he'd bring new artwork, posters, ceramics, even some jewelry that he had fashioned. These were always displayed in the front window of the shop. The customers seemed to look forward to the novel displays. Austin's card was always alongside to inform interested persons of his own store on Massachusetts Avenue.

"Austin has really been very good to us," Elyse remarked to Emerald one morning while they were having their coffee and muffins.

"I know, and I'm glad that there's someone like him. Like he said that day, you'll get better. I know you will. Now finish up that blueberry muffin, we've got work to do."

"Okay, my friend." Elyse smiled as she popped the last bit of muffin into her mouth.

She thought back to the day when Austin had held her in his arms at her request. She had felt strengthened by a man's strong arms, but did she have the strength she needed to go on living? Where would she find such strength?

Since Barry's death she had relied on support from Emerald and Ace. "Call me Ace, please," he'd said to them. "It's my nickname, all my friends do, and I'd like to think that you both are my friends."

So when the tears, deep sense of loss, feelings of fragmentation and abandonment overwhelmed her, it was one of them, or sometimes both, who offered food, a shoulder to cry on and encouraging words to help her face each day.

As she prepared to leave her car to go into Jay's office, she thought back to the support she was receiving from Emerald and Ace. There was no doubt in her mind that she owed them big time. Would the day ever come when she would be able to stand on her own two feet and face life again?

Her mother had been urging, "You should not be alone, Leese. Your father and I want you to stay with us, so we can keep an eye on you. Already you're too thin, not eating right. I can tell."

"No thanks, Mother. Got to weather this by myself," she'd said stubbornly.

CHAPTER 7

Jay got up from his desk, opened the small wall safe hidden behind a landscape. He retrieved an eight-by-ten brown envelope that bore his name on the upper left-hand corner. The front of the envelope had instructions that read *To Be Opened Six Months After My Death.*

Jay Collins placed the sealed envelope on his desk, then sat down and stared out of the window. It had turned out to be a beautiful June day, quite mild with plenty of sunshine.

On the intercom he heard his secretary announce, "Mr. Collins, Mrs. Marshall is here."

He punched the button.

"Send her in, please."

He greeted Elyse at the door, kissed her cheek and noticed that she looked quite attractive in a blue linen suit. The white silk blouse she wore, buttoned to the neck, gave her a slightly military appearance. Jay noticed, too, that she was wearing her husband's wedding band on a gold chain around her neck. *Good,* he thought, *she is no longer wearing it as a married woman.*

He offered her a drink. "What would you like, Elyse? Coffee, tea, or a cold drink?"

"Do you have Diet Coke?"

"Coming right up," he said. He reached into a small refrigerator beside his desk and poured the beverage into a Waterford glass. Placing it on a small tray, he set it on his desk where she could reach it.

First she unbuttoned her jacket, then picked up the drink. She took several sips.

"Guess I was thirsty."

"Right. It has gotten warm today. Seems all of a sudden summer is really here."

"Seems like it," she agreed.

"Elyse, how have you been? Is everything okay? Store doing well?"

"Yes, Jay, it's going rather well. Austin Brimmer, you remember him, displays his artwork at the store. It seems a natural enticement for customers."

He looked down at his desk at the envelope lying there. How would its contents affect the young widow who was waiting for him to explain why he had summoned her to his office?

He picked up the envelope.

"Elyse, I know you are wondering why I asked you to come here today. This packet," he tapped on the brown envelope, "was left in my care by Barry. He wanted you to receive this six months after his death." He handed it to her.

She pressed her hand on her chest. He saw tears well up in her eyes.

"Oh, my God, no!"

Jay could see how terribly shocked she was to see her husband's handwriting on the envelope she held in her hands.

"I don't know what's in it. You can see that it is sealed. BEM, Barry's initials, Barry Edward Marshall, are on the sealed flap."

As all the color drained from her face, Jay wondered if she would faint.

Taking a deep breath, Elyse picked up the envelope. Her hands trembled as she tried to break the seal. He stood up, prepared to leave. He tried to appear calm, matter-of-fact, hoping it would help her.

"I'll be in the office across the hall. Just call out and I'll come right away."

"Th-th-thanks, Jay," her voice quavered.

Finally, after he left, she was able to break the seal. She removed a single sheet of paper that had been torn from a yellow legal pad. Her husband's familiar cursive writing filled the page.

Barry's handwriting. *His hands were the last hands to touch this piece of paper*, she thought. She read very slowly, her eyes blurred with tears that she could not control.

She saw that the date was shortly before he was sent overseas. Her breath came in choking gasps as she tried to read. *My beloved, my darling Elyse*, it started, *if you are reading this, I was not able to come back to you as I promised. I am so sorry, because the last thing I ever wanted to do was to disappoint you. You were always the one constant in my life.*

She felt a distinct chill come over her entire body and at the same time her hands and face felt clammy, as if she had just touched something icy cold. Her breath came in short, rapid gasps as she tried to control the surge of emotion that engulfed her.

She wiped her eyes, swallowed some of the cold drink and again began to read her husband's last message.

However, my dearest, there is one final request I would like you to consider. This is the one thing that only you can do for us, for the love that we share.

A week ago, seems a lifetime ago now, I went to see Dr. Barnes. No, my dearest Elyse, there was nothing wrong with me. But, well, to make a long story short, as they say, I left a deposit with him. I deposited sperm to be frozen in case, well, you know. I am so sorry, my darling, that I had such selfish reasons for denying our wish to have our child. I cannot expect you to forgive me for putting my wishes before yours. Maybe you wondered if I really loved you. Please, I beg you to remember that I have never, ever loved anyone the way I have loved you. Please have our child. Only you can do this. I have explained to Dr. Barnes that this request is the only way I can atone for my selfish stubbornness. Always, your Barry.

She could hardly see. She shivered as a cool breeze blew through the open window.

"Oh, Barry, Barry," she sobbed as she clutched the letter to her heart. She could smell a faint whiff of his after-shave lotion. She closed her eyes as hot tears washed down her cheeks. She remembered their last night together.

"I will come home to you. I promise I will," he had insisted.

The thought flooded into her mind, *If I have our child, a little bit of Barry will come home to me.*

She knew what she had to do. First, she had to see Dr. Barnes.

Dr. Hollis Barnes's office was in a medical building not far from Massachusetts General Hospital.

A week after receiving her husband's letter Elyse called for an appointment, surprised when she was told that there had been a cancellation and that the doctor could see her within the next few days.

She dressed very carefully that morning, not really knowing why she felt she had to make a good impression.

She took the elevator to the fifth floor and walked into a pleasant waiting room. Several women were already present, each seeming to be in a different stage of pregnancy. She wondered what she would feel like . . . being pregnant with Barry's child. A few of the women acknowledged her with a brief smile, perhaps remembering their own once slim pre-pregnant figures.

She took a seat in the far corner of the room, somehow feeling as if she did not belong there, hearing her mother's voice echo in her mind. As usual, she had not hesitated to voice her strong opposition.

"Elyse! Girl, have you lost your mind? Why would you even consider having a baby? I know how much you're grieving for Barry, but, honey, he's gone. You don't want to be a single mother? Don't you know how hard that's going to be? Why on earth . . . what are you thinking? This is unheard of! Just nonsense, that's what."

Frances Joyce and her husband Jerome had discussed this new development in their daughter's life for hours on end. Elyse knew that. Her parents and her brother

Jack and his wife Marcella were solidly aligned against her.

Elyse shook her head as if to dislodge the negative thoughts her family had presented to her. She remembered her mother's face, flushed with dismay and anger that her only daughter could even *think* of trying to produce a child using her dead husband's frozen sperm.

"It's just unthinkable!" she had sputtered.

Seeking to end the discussion, Elyse had told her mother, "Mother, it's *my* life and my choice! If I want to have this child, and if my doctor says it's feasible to do so, then it will be my choice, not yours or anyone else's."

Now sitting in the waiting room, anxious to be called into the doctor's office, the uncomfortable, miserable scene with her mother reverberated through her mind.

Her mother was a tiny woman, but she never allowed her diminutive size to limit her in any way. She always spoke her mind, and her family's growth and success were due in no small part to her strength and no-nonsense maternal leadership. Elyse and her brother Jack always remembered how often even their father had deferred to their mother. "You'd better ask your mother," was their father's usual response to their questions. It was not that he was not a caring father, they knew he loved them, but they knew, too, that his response was easier for him. She wasn't at all surprised, however, when she received a call from her father one night.

"Elyse, honey, think it through, then make up your own mind. I love you and I want you to be happy."

"Thanks, Dad. I love you, too."

She sighed over the difficult memories that beset her. What would the doctor say? Would the procedure be difficult, painful? Would it be successful?

She looked at the stack of magazines on the table beside her chair. There was *Newsweek*, but she had already read that issue, so she replaced it and picked up a copy of the *The New England Journal of Medicine*. Perhaps she would find something of interest, she thought. She began to leaf through the pages. Most of the first few were medical advertisements. Then she reached the table of contents. On the list were reports of various studies and research. There was one that caught her eye. It was titled *How Can a Woman Determine if She Is Fertile, Able to Conceive?*

She began to read the article, hoping that she could finish reading it before being called into the doctor's office. Maybe she could take the magazine with her.

The article explained that women tend to believe that as long as they have menstrual periods they have healthy eggs. According to the article, even though eggs might be produced, they might not be of good quality. In addition, the article continued, a woman's fertility might be on the decline after age thirty-five.

Elyse, reading that fact, realized that her window of opportunity might be closing. She continued to read about a blood test that could predict a woman's fertility. Would Dr. Barnes want to do such a test on her?

"Mrs. Marshall?" a nurse called from an open doorway. Elyse hesitated for a moment, then decided to take the magazine with her. She walked toward the nurse, a young blonde who gave her a warm smile.

"How are you?" she asked, leading Elyse along a carpeted hall past several closed doors. "This is Dr. Barnes's office, Mrs. Marshall. He will speak with you here and then I will come in to prepare you for an examination. He'll be with you shortly."

The office windows overlooked the Charles River and Elyse could see sailboats moving gracefully across the quiet water. There were several diplomas and citations on the walls, and two large bookcases were filled with medical books and journals. Then the doctor came into the room.

Elyse thought that Dr. Hollis Barnes looked as if he could be anyone's uncle. He was a tall man with a broad, open, friendly face weathered to a leathery brown. But it was his eyes, dark yet warm, that greeted her and put her at ease. She relaxed.

Shaking her hand, he said, "First, I am very happy to meet you. Please let me express my deepest sympathy for your loss. I found your husband to be a wonderful man, and I do hope that I can help you to fulfill the dream that he had. It would be my distinct pleasure to help you achieve that goal. Your husband signed all the necessary forms, including the instructions to destroy his sperm if you decide not to use it. He wanted only you to bear his child . . . if, of course, that is what you wish to do."

"Right now I don't know what I really do want. My family has made very strong objections to my pursuit of this, especially my mother. But I, well, I loved Barry very much. And at first I thought how much I really want to have his child. He was my . . . my life, my reason for living . . . and now . . ." She sighed deeply.

"I understand. I am hoping that I can help you make that decision. It is yours to make, you know." he said quietly, all the while making direct eye contact with her. "No one," he continued, "can make this decision for you because you are the only person in the world who has this privilege to create a new life . . ."

"We were planning to have a child, but . . ."

"I see. Well, to start with I would need a complete medical history and a complete physical and gynecological workup. Afterwards, we could talk about the next steps and procedures if you decide to go forward."

Elyse nodded, tears of relief and hope in her eyes. Her voice was shaky when she finally spoke to the doctor.

"Dr. Barnes, my husband gave his life for his country, but he . . . he so wanted to live to start our family, build our home, and, well, if I can make part of that dream come true that's what I want to do."

"You loved him very much."

"Yes. I'm still in love with the memory of the wonderful man I married. And right now I feel that I'm no different than the many widows of the 9/11 tragedy who had to bear their babies alone."

"It's always a sad situation when a mother has to bear a child without the support of the child's father, but for centuries brave women have done just that. Any man on earth worth his salt has utmost admiration for mothers."

Then he reached into a desk drawer and retrieved a file folder.

"Before I begin, Mrs. Marshall, I must tell you that I was very impressed by your husband. He seemed very sincere, and completely focused on his wishes. And, yes, we do have his donation safe and secure. You need not worry. And . . . there is no hurry."

"So, when can you . . ." she started to ask.

He put down his pen.

"I understand your anxiety, Mrs. Marshall, but there are various steps we must take prior to fertilization. I'm going to put you through a series of tests. There will be certain hormones, medications you may have to take."

"And then?"

"Then we proceed. In the meantime, some medical questions. You don't drink or smoke?"

She shook her head in the negative.

"Good. I would like to see you gain a little weight. You seem a bit thin. Understandable, of course," he added. "And I'd like you to start taking multivitamins and folic acid. We want your body to be ready."

"For my baby. Mine and Barry's." She smiled at the doctor. "I can hardly wait," she told him. She had made her decision.

CHAPTER 8

Later that afternoon Elyse drove back to the store. She felt waves of stunning excitement race through her body as she thought of Dr. Barnes's last bit of advice.

"Be patient, be calm, and *believe* that all will be well."

She could hardly wait to share this news with Emerald, and Ace, too. As her friends, she hoped she would have their support.

She turned on the car radio, something she rarely did because she found it to be distracting. But today was different. Oh God, was it ever different! The sky was bluer, the air seemed fresher, and when the music came on it added to her happy, upbeat feeling. It was "Für Elise," a well-known sonata that she had learned to play on the piano. Her mother was a lover of classical music and had named her only daughter after that melody, changing only the spelling. Elyse listened to the familiar tune. Could that be a good omen? It had to be, from the way she was feeling. Dr. Barnes had said to be patient, and somehow she just knew that this miracle would come to fruition.

The store seemed busy when she opened the front door. There were a few customers at the checkout counter, and Elyse was glad to see that they were being taken care of by the two part-time workers, college students she had hired who were glad to have the jobs. Tia Spencer, her high school volunteer, was busily stacking books as Elyse hurried past her to the back room. She smiled and waved an acknowledgement to all of them and fled into her rear sanctuary, hoping that Emerald was there.

Emerald looked up from her computer as Elyse rushed into the room, throwing her handbag on her desk. She flopped into her chair, swinging her seat around to face her friend.

"So," Emerald asked, "how was your annual physical? Everything okay?"

"Better than okay. Perfect. Just perfect!" Elyse told her, then added in a quiet, matter-of-fact voice, "I'm going to have a baby."

Emerald dropped her pen on the floor, jumped up from her chair and stared, wide-eyed, disbelieving what Elyse had just said.

"You're going to have *what?*"

"I said I'm going to have a baby."

Disbelief, shock, and even horror widened Emerald's eyes as she wondered if Elyse had gone crazy.

"Girl, what on earth are you talkin' 'bout? Barry was overseas over a year." Then a light bulb went off in her head. "Leese, who you been sleeping with?"

"Nobody, *nobody, nobody,*" Elyse answered, sudden tears cascading down her face. "It's not like that!"

"Well, it's gotta be something! I know it's not the Immaculate Conception, so explain!"

She reached for her chair at her desk, knowing that if she did not sit down she would fall to the floor. Her legs had turned into jelly. She continued to try to understand.

"I know you've been under a lot of stress lately, but this sounds as if you've lost your mind! Girl, what in God's name are you talking about? Adoption? And why? Don't you have enough to keep you busy?"

Emerald's eyes flashed with incredulity and it seemed to her that Elyse had now somehow reached a precariously high level of insanity. She continued to stare at her friend, searching for some sign of craziness. But all she saw in front of her was a calm, serene woman who presented the usual clear-eyed posture that Em had always seen.

A bewildered, confused Emerald flopped back in her chair, waiting for an explanation of something she was finding very hard to believe.

Calmly, Elyse began to explain.

"I know this is hard for you to understand. It's been real hard for me. I didn't tell you before because I was real upset when I got a call from Jay Collins—"

"Your lawyer, I remember. What did he want to see you about? I thought all of Barry's affairs had been settled."

"I thought so, too, Em. That's why I was so mystified and upset. I didn't want to say anything until—"

"Come on, Elyse, why *did* Jay want to see you?"

"Well, you won't believe this . . ."

"Try me. At this point I'll believe the moon is made of green cheese," Emerald sputtered.

Suddenly Emerald saw tears welling up in her friend's dark eyes. She leaned forward, placed her hand on Elyse's knee.

"Tell me," she said softly. She reached for a tissue and placed it in the tearful woman's hand.

"Em, he . . . he had a letter that Barry had left . . . to be . . . to be opened," she choked, "six months after his death."

"A letter? For you?"

"Yes, a letter for me."

"You *are* going to tell me what it said, aren't you?" Emerald prompted, anxious to hear the whole story.

Elyse wiped her eyes, took a deep breath and exhaled slowly.

"Emerald, he had written this letter to me shortly before he was deployed overseas. He always promised me that he would come back to me, that we would build our house . . . start . . . start our family," she said quietly. "The letter was not to be opened until six months after he died. Jay had the letter in his safe."

"So he called you to his office to give you the letter? Go on," Emerald said.

"Well, like I said, he . . . he wrote this letter before he went overseas and . . ."

"And what?"

"He had deposited semen in a sperm bank and wanted me to use it . . . to have our child . . ."

"And you've decided to do this? Isn't this some kind of gamble, a crapshoot? Why on earth would you want to do this? Why?" Emerald could hardly contain her strong feeling of dismay. "Tell me, Elyse, why you want to do such a thing?"

"Because I am the only one who can," she said quietly.

"But Barry is dead! You'd be a single mother, with a lot of responsibility. Have you thought about that?"

Emerald sucked her teeth, shook her head as she thought about Elyse's announcement.

"I know. I hear you sucking your teeth. You've the same mindset as my mother."

"She thinks you've lost your mind, and so do I."

"Em, I'm not about to try to convince you, my mother, or anyone else because I am going to go ahead with this. Dr. Barnes . . ."

"You've already seen a doctor?" Emerald interrupted.

"Yes, I have, and he has assured me that I have a chance to have a healthy child. I have to face a lot of tests and there are many procedures that have to take place. But he says it can be done. Look, Emerald," her voice grew stronger, "my husband gave up his life, but we both wanted children. If I can have his child . . ."

"A child can't take his place," Emerald interjected soberly.

"I know that, but because of Barry a new life will come into the world. He or she will have a life because of Barry and the love that we shared. I want to do this, Em. Really I do."

Her tearful eyes implored her friend to understand, to support, to care.

Emerald reached for Elyse and placed her arms around the tearful young woman. Her heart understood.

"Don't cry, don't cry. Don't worry 'bout a thing, 'cause I'm going to be with you every step of the way. This will be about the biggest project we've ever done, but we can do it!"

"Oh, Em! What would I do without you?"

"Told you before, I'm in it for the long haul. Just sit there for a minute." She pushed the teary-eyed Elyse back in her chair.

"Got some wine here in the fridge. We're going to have us a toast to get this action going!"

She raced to the back room. Elyse smiled as she heard the wine cork pop and the sound of glasses being filled. She prayed silently, *Dear God, help me, please help me.*

Can I do this? Should I? Or am I just being willful and stubborn? She prayed silently for guidance, knowing full well how much she *wanted* to be a mother . . . to have *this* child. She swore to herself that she would be a more loving, warmer mother than her own had been. This child would know love.

CHAPTER 9

"Dr. Barnes said that I should not drink or smoke," Elyse said to Emerald when she returned with the chilled wine on a tray, "but since I'm not pregnant yet, this shouldn't count."

She sipped the wine, slowly thinking about her new situation.

"What else did he say?" Emerald asked.

"Mainly that there are a lot of tests. Check my ovaries, my egg count, and that I should try to gain a little weight."

Emerald nodded in agreement.

"I should start taking multivitamins, folic acid, and he said he's going to start me on birth control pills to stop my menstrual cycle. Then he will be able to regulate my egg production to determine the proper time for fertilization."

"God, sounds like there's a lot to this."

"I think there is, and I'm sure the doctor is only telling me what I need to know for the time being. I'd be just overwhelmed otherwise. Listen, I'm going to wash my face and get out front. Seems a fair number of customers out there."

"Okay, and if you need my help, let me know."

Elyse got up from her chair, stretched out her arms and shrugged her shoulders as if making a fresh start.

She'd started to walk to the small lavatory tucked in the room's far corner when she stopped, turned to look at Emerald.

"And oh, Em . . ."

Emerald put her fingers to her lips and made a key-locking gesture.

"You don't have to say it, kiddo. This conversation we just had never took place. You *know* that. Don't have to reckon nothin' 'bout it."

"Thanks, Em."

"No problem, hon."

Because he had been very busy at his store, Ace Brimmer had not made any recent visits to The Kwanzaa Book and Gift Shop. He had designed some animal molds from clay, fired them and then decoupaged them.

He had created a figure of a giraffe that stood about eighteen inches tall, and a hefty elephant with ivory tusks. It was about twenty inches high. Each piece had been decoupaged with the appropriate markings and coloring.

The idea in Ace's mind was that these ceramic figures would enhance any African-American's home. He decided to share the pieces, along with a zebra figure, with Elyse and Emerald to get their opinions. Perhaps he would even exhibit one in the store's front window.

When Ace appeared at the front door, his arms full, Emerald met him at the door and opened it, noting his awkwardly shaped packages.

"Ace, man! Where have you been?"

"Whoo," he panted, "just let me put these down. How are you?"

"Oh, I'm fine. Everything's going good."

He smiled at her as he set his bundles down on a nearby book table.

"That's good to hear, Em. Look, I brought some figurines that I want to show you and Elyse. She here?"

"Elyse?" Emerald called out to the back of the store. "Ace is here. Has something he wants to show us."

"Coming, one moment," Elyse called back.

Ace could hear her high heels tapping on the floor and when she came into view from behind the book stacks he was awestruck. She looked so vibrant, so alive. Her eyes were bright and her hair . . . She had cut it short and wore it with sleek, wispy curls around her face. She looked at least five years younger than when he'd last seen her. He didn't know what had changed her but she *was* different. Before, a heavy dark aura of sadness had seemed to hover over her. Today that sadness was gone and in its place he saw an almost incandescent glow.

"My God, you look wonderful, Elyse! Mind if I put my arms around you once more? You look so good. Maybe you don't need a friendly hug."

"A friendly hug is always welcome," she said as she walked into his embrace. "Good to see you, Ace."

For Ace the moment became an epiphany, a revelation. This woman was becoming very important to him. Quickly, he let her step away, afraid that his feelings might show and he knew it was much too soon for that to happen.

His face flushed from the emotional tension he was undergoing at that moment, so he turned quickly to his wrapped packages. He knew both women had their eyes on him, watching as he unwrapped each one. First, the elegant giraffe, its long neck stretched up from its sleek but muscular body. The decoupaged effect, shiny gold with glistening black spots, was striking. Both Elyse and Emerald gasped with delight as Ace placed the figure in the front window.

"Ace, it's beautiful!" Emerald said.

"This is my idea of *zirafah*, an Arabic word for giraffe, although its origin is probably African," he told them.

Then he unwrapped the elephant figure, its thick muscular trunk raised in a triumphant gesture.

He saw the delight in Elyse's eyes when he revealed the statue.

Elyse picked up the figure. "Oh, Ace, I must have this one! Got to have it! It's one of my sorority's symbols!"

He grinned, pleased with her reaction.

"Then you shall have it!"

"How much is this beautiful treasure?"

"The delight in your face is all the pay I need. It's yours, with my pleasure."

Standing by watching the two, Emerald sensed a distinct change in the budding relationship between them. For a brief moment it was as if she was not even in the room.

Then, seeming to remember that Emerald was quietly observing them, Elyse said to her, "Do you like it, Em?"

"I do. Really, I do like it. Ace," she winked at him, "you know how to create magic with that artistic talent you have. These pieces are so original, so unusual, one of a kind. Go *on*, my brother!"

CHAPTER 10

Holly's new assignment was proving to be rewarding. She was excited and motivated by the new experiences of working with occupational, physical and speech therapists. She found that she was anxious to get to her job. Each day presented new challenges, and she realized she felt eager to meet them.

Branch was delighted with the positive change he saw in her. He had stronger hopes for their future together now that she was so much happier.

"Holly, hon, I'm so glad you're doing so well in this new job of yours. You really like it, don't you?"

"Branch, it's finally the way to a better future. I see positive changes in the patients. I see them make steady improvement, and they are so happy, making plans to go home. It's not at all like the patients I took care of before. Of course, I do miss my old patients, like Mr. Harkins. And I do stop in to see him when I can."

"I'll bet he misses you."

"Well, he does scold me sometimes. Says 'Not the same, child, when I don't see your young face round here.' But he did say he was happy that I was 'movin' on up.' I miss him, too. He was one of my favorites."

Branch had negotiated a turn into a street that would take them to Columbus Avenue in the South End. They had agreed that morning that, since it was Friday, they would go out to dinner. They were headed to Papa Joe's Ribs and Soul, a down-home restaurant. Although located in a small strip mall, the building stood alone, a one-story sandstone-colored brick building with a five-foot-wide swath of green grass on its front and sides.

A green awning with a scalloped border proclaiming that this was Papa Joe's hung over the entrance.

Holly and Branch got out of the car and walked to the wide wooden door that had decals of American Express, Visa and Discover cards posted on its stained glass window.

The pair stepped into a small alcove, breathed with relief as the welcome air conditioning swept over them. There were several chairs where patrons could sit while waiting for a table. They walked up to the lectern to be greeted by a young black man dressed in a black tuxedo.

"Good evening, sir, ma'am," he said.

"Good evening," Branch answered.

Knowing how busy Friday nights were at the restaurant, Branch had already made a reservation.

"A diner reservation for Adkins," he told the maitre'd.

The man checked his list, picked up two menus from a slot beside his lectern, and after making a check mark beside the name Adkins, said, "Please follow me, sir. Your table is ready."

He led them to a table on the right. A window looked out to the street, but there was little foot traffic on the sidewalk.

"Is this acceptable, sir?"

"This is just fine," Branch said as the maitre'd seated Holly and handed each a menu.

"Enjoy your dinner. Your server will be with you shortly."

Holly looked around the room. Pictures of famous black people formed a montage on the walls over the booths. There were black and white photos of Quincy Jones, a smiling Count Basie, Louis Armstrong and his trumpet, Ella Fitzgerald, Nancy Wilson, and even younger persons such as Wynton Marsalis, Stevie Wonder and Queen Latifah. Many of the photos showed Papa Joe posed with the entertainers. His white starched uniform hid some of the bulkiness of his large, muscular body and the pleated toque on his gray head added distinct authority. This was a man who knew who he was and exactly what he was doing.

A jazz trio, piano, drums and bass guitar, were seated on a raised platform. In front of them was a small parquet dance floor. A few couples were making good use of it. The music invited them to do so.

"This joint is jumpin'," Holly said to Branch.

"Sure is."

Papa Joe's place smelled really good. Word of mouth had made him justifiably famous for his southern cooking. It was well-known, for example, that he marinated his barbecued ribs overnight in a secret recipe containing bourbon and rum. The swinging door from the kitchen sent enticing scents of freshly baked cornbread and cinnamon- and brown sugar-candied sweet potatoes.

Holly was glad to see their waiter approaching their table. She was hungry.

"Good evening. My name is Lucas Anthony. I will be your server tonight. May I get you something to drink?"

"A light beer for me," Branch said.

"Water with a slice of lemon, please," Holly said.

"I'll be right back and then I'll take your orders."

"Seems like a nice young man," Holly observed, watching the waiter move away. He was tall, with the slender, leggy body of a tennis player. His brown skin had a healthy bronze glow, as if he'd spent many hours outside.

"Could be a college student working his way through."

Holly nodded her head in agreement.

"I know what it's like to have to work so hard. Thank God I don't have to do *that* anymore."

"Holly, you don't know how glad I am to see you so happy. I was really worried about you one time back there, but now . . ."

"I'm very lucky, Branch, and I know it. Believe me, I'm going to do my very best to make the most of this opportunity. Somehow I feel that I have a better chance of making it now."

Lucas, their waiter, brought their drinks to them and took their orders.

"I would like the home fried chicken, the breast, please, and peas and rice with a side order of candied sweet potatoes. And may I have a house salad, vinaigrette dressing?"

"Yes, ma'am," Lucas said, turning to Branch. "Sir?"

"Please bring me an order of ribs with red beans and rice. Do you have scalloped tomatoes?"

"Indeed we do, sir."

"Good. I'll have a side order of that and the house salad with Thousand Island dressing. Oh, and another 'light,' please."

"My pleasure, sir."

They sat quietly, listening to the music and watching the couples dancing.

"Know what, Branch?" Holly asked.

"What?"

"I'm thinking that maybe I can start taking some college courses part time at night."

"Good idea!" he agreed. "There's nothing wrong with night school as long as it doesn't interfere with your day job, and you don't try to overload. Maybe one or two courses a semester."

"I understand. Probably go slow, rev up my study habits."

"You know, Holly, you're an inspiration. I might try to do the same thing. I always wanted to go to med school."

Holly's face brightened. "Let's see what we can figure out. Maybe go to the same school . . . that is, if you're willing to provide the transportation. I'd help with the gas."

"To be with you, my girl, I'd drive you anywhere, and don't worry about the gas. Are you kidding me?"

"The more I think about it, the more I think I should try. Maybe, Branch, we should check, see what's available out there. Get some catalogs, go online . . ."

"Right. What would be your major, your goal?"

"I think nursing, perhaps make geriatrics my specialty. People seem to be living longer these days, and since I already know about working with the elderly, that's a place to start. What do you think?"

"Sounds practical to me. You've been working in that field so I'd say you have a leg up."

"What about you, Branch?" Holly asked as she twisted her stemmed water goblet. "What do you want to study?"

"Always wanted to do something in the medical field. I like what I'm doing now in the OR, but there are limits, and I won't be able to go any farther than I am right now. But I do know there is a career that I'd like to look into."

"What is it?"

"It's called physician's assistant."

"I've never heard of that. What, you're like a doctor or something?"

"No, not really, but you can do some of the things doctors do now."

"Really?"

"Yeah. You can provide a diagnosis, some therapy and preventive health care under the supervision of a physician. You can examine the patient, take medical histories, order and read lab tests, lots of stuff like that. But I'd need to get my bachelor's degree. Already have a couple of semesters under my belt. I think I'd be happy if I could become a PA. They make good money, too."

"You know, Branch, it seems to me that we should do something with our lives that we want to do, not *let* our lives just happen."

Branch felt his heart lighten up, and a feeling of hope and well-being swept over him. Just perhaps this new, more optimistic attitude would be the path to the other major goal he sought, that of a loving, lasting relationship with this girl, Holly Francis.

Their meal came then and they were both hungry, so for a few minutes they ate in silence.

Finally Holly took a deep breath, leaned back in her chair.

"I didn't know how famished I really was," she said. "This food is great, isn't it?"

"Glad you're enjoying it."

Holly saw the friendly warmth in his eyes and knew that she had never had a better friend than Branch Adkins. She picked up her fork and returned to her food. She noticed a family being escorted to a table near where they were seated. She watched as the younger of two boys pulled out the chair to seat his mother. The lad looked up at his parents, smiled at the words of praise his family gave him. He acted real grownup as he took his own seat. Holly thought he could have been about eight years old.

"Branch, did you see that? That little boy was so proud to seat his mother."

"Yes, I did. Shows that those two boys are being well brought up. Most black families expect good manners from their kids."

She agreed, nodding her head.

"I'm thankful that my mother and grandmother wouldn't tolerate any nonsense from me. And not having a father, well . . ." Her eyes softened.

"You missed that, didn't you?"

"I guess. I always wondered what he was like."

"What do you really know about him?"

Branch didn't want to upset Holly, but he sensed she wanted to broach the subject of her dad.

"My mother said that he was eighteen, a college student, and that they both decided to give me up for adoption. Mother was sixteen, and both thought too young to start a family. She said that my father signed away all responsibility so that I could be adopted, but she said my grandmother talked her out of that and the two of them raised me."

"Do you ever think about finding him?"

"When I was younger, but not so much anymore."

"Know his name?"

"Mother once told me . . . Barry. Barry something. I'm not sure."

"Probably could find him if you went online, made a search."

"H-m-m-m. Maybe, maybe not," she said quietly.

Wisely, he decided not to pursue the topic. He had noticed a sadness in her face. Maybe later he'd bring up the search business again if and when she seemed more amenable to the idea.

CHAPTER 11

It turned out to be a warm summer morning Elyse drove Barry's Volvo to keep her appointment with Dr. Barnes. She left Mattapan Square and drove down Blue Hills Avenue, noticing and thinking about all the changes that had taken place in the area. Formerly the area had been the core of Jewish families; now it was redefined by new residents, mainly African-American.

There was the former delicatessen known as the B&B, named for two brothers. It was famous not only for its fine food, but had become legend as the place for politicians to meet and greet. Elyse smiled as she drove past the building, now a Caribbean food mart. She recalled being told that presidents from Roosevelt to JFK had made stops at the well-known spot.

She continued down Warren Street to Melnea Cass Boulevard, named for an African-American woman who had been active in civic affairs. Soon she found herself merging with traffic entering the city and she breathed a sigh, releasing the tension she had been feeling as she exited Route 93 onto Cambridge Street. Within minutes she drove into the parking lot beside the medical building.

It was such a beautiful day that Elyse felt her spirits soaring with hope. She took the elevator to the fifth floor. Her mother's admonitions still echoed in her mind.

"I hope you know what a burden you're taking on, one that you don't need, just to prove a point. Whose, I don't know," her mother had railed at her. "And," she had hammered at Elyse, "how are you going to pay for all these tests and stuff you have to go through?"

"Don't worry, Mother, my medical insurance will cover it. And I have Barry's life insurance as well," she explained, knowing that if she didn't, her mother would keep nattering at her.

As she exited the elevator, she shook her head as if to release the negative thoughts. Today was not the day to be burdened with troublesome thoughts.

⁓◎

"Good morning, Mrs. Marshall, how are you?" Dr. Barnes said when he entered the examination room.

Elyse was sitting on the exam table, feeling quite undressed as she was clothed only in the obligatory hospital gown called a "johnny." She wondered how it had gotten that name. She accepted the doctor's warm handshake, buoyed by his friendly approach. His touch was businesslike and firm as he completed his examination.

"Everything is just fine." He smiled at her as he washed his hands at the sink. "You may get dressed, and I'll speak with you in my office."

In his office he directed her to a comfortable chair and opened her file.

"First, everything looks good. We're right on track. First, I'm going to start you on medication that will stop your periods. Then we'll place you on hormones to increase your egg production. And we do need to regulate your ovarian cycle. We have to determine the optimum time to perform the sperm implantation. Okay?"

She nodded.

"You're going to be a fantastic mother, I just know it," he added.

"Thank you, Doctor. I hope so."

"Not to worry, you will be."

"Could I . . . could I ask you a question?"

"Oh, of course, by all means, my dear. What's on your mind?"

"How long will this preparation be? Will I be pregnant this time next year?" she wanted to know.

"Possibly, but we really can't set a timetable until we see how your body responds. We will move forward quickly and steadily as dictated by the progress we make. Remember, I said 'be patient.'" He smiled as if he wanted to put her mind at ease. "I realize this is a new experience for you. But I want you to be excited and, yes, happy, too, as you go through the most extraordinarily rewarding experience in your life. It happens every day, but it is still magic, still unbelievable. You'll see."

"Just hope I can do it. So many of my family . . ." She thought again of her mother, whose support she so badly needed and wanted. "So many are against . . ."

"But it's what you want and your husband wanted, so that's all that matters," he said. "You are feeling well?"

"Quite well, Dr. Barnes."

"Not having any difficulties?"

"None, but I have gained five pounds."

"That's fine. I should tell you that it's very possible you may experience some mood swings from sadness to euphoria. Don't worry if that happens. It is to be expected. The hormones, you see."

" 'Forewarned is forearmed,' right?"

"I've always thought so, and I try to educate my patients, give them any information I think would be helpful."

Elyse was feeling optimistic, hopeful that Dr. Barnes was more than capable . . . would help her fulfill her dream of bearing a healthy child.

She waited for the doctor to continue his instructions, acutely aware of the importance of what he was telling her. Both hands clenched in her lap, she focused on his next words of advice.

"As I told you, so far everything indicates that we move forward. When the time comes to start your hormone injections, I will refer you to a nurse. She will administer the shots, and hopefully will be able to instruct someone to give them to you. Do you have such a person?"

She thought of Emerald. Could she, would she, be willing to learn how to do such a procedure?

"Yes," she said, "I think my co-worker might be able to do it. She's quite capable, levelheaded, not easily rattled . . . most of the time. If it's something she can do to help, I think she'd try."

"Fine, there's no rush. We'll cross that bridge when we come to it."

He stood up to shake her hand, and as he walked her to the door, he said, "Stay well and I'll see you next month."

CHAPTER 12

Khaleda Hubbard arrived at the bookstore on time. Elyse had made the appointment, suggesting her store as the place where she would be available for the series of intramuscular injections.

"I have a sort of office lounge and small bathroom at my store if you wouldn't mind coming here," she explained when she called the nurse. "My store opens at ten, but I'll be here at nine, and my friend Emerald will be here to observe."

When she came in that morning, Elyse saw a short, robust-looking young woman dressed in jeans with a blue floral smock. She wore white socks and white Birkenstocks. She flashed a wide, friendly smile as she entered the store.

"Good morning. I'm Khaleda Hubbard, but please call me Khali," she said brightly. Elyse relaxed, sensing at once that she was in capable hands. Khali's soft brown skin and dark eyes added to her patient's sense of well-being. Elyse saw the nurse's interest in the store as she looked around at the elephant statue in the front window, which Emerald had positioned on a patch of grass. The nurse admired the books, posters and the children's nook with its low chairs and rocking chair.

"This is a beautiful store that you have. How long have you been here?"

"About four years," Elyse said with pride.

"Good for you! I always like it when I see a sister making it."

"Thanks. Won't you follow me? I'll show you where you can set up. My office is right back here at the rear of the store. We have sort of a lounge, and a bathroom, too."

"Lead the way."

The nurse seemed like a real no-nonsense person and Elyse liked that.

"Here we are," she said. "And this is my friend and confidante, Emerald Stokes." She introduced Emerald, adding, "I'm hoping you can teach her how to give me my injections."

The two women shook hands.

"Nice to meet you, Emerald."

"Nice to meet you, too. So, you're going to turn me into a nurse?" Emerald teased.

"Not to worry, no problem. By the time I get through with you, you'll be Florence Nightingale personified!"

The concrete walls of the store's back room had been painted a cheerful creamy pale yellow. In front of the wall was situated a dark blue chenille sofa with inviting throw pillows of blues, golds and reds. The tiled floor of muted grays had been enhanced by one Oriental rug directly in front of the sofa.

At a right angle to this wall, two desks with office chairs had been placed side by side. Computers, printers, desk lamps and other office equipment indicated that this area was the heart of the bookstore.

A section of three panels with a black and white silk screen, Khali was told, hid a microwave and refrigerator.

High cellar-type windows with tan Roman shades added to the room's comfort and serenity. There was even a leather recliner with a table and lamp beside it.

"What a lovely room," Khali observed.

"We like it. It's our home away from home," Elyse told her.

"Is it okay if I put my bag here? I need a place to lay out my equipment."

"By all means. I'll move the computer back to make room."

"That's fine."

"I take it you have a bathroom nearby?"

"Sure do," Emerald said. "I'll show you."

She led the way to the small bathroom with toilet and sink in the back hallway.

"This is perfect, Emerald." She proceeded to wash her hands.

"Although I'll be wearing gloves," she explained, "it's still very important to wash your hands thoroughly before starting the procedure."

They returned and Khali opened her nurse's bag. She took out a sealed packet and opened it to remove a sterile towel, which she placed on the space Elyse had cleared for her. She laid out an ampoule, alcohol swabs in sealed packets, a sterile capped syringe with an attached needle, a small metal file and latex gloves.

As she watched, Elyse thought about her family's fierce disapproval of what she was doing.

"You're just hardheaded and stubborn," her mother had thundered at her when she learned that her daughter was about to begin the assisted reproduction treatment.

Elyse remembered her mother's angry face when Elyse responded, "This may be my only chance to become a mother, and it's what I *want* to do. And, Mother, you have to accept *my* decision whether you like it or not."

As she watched Khali lay out the equipment, she had to ask, "Do you have many patients getting this treatment?"

"Oh my, yes. You'd be surprised at the number of women undergoing this procedure."

"Married women?"

"No, not all are married. A great many are single women who want to be mothers but have not met Mr. Right. Their biological clocks are ticking, so many of them decide to use donated sperm as a means of having children. You'd be surprised at the number." She gave Elyse a warm smile, sensing her patient's anxiety.

She turned to Emerald. "I want you to observe what I do and then later I will have you practice with an orange."

"An orange?" Emerald's eyebrows rose in question marks.

"Yes, an orange will give you the feeling of the muscle's resistance. And I'll show you the proper site for the injection and observe you until you feel comfortable doing it."

"Good," she said to Elyse, "you're wearing slacks. Why don't you pull them and your panties down. Lie face down on the couch and we'll get started. I know that you've been on medication to stop your menses, and today we'll start you on a hormone to increase your egg production. We want you to have a reasonable number of eggs so that fertilization with the sperm donation will be effective."

Raising her head from the pillow, Elyse asked, "How will you know that?"

"Usually the doctor does a needle sonogram . . ."

"Isn't that painful?"

"Oh no, it's done under general anesthesia. There's no discomfort. Now," she said briskly, "let's get the show on the road. Emerald, I want you to stand right here so you can look over my shoulder."

The procedure was accomplished quickly and Elyse seemed to tolerate it well.

"I usually stay around for twenty minutes or so to monitor any reactions you might have, although you did very well. Do you feel all right?"

"Yes, I feel fine."

"Just to be sure, lie still for a moment or so."

Emerald had disappeared soon after the injection had been completed. She came from behind the screen with a tray containing three coffee mugs and slices of coffee cake, plus packets of sugar and a small bowl of creamers.

"Let me get the coffee," she said as she hurried back to the makeshift kitchen. "This is not the way it's usually done, but folks, we're going to have us a baby!"

"What's today's date?" Elyse asked.

"June fourteenth, Flag Day," Emerald said.

"I calculate, with good luck in your cycles, you could be pregnant by August and have our baby in April. How about that?" Khali grinned.

Elyse shook her head and her hands trembled as she put her coffee mug down on the coffee table. "It will be the miracle that I always wanted," she said quietly.

"And if it will help you any," Khali said, "you are not the only patient that I have who is having her deceased husband's child. So take heart. And if you need me, just let me know, anytime."

As she watched the confident friendly nurse leave, Elyse thought, *Maybe this is not happening in the usual way, but I'm going to have a baby, a part of Barry, and that's what I want.*

CHAPTER 13

After a few more days of instruction, Khali felt that Emerald was quite proficient in administering the injections Elyse required. She also told Elyse not to be alarmed if she should experience mood swings from elation to depression. "It's only because of the increased hormonal activity, so just ride it out. It's not something that will last. Most all mothers go through episodes like that. And remember, you have my cell phone number. Call anytime."

Emerald had just completed the injection for the day.

"Four more to go, and I'll take off my nurse's uniform," she told Elyse.

"And a good thing, too. My behind feels like a pin cushion." Elyse rubbed her right buttock, scowling as she did so.

"No pain, no gain. You know the drill, my friend."

"Wonder what they'll put me through next?"

Elyse adjusted the rubber ring on her chair and sat down gingerly.

"When's your doctor's appointment?"

"A week from Thursday."

"Dr. Barnes will probably tell you then."

"I expect he will, but whatever it is, I'm ready to keep going. I've made my decision to fulfill Barry's wishes."

"Look, honey," Emerald said as she handed Elyse another book. They were stacking an order of new books on the display rack. "I know this is a new experience for you. Can't be easy, and I admire your spunk in taking it on. Remember, you have to be strong and think ahead to the wonder and love you will feel when you hold your baby in your arms, a real manifestation of the love you and Barry shared. A whole lot of folks never have that chance. Consider yourself blessed."

"Oh, Em, I do, I do. I'm blessed to have a friend like you," she insisted as she hugged her.

The telephone rang then, interrupting their work rhythm.

Emerald answered the phone on the store's front counter.

"The Kwanzaa Book and Gift Shop. Oh, good morning, Ace. How are you?" Elyse heard her say. "Oh, we're fine. Working hard, you know. Yes, she's here, one moment."

She handed Elyse the phone and went to the back room, not wishing to intrude on the conversation. Ace's interest in Elyse was evident to her . . . but to Elyse?

"Good morning, Ace. How are you?" In answer to his first question she said, "I'm well, thanks." In answer to his next question, she said, "Not tonight, Ace. I've promised to . . ." She broke off as Ace, obviously disappointed, interrupted her.

"Right, Ace, keep in touch. By the way, many customers have admired your new figurine. I've given out many of your cards to interested folks."

He must have thanked her because she said, "No problem, Ace. Stay well."

She hung up, keenly aware of Ace's letdown, but at the moment she had enough on her plate to consider.

Emerald was drinking coffee when Elyse returned to the back room. She raised her cup in question, asking if Elyse wanted a cup.

"I'd better have milk. No coffee, doctor's orders."

"So, when are you going to tell him?"

Elyse shrugged. "Not yet. As far as I'm concerned, it's a 'need to know' situation. And," she reflected, "there's no need for him to know. Not yet, anyway."

In a dry tone of voice, Emerald said, "Better think about when you're gonna tell him. He wants to be more than a friend. Any blind man can see that."

"Em, you know I've never encouraged him. You know that. Never! All I have on my mind is Barry. It even seems to me that he's closer to me than ever, planning and . . . trying to have this baby. It's all that I can deal with right now."

"Just ought to be prepared, is all I'm sayin'," Emerald added.

"I'll decide after I see Dr. Barnes next week."

When she kept her appointment with the doctor, she was not surprised when he greeted her in his usual cheerful manner.

"We're right on track," he told her. "The needle sonogram revealed that you have a healthy egg supply. You didn't have any problems after the procedure, did you? You seemed to tolerate it well."

"Only a bit of anxiety, but no real discomfort," she told him, adding, "What's next?"

"As I outlined to you when we started, Mrs. Marshall, I believe the in vitro fertilization, IVF . . . simply bringing together the egg and sperm in the lab, in vitro, is the most expedient method to use in your case. We perform intracytoplasmic sperm injection by puncturing the egg directly under a microscope and injecting one sperm into it."

"When do you put the . . ." She was very anxious to know when she would finally be pregnant.

"We check to determine if fertilization has taken place under the microscope. We usually do this for a few days. Most times we transfer three or four eggs into a catheter. But this time, three days or more, the embryo has developed into six to eight cells. We transfer these embryos through the cervix and into the uterus. In about two weeks I will do a pregnancy test, and in another two weeks an ultrasound can be performed and we'll be able to hear a fetal heartbeat."

"I can't believe that I'm going to have a baby. When . . . when I found out that Barry had been killed, I wanted to die myself. All the hopes and dreams we had were gone . . . all gone. But now it's possible that I can do something that we both wanted, have our child. Life is worth living now, thanks to you, Doctor Barnes."

"Mrs. Marshall, my dear, it's times like these, bringing joy to patients, that makes my work so rewarding."

He sat down at his desk to check his calendar. "I want to see you next Thursday. Report to the outpatient department at the hospital at eight in the morning. Remember, nothing by mouth. And I suggest you have someone to drive you home."

Elyse left the doctor's office, buoyed by his optimism. He had informed her that Barry's donated sperm, cryopreserved, would be removed from storage, incubated to thaw the frozen sperm, then used to fertilize her retrieved eggs.

She reached her car. Actually it was her husband's treasured Volvo that she usually drove to her appointments with the doctor. It made her feel closer to Barry. After all, she reasoned, they were truly in this adventure together. Her hands caressed the leather steering wheel cover as she had seen Barry's strong, capable hands do so many times before.

"We're on our way, honey," she whispered as she belted herself in the car. *"Can hardly wait,"* she said under her breath. She could almost hear his voice, *"That's my girl, my beautiful Elyse."*

She could see his handsome face smiling at her with love and approval. He had always been her hero.

CHAPTER 14

Holly met Branch on Saturday morning at Summit University's library. Saturday morning was a good time to do so because so many students slept in after Friday night parties and all-night drinking sessions.

Holly had worked the night before at the nursing home to fill in for one of her friends who needed the time off to attend a family funeral out of town. She was happy to earn the extra money.

"It was really an easy babysitting gig," she told Branch. "The patient's family was so guilty about putting Ma in a nursing home, they wanted her to have special care around the clock. She slept all night, and to tell you the truth, so did I," she laughed. "Did get some homework done, though."

"That's great! What are you working on now?" Branch wanted to know. He dropped his book bag on the table next to her stack of books.

"I'm doing a paper on chronic illnesses found in the geriatric population. You know," she ticked off on her fingers, "hypertension, diabetes, stroke, cardiac conditions, etc."

"Right. That information should not be hard to find. Be sure to put in a lot of statistics. That always impresses the professors."

"I'll do that. What are you working on?"

"Me? I have to get ready to do a one-on-one with a patient."

"One-on-one. What does that mean?"

"What I have to do is interview a patient, perform a physical exam, make an assessment, then present my findings to the doctor. Something like I'd be expected to do, say, in the triage area of a hospital."

"Well, all right then!" Holly cheered. "Almost like a real doctor."

"Don't I wish?" Branch replied soberly. "Don't I wish?"

"Never mind," Holly tried to comfort him, "you never know what's down the road for you, Branch. I say never give up hope, and go after whatever it is that you want."

"Even if it takes years?"

"Of course. Even if it takes years."

"You're probably right, Holly. We didn't, either of us, know we'd be in college. Weren't we lucky that Summit University gave us so many credits for our work experiences? You know, if we take courses this summer, we'll be much closer to getting our degrees."

"Now you're talking!" Holly gave him a wide grin and a high-five. "Let's hit the books. Time is marching on, you know."

"That's what I love about you, girl," Branch said as he pulled books out of his book bag. "All you ever need is a chance and . . ."

"That's all any of us need. You know that. Just a chance. Branch?" Holly asked.

"Yes?"

"When we leave here today, can we stop at The Kwanzaa Book Shop?"

"Of course, don't see why not."

"It's Mr. Harkins. He's becoming quite a reader. Now he wants to read some books by black authors."

"Good for him."

"It's really amazing to me, the excitement he shows about reading, current events, *all* that stuff. Wonder what he did for a living?"

"You should ask him. Be interesting to find out."

Ace was deeply disappointed by Elyse's refusal to go out with him. He realized, however, that she was still grieving for her dead husband. Who wouldn't? But *all* he really wanted to do for now was to give her a change of pace.

He hung up the phone and went to the basement to check on his kiln. He had some new pieces that he had already fired, and by now the kiln was cool enough for him to retrieve them. There were small gift boxes and some ceramic pins, and he tried to duplicate some of the tribal masks he had seen in Africa.

He had even replicated some of the ornate shields from Cameroon. There were also tiny bud vases, and he had experimented with a set of nesting bowls that he planned to decoupage much like his earlier work.

As he worked, he wondered if perhaps he should *not* pursue the young widow. But remembering the feelings he'd had when she had stepped into his arms, it seemed she belonged there. As he thought about her beauty, her dark eyes with their slightly oriental slant, her lovely soft skin, her regal stature like a Nubian queen, he knew he had to get to know her better. Perhaps, he thought, time was what she needed. He remembered the phrase that time was a healer. He reasoned that perhaps time and patience would be on his side. And, as he recalled, she had been looking much healthier the last times he'd seen her at her store. The thought encouraged him. It could be that as she became healthier, her grief would subside and he would be there for her. One thing he did know, was positive about—he had never felt this way about a woman before.

The more people like her parents and brother were against her decision, the more determined Elyse was to go ahead with her plans.

For over a quarter of a century, since those two English doctors had successfully succeeded in an effective fertility procedure, more than 20,000 babies had been born in England by that method. So why shouldn't she have a baby that way? Elyse thought, reviewing in her mind what Dr. Barnes had told her. She surmised, too, rightly or wrongly, that despite her education and her successful business, many people viewed her as needing protection, needing to be sheltered from adversity, coddled, as it were. She had always had to try to make her own way, stand on her own ground; even her own husband had made it his personal goal to overprotect her. Why was it that no one saw the steel in her? The singular drive that she had always had, that no one could squelch?

Finally Barry had given in when she opened her bookstore.

"Got to hand it to you, babe," he admitted. "You knew what you wanted, didn't stop 'til you got it."

"So," she teased him, "are you proud of me, or what?"

He had held out his arms to her, held her tightly, whispered, "Proud! I'm more than proud. I married me a very special woman. Just hope I can keep up with you. Leesy, you take my breath away. I'm the luckiest man in the world, and don't you forget that!"

Then his lips had closed over hers as he kissed her.

She recalled that moment as if it were yesterday. She had lost the man she loved, but now it was possible not only to fulfill their dream, but to have a part of him. A real, tangible part, because he had loved her. She vowed that no amount of adverse advice from family or friends was going to stop her. *God willing,* she added in her mind.

By the time she reached the store, she had decided to bring Emerald up to date on her progress. One thing she knew for certain. She had never before had a friend who was as selfless, always willing to help, smart and wise in the ways of the world as Emerald Stokes. Elyse realized what a treasure she had in this loyal friend. She hoped to God nothing would ever come between them.

"Next week?" she announced jubilantly as she walked into the back room.

Emerald took off her reading glasses and looked up at Elyse.

"Next week?" she repeated. "What's going to happen next week?"

Elyse grinned at her friend, sat down at her desk, shed her shoes and whirled her chair around to face her friend. Their knees practically touching, she made direct eye contact with a puzzled Emerald.

"My dear, dear friend, next week I have a big date with my beloved husband's sperm! All systems are go, and we will be in the process of making a baby! His sperm and me!"

Emerald shook her head, speechless for a moment. Then she saw the glint of tears that had welled up in her friend's eyes. Impulsively, she slid her chair toward Elyse, wrapped her arms around her.

"Oh, hon, I'm so happy for you. Your dream is coming true."

"So why . . . why," she hiccoughed, "why am I crying?"

"Shush, shush, all mothers cry. It's almost part of the process, bringing a new life into the world. It may be an everyday thing, but it's still an awesome, miraculous happening. So cry all you want."

The next few days went by in a blur of activity. Elyse had decided not to have Emerald accompany her for the fertilization episode. She had determined that she did not want to have anyone in the room. It was enough that there would be Dr. Barnes and the nurse. She planned to tune them out and focus only on Barry and their baby.

With both legs in the cold metal stirrups, the whole episode seemed to her much like having a pap smear. When her legs were lowered, soft blankets were gently placed around her body as if she were a precious gift in a protective cocoon.

Dr. Barnes appeared at the head of the gurney.

"It's all done, my dear. Rest for a while, then we'll send you home. My secretary will call you for an appointment so we can do a pregnancy test. Then two weeks after that we'll check to see if we have a fetal heartbeat. Okay?" He smiled and patted her shoulder. "You did just fine. I'm proud of you."

CHAPTER 15

It was August, a very hot day, when Elyse first heard her baby's heartbeat. Actually it was August eighth, a whole year since she had marked the calendar, checking Barry's expected return home. Fleetingly, she wondered if she should attach any special meaning to the date.

Dr. Barnes's technician had come into the darkened room to prepare her.

"This will only take a few minutes, but I promise you it will be one of the most exciting few minutes of your life." She smiled at Elyse as she helped her get on the examination table.

After positioning her on the table, she said, "We need to expose your abdomen." She pulled Elyse's blouse up toward her chest, lowered her slacks and covered her body's lower half with a white sheet.

"Now," she explained, "this jelly will feel cool to the touch, but it makes it much easier for the sonar probe."

Dr. Barnes came in, his face wreathed with a warm smile.

"How are you feeling, Mrs. Marshall?"

"I'm feeling well."

"Good. Now, let's get on with our next step, shall we?" He asked the nurse for an instrument.

He moved the fetoscope over her lower abdomen, and then she heard it. It roared into her ears like the thundering, repetitive pounding of the ocean as it beat against the shore.

Tears welled in her eyes as she looked at Dr. Barnes for confirmation.

He nodded, a smile of reassurance on his face. "All is well," he said softly.

"Awesome . . . it's awesome," she whispered.

"You're on your way now to becoming a mother, my dear. My work is done, and I've made an appointment for you. I'm turning you over to the best OB GYN man in the city. Dr. Anthony Kellogg is board certified, one of the smartest, nicest young men I've ever known. I guarantee he will take very good care of you. And please . . . keep in touch. If there's anything I can help you with . . ."

"Dr. Barnes, I don't know how to thank you."

"Just be happy, stay strong. I'm proud of you and I know you're up to the challenge ahead."

"Elyse? Ace called while you were out. Says he'd like you to call him back. How did it go at the doctor's?"

"Em, I heard it! The baby's heartbeat. It was . . . like I told Dr. Barnes, awesome! I really can't describe it to you. Wait until *you* hear it!"

"When are you going to tell Ace about the baby? You know, don't you, that he really cares about you."

"He has been a good friend to me . . . to us both, and I'll have to tell him."

"I don't mean to butt into your business, Leese, you're a big girl now, have already made some real monumental decisions," Emerald waved her hand in an all-encompassing gesture, "and you certainly don't need to listen to me, but . . ."

"I know, Em, I know. I'm not trying to be evasive, but now that I've heard the baby's heartbeat it's all becoming real to me and, well, I'm trying to . . ." She hesitated for a moment, then sat down at her desk and turned to face her friend. Then she sighed. "I'll call him tonight. You're right, of course. He's been nothing but kind and supportive and I owe him the truth about our relationship. I'd like to keep him as a friend. He really is a nice guy."

"I know that's the truth," Emerald said. Then she added, "By the way, that young girl was back in the store today. I think she's a college student. Bought a thesaurus, and she asked me about ordering some nursing textbooks for her. Something about reference material."

"What girl are you talking about, Em?"

"Remember the one I said that looked like someone I thought I knew but can't place?"

"Did you get her name?"

"Holly Francis."

"Hm-m-m. Don't think I know anyone by that name. You say you think she's a college student?"

"I do, Leese. Maybe you'll be here the next time she comes in."

"Could be. You can point her out to me then."

As soon as she arrived home, Elyse changed into a comfortable robe and slippers. "It's been quite a day,

Sebastian," she said to the cat, who had greeted her with a deep throaty purr. She wondered how he would react to a baby in the house. She'd heard something about the jealous nature of cats. Well, she'd cross that bridge when she came to it. Perhaps as her belly grew, the cat would accept the change in her body. She'd see.

He watched her open a can of tuna from his vantage spot on the floor near her feet. His heavy tail fanned the floor in a wide circle as he kept his eyes focused on her task.

"Here you go, my man," Elyse said as she placed his feeding dish on the floor. She watched him for a moment as he greedily devoured the food.

Her mind turned to Ace. She knew she had to call him. She wondered what he would he say when he learned about the baby. He had been so supportive in her bereavement, she hoped he knew how much she had appreciated that. She punched in his number, uncertain of what to say to him.

"Yes, Ace, it's me Elyse. Em said you called, wanted to talk to me. How are you?"

His voice came back sounding warm and friendly.

"Elyse! How you doin'? I've missed seein' you."

"I'm fine, Ace. You sound good."

"Oh, I'm okay. Busy as ever, but I'm not complaining. Look, Elyse," he stuttered, "I . . . I . . . I wonder if you'd like to have dinner with me sometime soon."

Surprising herself, Elyse answered quickly, "Yes, Ace, I would like that."

"Great! A curator from South Africa has brought South African artifacts to the Boston Museum of Fine

Arts and I'd like to take you to see them. Then we can have dinner later. You've been on my mind so much," he confessed breathlessly, as if he could not hold the thought back another moment. He waited for her answer.

"Ace, a visit to the museum sounds just fine."

"Great, I'll pick you up. What day and what time, Elyse?"

"Let me think." She hesitated for a moment because she needed time to think about the news she would share with him. Finally she said, "Today is Wednesday. Would Friday be a good evening?"

His answer came quickly. "You bet!"

Now that Elyse had tangible evidence that she was truly pregnant, she wanted Ace to know the truth. He was a warm, decent, friendly guy. Bright, interesting to be with, with lots of experiences to share, like his tales of his time in Africa.

So how should she tell him? Would he remain a friend or . . .

But now her baby, hers and Barry's, was the major focus of her life. No one, nor anything, was as important. Her thoughts raced to her husband. He would be so happy.

Emboldened by her decision, she made one other one.

"Ace, I'll meet you Friday in the museum lobby."

"I can pick you up," he interrupted quickly.

"No, this will be best for me, Ace. I'll be there at seven."

CHAPTER 16

When Elyse went to bed that night, her thoughts were on her date with Ace. She settled into a sound sleep, but it was Barry that came into her dreams.

In her dream he explained to Elyse that he had come to a decision.

"This night is going to be special. I've been thinking," he said as he flung his jacket and briefcase on the sofa.

"Why?" Elyse looked up at him as he bent over to kiss her. "Why special?"

She had been looking through a new copy of a Victoria's Secret catalog. With her forefinger holding open the page she was interested in, she waited for his answer.

"It's like this, honey. I want to spend as much quality time with you as possible. You know how much I love you, don't want to be away from you for one second, but . . ."

"I know, Barry. I hate the thought that you will be so far away from me . . . don't know how I'm going to make it without you." She teared up. It seemed to her that the closer they got to Barry's deployment day, the more frantic their lovemaking became, knowing their time was limited.

He knelt down in front of her, took the catalog from her, placed it on the floor, took both of her hands in his.

"You will make it, sweetheart, because you are strong, and our love will see you through. And we'll both have our memories to help us get through this temporary situation. Just be strong, honey, be strong."

Elyse showered quickly, found her excitement building as she wondered, would this be the night? She was tempted not to wear her diaphragm, but even under these circumstances, she would not cheat.

On her return from the bathroom, Barry had drawn the sheets on their bed and invited her to join him. That memorable night began with touching, exploring, sending and receiving sensuous stimuli that paired them in an emotional and physical bond. They reached the pinnacle of rarified ecstasy that only true lovers experience. Then they slept again, secure in each other's arms.

Elyse woke up feeling a stunning sense of happiness. Barry's sensitive lovemaking had left her with such feelings of fulfillment, her whole body throbbed. She reached over to touch him. The space was empty . . . it had all been the cruelest of dreams. She was alone. Tearfully she stroked her abdomen, sliding her fingers over her silk nightie. The baby . . . it was still there, safe and secure. Barry's child. She was not alone.

For her dinner with Ace Elyse wore a black silk blouse with a white pleated skirt that ended just below her knees. She took with her a yellow cashmere cardigan sweater as insurance against sudden inside air conditioning. She wondered if she looked matronly . . . or when she would begin to look pregnant.

Dr. Kellogg had given her a tentative due date of April twentieth. "You will have a spring baby," he'd said. She found that Dr. Barnes had been right. She liked Anthony Kellogg the moment she met him. Tall, with warm brown skin, his youthful appearance was lessened somewhat by his bald head. But he welcomed his new patient with caring eyes, and his manner was alert and professional.

The taxi driver dropped her off in front of the Museum of Fine Arts and Elyse found her way into the lobby, following the excited crowd of well-groomed, well-dressed black people. There were few dressed in African garb, dashikis, head scarves of Kente cloth, but most were outfitted in elegant clothes.

She looked around and finally spotted Ace at the ticket counter. She watched as he approached the ticket seller, paid for his tickets, slipped them into his jacket pocket. He turned around and she could see him scanning the room. She had to admit to herself that he was one of the handsomest men in the crowd. When she saw his eyes move in her direction, she waved her hand. His face lit up and he hurried to her side.

"Elyse, good! Glad you made it. You look wonderful!"

His green eyes flushed in a warm welcome.

He kissed her cheek.

"You look great yourself, Ace. It's good to see you."

"Come, let's go on up to the gallery. Do you mind the stairs, or do you want to use the elevator?"

"The stairs, fine with me."

He led her up the grand marble staircase to the gallery set aside for the African exhibit. They followed the crowd into a well-lit room. There were colorful, exotic ceremonial masks on the walls, Ashanti stools from Ghana, Tanzanian drums, shields from Cameroon, strange-looking fertility dolls. But it was the magnificent gold and gemstone jewelry that caught Elyse's eye. Displayed on black velvet, the pieces were breathtaking. A uniformed guard stood near the glass enclosed case. Elyse was sure there were several alarms hidden to protect such a valuable collection.

Ace took her elbow and led her to a display of miniature carved heads from Nigeria. Some had gold threads around their elongated necks.

"These pieces are fascinating, Ace."

"They are, no doubt about it. I think they sell very well because they are small but bring a bit of authentic Africa into anyone's home."

"Part of our *roots*, eh?"

"You could say that. Seems to me it's becoming quite crowded. Have you seen enough? Want to leave now?"

"I'm ready whenever you are, Ace."

"Okay, we're out of here."

He took her elbow. A noisy crowd was moving up the staircase, so Ace suggested they take the elevator down to the lobby.

He stopped in front of the entrance to suggest to Elyse that she wait for him there.

"I'll bring the car around."

"I don't mind walking, not at all."

"No, it's a bit away. Just wait here."

A few minutes later he drove up, hopped out of the car and helped her into the front seat.

"That was really a very interesting exhibit, Ace. Thanks for taking me," she said as she fastened her seatbelt.

He buckled up, saying to her as he did so, "It was my pleasure, Elyse. So glad you enjoyed it."

He drove out of the parking lot onto Huntington Avenue on his way to Massachusetts Avenue. He was so pleased to have Elyse with him at last. He truly hoped this would turn out to be a momentous evening, and the first of many more to come.

"There's this new restaurant in the South End. I think you might enjoy it. Do you like Greek food?"

"Yes, Ace, as a matter of fact I do. Used to go to one in Central Square in Cambridge."

"I know the one you mean, Tomaso's, a dining-car type. Good food, cheap, for students." He laughed.

"That's the one. Kept me from starving many a day."

"This one is fairly new, but already seems to have a busy clientele. People will go to a place that serves good food. I did make a reservation because it's Friday. Hope you're hungry."

"As a matter of fact, I am."

"Good. You'll be able to order anything from pizza to steak. I'm partial to the lamb, cooked Greek style."

"I *love* lamb, Ace. You couldn't have chosen a better place."

"Great! I'm glad. Here we are."

Ten minutes later they were seated in the ornate Gold Room of the restaurant. Their waiter appeared as soon as they were seated. He took their orders.

Ace asked for a light beer and Elyse ordered water with a slice of lemon. They each requested the lamb dinner, which included a Greek salad. Ace asked for extra feta cheese on the side.

Ace smiled at Elyse. "I hope you enjoy your meal."

"This salad is delicious," she said, thinking, *When do I tell him I'm eating for two?*

She bent her head and decided for now to concentrate on her food. The lamb was succulent and savory with the meat falling away from the bone, tender and delicately seasoned.

He looked across the table at her, pleased to have this lovely woman with him for the evening. "I'm glad you agreed to spend this evening with me," he said to her as he watched her take a sip of water. "It was a pleasure to share the exhibit with you. Someday I'd like to show you the exciting Africa I learned to love."

He reached across the table to touch her hand.

Quickly she pulled it away from him.

He raised his eyebrows at the unexpected response.

"I . . . I . . . I'm sorry, Ace, that would not be possible for me to do . . . go to Africa with you."

"Why not?"

Tell him now, she thought.

"I, well, I'm having a baby."

He fell back against his chair, his eyes widened in disbelief at what he'd just heard. His cheeks puffed as he exhaled.

"But, but, I didn't know you were seeing anyone."

"I'm not."

"But how . . ."

She put down her fork and spoke slowly, as if forming her response so that this bewildered young man could understand.

"I should have told you before," she said as she wiped the frost from her glass of water, "but I couldn't, not until I knew for sure. But a few months back I received a letter from my husband that he had written some time ago, before he went to Iraq. In the letter he said that he had left a sperm donation so that I could have our child." Tears welled up in her eyes and she choked out the words, "In case he did not come back, as he promised to do."

Still confused, Ace asked, "But how . . ."

"For the past three months I've been undergoing treatments by a fertility specialist. And now," she hesitated, then spoke softly, "I expect to have our baby sometime in April."

Ace was quiet for a moment. This time when he reached for Elyse's hand she let him hold it. He rubbed his thumb over her knuckles.

"Elyse, I'm, I'm, well, I'm speechless. I know how much you loved your husband. And I know now that he must have been a very unusual, special guy, and very lucky to have a woman like you to love him."

"He was very special to me," she said quietly.

Then Ace asked, "Are you feeling all right? Anything you need? Anything I can do for you? Anything? You have only to ask, anytime. I really mean it, Elyse. Wow! A baby . . ."

She could see the bewilderment on his face.

"I appreciate your kindness, Ace. Really, I do. I need all the support I can get. Don't know what I've got myself into, but I *do* want this baby, badly. It's all I'll ever have of Barry."

Elyse wanted to take a taxi home, but Ace would not hear of such a thing. He drove her to her condo. There was little conversation between them. It seemed to each that the bombshell news had knocked any conversation far away from ordinary thoughts.

"Keep in touch, Elyse," Ace said as he walked her to her front door. "Please let me know if there's anything you need."

"I will, Ace, I will. Thanks for everything, and goodnight."

"Goodnight, Elyse. Take care." He kissed her on the cheek and returned to his car, waiting until he saw her safely inside.

Never in God's green earth had he expected the evening to end this way.

God, not only was he in love with a dead man's wife, she was going to have her dead husband's baby!

CHAPTER 17

"So you finally told Ace about the baby?"

Elyse nodded, "Em, I had to."

"How come? What happened?"

"He was so excited about the African exhibit, went on and on about it. It *was* nice, and then he said, out of the blue, that he'd like to take me to Africa, so that's when I told him. I certainly didn't want him to go ahead with plans for a trip like that . . . had to explain why I couldn't."

"What did he say when you told him?"

"At first he just stared at me, dumbfounded. Then he said that he didn't know that I was seeing anyone."

"He was really shocked, wasn't he?"

"He was. I'll never forget the look on his face, Em. I tried to explain about the in vitro fertilization process, but I don't think he took in what I was saying. He just stared at me, open-mouthed. Then he sort of shook his head and said that he didn't know what to say."

"I can believe that."

"Em, for a while he just stared at me. It was like he was so stunned he couldn't speak."

"I can imagine. Then what?"

"Then I began to tell him that I'd been undergoing treatments for the past few months and that I expected to have my baby, mine and Barry's, next spring."

"And then?" Emerald prompted.

"He said that he knew that Barry and I were a special couple with a very special strong bond of love, and he asked me if there was anything he could do to help me, in *any way*, he said. I had only to ask."

"And you said?"

"Told him I would always need a friend, that this was an entirely new experience for me. We didn't talk much after that. He drove me home, kissed my cheek, wished me well, and said if I needed him to give him a call."

~⚬~

"Yes, Mother, I'm fine. How are you and Dad doing?"

"We're both fine, Elyse. How are you feeling, really?"

"Good, Mother."

"No morning sickness?"

"Not yet."

"If you don't have it, you're one of the lucky ones. I didn't have it with you, but your brother, now that was a different story, let me tell you. Anyway," her mother went on, "you've got a long road ahead of you. I know you think you know what you're doing, but, my dear, you don't know the half of it . . . of what's ahead of you."

As she listened to her mother, Elyse wondered why her mother always disapproved of anything she tried to do.

She stopped speaking abruptly before Elyse could even get a word of protest in. That didn't surprise Elyse because her mother always seemed to be rushing about, pushing her own agenda, not caring if you kept pace with her or not.

"Anyway," her mother went on, "I'm glad you're okay so far. I'm calling because your father's birthday is coming Saturday. Your brother and Marcella are coming for the weekend, so I thought I'd have a few friends and family for dinner Saturday night. He'll be seventy, you know. Can you make it?"

"Of course. What time? Can I bring anything?"

"Bring yourself, and come early so you can visit with the folks."

"Mother?"

"What?"

"Have you told anyone about . . . ?"

"Only Jack and Marcella. It's up to you when you want other people to know about . . . this crazy thing you're doing."

When she hung up the phone, Elyse thought about the relatives she would see at her parents' home in Milton, a Boston suburb.

She would see her brother, Charles, and his wife, Carla. Because of the similarity of their first names, Aunt Carla was called Aunt Cecci. The other family relative that she expected to see was her mother's older sister, Virginia. Aunt Ginny was a vibrant seventy-two-year-old widow who had always encouraged her niece to be strong, to follow her own mind. It was with her encouragement that Elyse had been able to fulfill her dream of owning her own book and gift shop.

～◎

She wanted to look nice for her father's birthday. Because she was not 'showing' yet, she decided to wear a pair of black silk slacks and pink cotton sweater set. If she became uncomfortably warm, she could remove the cardigan. She set out for Milton in Barry's Volvo.

"Daddy!" She hugged her father when he greeted her at the front door.

"How's my girl doin'?" he asked as he twirled her around so that he could look her over.

"Daddy, I'm fine, and happy birthday to you!" She handed him a bottle of wine.

"Thank, hon. You didn't have to bring me anything. Just having my baby girl here is good enough. Come on in, the folks are out on the back patio. Everybody's here," he went on as they passed through the kitchen and he put the wine in the refrigerator. "Your aunts and uncle, the Jennings, Dr. Litchfield and his wife, Muriel."

He kept his arm around her shoulders. "You look good, hon. Feel all right?"

Impulsively, she squeezed his right hand draped over her shoulder. "Dad, I've never felt better. I'm so excited about . . ."

"You know something?" He winked at her. "Me, too. My first grandbaby. Here she is!" he announced as they moved out to the back patio.

Her brother Jack and his wife Marcella were the first to reach her side as the assembled group all greeted her.

"How are you, sis?" Jack kissed her cheek.

"Hello, you guys," she said as she included her sister-in-law in a group hug. "Good to see all of you," she said, waving her hand to include all in the group.

Her mother came up to greet Elyse, saying, "Everyone has been waiting for you to get here. I must say you *do* look pretty good."

Despite her mother's lukewarm greeting, Elyse did feel the warmth and caring she was receiving from her relatives, as well as her parents' close friends. She had always been close to her brother Jack, and now she continued to hold on to him fiercely as if she would stumble if she should let him go.

To Marcella she said, "I'm feeling fine, just fine."

Her sister-in-law answered, "You do look good."

"Thanks, so do you."

She felt a pull at her elbow and turned to see her favorite aunt smiling broadly at her.

"Aunt Ginny! Am I glad to see you!"

"Well, child," her aunt hugged her, "it's good to see you, too. How are you?"

She stepped back to give Elyse a good look, a once-over to be exact, Elyse thought. She wanted to give her aunt the news of her baby, but hesitated. It would cause the focus to be on her, all sorts of questions, and she did not want that to happen, not on her dad's birthday.

"I think," her aunt said, looking her niece up and down, "that you've put on a little weight."

"Think so, Aunt Ginny?"

"Yes, you're looking a lot better for the first time since Barry's death. I'm so sorry that you had to go through that," her aunt said softly.

"It, it was hard . . . still is."

"I'm sure, but I'm proud of you, Leese, working hard at your store. Doing well, I understand."

"It is."

Suddenly she made up her mind. She decided to share her news with her aunt.

"Aunt Ginny, could you step into the house with me?"

"Of course, honey."

They linked arms and moved back into the house. They went through the kitchen and dining room and past the living room into Elyse's father's den, where she knew they were not likely to be disturbed, especially if they closed the door.

"I didn't want to say anything outside," she confided to her aunt, whose wide-open eyes attested to her excitement over what Elyse was about to tell her.

Elyse watched her aunt's face as she told her about the baby.

"Oh my God, Elyse! That is wonderful! Just wonderful! I'm so happy for you!"

"Really, Aunt Ginny?" she questioned.

"Girl, it's the best news I've *ever* heard. I'm proud of you, accepting a challenge like this!" She hugged Elyse, tears flooding her eyes. "It's mind boggling, that's what it is!"

"Mom, Dad, Jack and Marcella are the only ones I've told. Can you keep mum a while longer, Auntie?"

"I'm so pleased you told *me*. My lips are sealed. But let me know if you need me . . . for anything!"

"Thanks, Aunt Ginny, I will." She thought, *Why couldn't my mother show some enthusiasm about the impending birth of her first grandchild? She'd be more excited if it were my brother. She's always favored him.*

CHAPTER 18

Ace's feeling of disappointment when he thought about Elyse and her baby had made him physically ill. His head throbbed, he could not concentrate on his work, and his stomach roiled with nerves.

For the next two weeks he found it difficult to work. He had no desire to create any artwork. His kiln remained cold. He rarely went to the store. Stanley Benjamin, whom he had hired as a part-time helper, kept him aware of the business by phone.

Finally, Ace decided he had to get away. He could not face the fact that the woman he loved was unattainable. Not only was she still very much in love with her dead husband, she was going to have his child. Under those circumstances, there was no room for him in her life. He called Stanley.

"Hi, Stan, Ace here. How are things going?"

"No problem, sir. Everything's shipshape."

"Good. Look, Stan, I'm going to be away for a while, actually, out of the country. Could you manage to take care of the store while I'm away?"

"Of course. Will I be able to reach you by fax or e-mail?"

"Yes. Tell you what, I'll stop by this afternoon and we'll go over the particulars. I'll leave some signed checks so you can keep up with my bills, etc. I have something that I have to take care of." His sanity, he thought. "See you later this afternoon."

At the airport, Omar Eugendidi spotted his friend. He was stunned at Ace's appearance. He was much thinner than Omar remembered from four years ago when they were both teachers at the high school.

Something has happened to Ace, he thought as he moved with outstretched arms to greet his friend.

"Ace, my man! Good to see you!"

The two men greeted each other with bear hugs and back slapping.

"Omar! It's great to see you, and thanks for picking me up."

"No problem, happy to do it." He picked up a satchel that Ace had. "Follow me. You remember my old Citroen, my French car?"

"Sure do. She's still running?"

"Like a bunny. I take good car of her."

"Expect you do, being someone who taught auto mechanics at the high school."

"Tell me, how are things in the good old USA? I was surprised when I got your e-mail that you were coming."

"I have my own art store in Boston, and I'm looking for new art pieces to sell. Interest in African art is high in America. And besides, I always said that I would come back, so here I am."

"For how long?" Omar wanted to know.

"'Bout two weeks. Want to see some of my old students, if possible."

They reached the car in the airport's parking lot and Ace grinned when he saw the aged, faded yellow four-door sedan.

"Hello, old friend," he said as he got into the passenger seat. He tapped the cracked leather dashboard, telling Omar, "Good to see the old girl again."

"She's glad to see you, too," Omar said.

They both buckled up and Omar put the car in gear, heading for the airport exit.

"Wish you could stay at my place, Ace, but my landlord has restrictions."

"That's okay. I have a reservation at the hotel in the city, but we'll get together."

"You picked a great time to visit. The next two weeks are school holidays. Couldn't have planned it better."

Omar focused on the busy traffic as he drove away from the airport, but he was anxious. *My friend has a reason for this unplanned visit,* he thought. *Eventually I'll learn what it is. He is not the cheerful, ebullient friend that I remember from years past.* Wise in his own way, Omar decided not to question but to wait. But from the outset he knew there was a problem. He hoped he'd be able to help Ace sort it out.

Soon they reached the city of Dualla, and Omar pulled up in front of a small two-story hotel much like the motels found in rural sections of the United States.

Ace was pleased to have been able to get a room, ordinary or not, in this busy city.

"So, what have you planned, Ace? When I got your e-mail I was surprised, couldn't believe you were coming back."

"After I sleep off this jetlag, I hope to check some of the bazaars and marketplaces to see what I can pick up for my store."

"Anything I can help you with, you'll let me know?"

"Will do."

Emerald had not seen Holly Francis for some time and she was pleased when the young student came into the bookstore.

"Hello, how are you, and how's school?"

"Oh, hello. School is good, getting ready for exams at the end of the semester."

"In the books, eh?" Emerald smiled. "How can I help?"

Holly's eyes widened. "Believe it or not, although I'm taking a nursing course, my curriculum also includes a few liberal arts courses like English and music appreciation." She laughed and shook her head at the idea. "Guess they want us to be well-rounded or something. I've got to do a paper, get this, on Chaucer's *Canterbury Tales*."

"Oh, I can help you with that. Though it was written in Old English, I have a modern version right over here."

She beckoned Holly to follow her and went to the back of the store to the reference section.

"I know right where it is," she said. Kneeling down to one of the bottom shelves she found what she was seeking.

"Here you are. Anything else I can help you with?"

"I'll always need all the help I can get, but this is wonderful. Thanks so much," Holly said.

During the sales transaction, Emerald kept hoping that Elyse would get back to the store from her doctor's appointment. She couldn't think of a reasonable way to detain Holly. She wanted so much for Elyse to meet the girl, to see if she resembled anyone they both knew.

When Elyse finally returned from her appointment with Doctor Kellogg, Emerald told her, "You just missed her! She left about five minutes ago."

"Missed who?" Elyse asked.

"You know, the student that reminds me of someone."

"Oh, her."

"Yes, her. How was your doctor's visit?"

"Fine. He said I'm okay and the baby is, too."

"I know you feel good about that."

"I do, Em. And guess what, on my next visit he's scheduled a sonogram. I'm so excited because he said then I will know whether I'm having a son or a daughter! I can hardly wait!"

"Boy, that's amazing! Leese, I've never asked you whether you want a boy or a girl."

Elyse shook her head. "As long as it's healthy, that's all I care about," she said. Suddenly, a scowl on her face, she asked, "Do you think it makes any difference that Barry's sperm had been frozen? I've wondered about that."

"Oh, I think the doctor would have told you. From what I read in the material he gave you, the first in vitro fertilization was in England in 1978. And since Louise Brown's birth, there have been more than 300,000 live births in the United States. I wouldn't worry, hon. You are one among many."

"Guess you're right. I do know one thing, there's no turning back for me."

"Right on, Leese! Hey, I was just thinking, we haven't heard from Ace since you guys went to the museum. What has it been, about two, three weeks?"

"'Bout that. He's probably busy working on some new ideas."

"Maybe," Emerald conceded, but she was thinking to herself, *You, my dear friend, knocked him off his legs with your news.* She decided to find out for herself. She'd make a phone call and put her mind at ease. However, it might be prudent to do so when Elyse was not around.

The opportunity came a week or so later when Elyse had to do some banking. Emerald made the call and was surprised when she did not recognize the voice of the man who answered. She questioned, "Is this the African Art Store?"

"It surely is, ma'am. How may I help you?"

"I'm looking for Austin Brimmer . . . Ace. Is he around?"

"No, ma'am, 'fraid not. He's out of town at the moment. May I give him a message for you?"

"Perhaps you could tell him that Emerald Stokes, from The Kwanzaa Book and Gift Shop, called. Do you expect him back soon?" Emerald wanted to know.

She almost dropped the phone when the man said his name was Stanley Benjamin and that he was managing the store for Ace, who was in Africa.

After she caught her breath, she asked again if Stanley knew when Ace planned to return.

"I'm not sure, Ms. Stokes, but I expect maybe in a couple of weeks."

"Thank you very much," Emerald said, her mind racing with the news she had just received. It told her a great deal about Ace's response to Elyse's news.

"I'll try to reach him later on this month. Our store has some of his work on display and I wanted to speak with him about some new pieces."

"I see. When he returns, I'm sure he'll get in touch."

"That would be fine," Emerald said. She said her goodbye and hung up the phone.

She sat for a few minutes, her mind focused on the news she had just received. *What will this mean to Elyse?*

"I have no problem dropping you off at The Kwanzaa Book Shop," Branch said to Holly. "My barber shop is a few doors down. I can stop in for a trim while you're in there. Take all the time you need. The folks that run that store have been mighty nice to you."

"They have, Branch, especially Ms. Stokes. She always seems to be able to find what I need whenever I go there. She helped me so much on that Chaucer project. I'm going to show her . . ."

"Goin' brag about that 'A', right?"

"You better believe it!" Holly exulted.

Branch was extremely pleased with the change in Holly. She was no longer the frustrated, depressed Holly that he had loved for so long. Now her increasing self-esteem, her confidence, made him happy and increasingly hopeful that they would have a future life together.

"I've got news," Emerald announced when Elyse returned from her banking errand. She went on without Elyse asking what her "news" was about.

"Ace is in Africa."

Elyse responded with a wide-eyed, shocked stare.

"What? How did you find that out?"

"I called his store," Emerald said calmly, knowing from the look on Elyse's face that she was stunned by the information. She continued, "A man, said his name was Stanley Benjamin, told me. Said he's been away for two weeks, but that he expects him to be back in another two weeks."

"I can't believe it. He really went to Africa."

"Honey, you know you knocked him right off his feet with your news."

Elyse sat down at her desk, shook her head in disbelief. Emerald sensed her consternation.

"Want something to drink?"

"Thanks. If I weren't pregnant, I'd say bring me something strong, but being as I am, a Coke will do. I still can't believe it." She rubbed her eyes with both hands and sighed deeply. Emerald left to get their drinks.

Elyse sat quietly, thinking about the Ace Brimmer she knew. She had found him to be a good friend. He had been so supportive in helping her, not only with Barry's death, but with the store. His artwork attracted clientele to her store. But she was sure she had not encouraged him to view her in a romantic way. He knew how devoted she was to Barry and his memory. She felt no guilt in any way toward Ace. On his return from Africa, how should she react? Will he try to pursue a relationship with her, a pregnant woman?

Emerald came back with a tray on which were two glasses of Coke and a plate of cookies.

"Here's your drink, Leese, and I made the molasses cookies. The iron in the molasses is good for you."

"Thanks, Em. You know this news about Ace is upsetting to me. I've *never* thought of him except as a friend."

"Except that you did walk into his arms the first day you met him."

"Well," Elyse bristled, "anyone could see that was my overwhelming grief I was feeling. I was missing the physical touch of my husband. Even you should understand that, Em!"

She reached for a cookie, bit into it and chewed slowly, her gaze fixed on her friend. She sipped her drink before she spoke again.

"Let me tell you this, Em. Right now my whole attention, my whole being is set on my baby."

"That's fine for now," Emerald interrupted, "but you have to consider this. Your child will have a life of its own, one that you and Barry have made possible. It will not, will *not*, I repeat, be your life, and you will have to allow *that* to happen. Which means you must live your own life, which might mean, someday down the road, another man in your life. It may not be Ace Brimmer, but . . ."

She raised her own glass to Elyse and took a long swallow. She continued with her advice.

"You should think about what I'm saying. Your future will include your child, but after awhile, as life moves on, that child will become an adult with his or her own future goals. It's the way life goes, Elyse."

"Don't you think I know that?" Elyse bristled. "But right now, all I can think of is the baby, Barry's and mine!"

"Fine," Emerald warned, "But don't close the door on the possibility of a warm loving relationship with someone like Ace Brimmer."

That night when Elyse got back to her condo, she greeted Sebastian, who, purring loudly, met her at the front door.

Still smarting from Emerald's strong admonitions, she leaned over to pet the cat. "It'll be you and me and the baby, Seb. We won't need anyone else, right?"

The cat stared up at her, then moved into the kitchen to stand over his empty food bowl on the floor.

"You're just like all men, aren't you . . . want to be stroked and fed."

She reached into the cabinet for a can of tuna. As she went over to the wall-mounted can opener, she felt a sudden fluttering sensation in her abdomen. She dropped the can and her hand flew to her round belly. The baby! It had moved! She sat down at the kitchen table with both hands pressed against her abdomen, but felt nothing more. She wondered if it would happen again. She remembered reading in the obstetric book Dr. Kellogg had suggested that she should expect this sensation from the baby.

Dr. Kellogg was not surprised at her news when she kept her next appointment with him.

"I expected that to happen," he reassured her. "You're right on time. Let's get you ready for your sonogram."

The technician prepared her for the procedure, helped her onto the examination table and applied the sonogram gel to her abdomen.

"This feels cold at first," she said, "but you'll get used to it. Watch the monitor to your right."

It looked like a television screen to Elyse, a totally black screen. At that moment the doctor came in. The lights were dimmed and he took the probe, began to press down on Elyse's now distended belly.

At first she saw only a blur on the dark screen. Then Dr. Kellogg pointed out to her the baby's head, arms and legs.

"What is it?" Elyse gasped.

"It's, it's, one moment, I want to make sure." He continued to move the probe around. "You are having a daughter," he said.

"Really?" Elyse's voice quavered with disbelief.

"Really, it's a girl. Are you happy about that?"

"Oh, yes, doctor, I am. As long as she's healthy."

"I'll have a copy printed out for you. Your baby's first picture."

As soon as she left the doctor's office and got into her car, the sonogram picture in her handbag, she called her father on her cell phone.

"Dad! I just found out! You're going to have a granddaughter!"

"Ah, babe, wonderful! Wonderful! You just found out?"

"Right, and I have a picture to prove it! It's hard for me to see, but the doctor says it's a little girl."

"Wait 'til I tell your mother. She'll be shopping like crazy, count on it!"

CHAPTER 19

Omar and Ace met for dinner the night before Ace was due to return to Boston. They had not been able to spend as much time together as they had hoped, mainly because Ace was shopping, particularly in areas outside the city. He had been seeking unusual artifacts crafted by natives. He had already shipped several cartons of his purchases to Boston and had more to ship.

"Omar, would you be able to forward a few crates of goods for me?" he asked as they waited for the waiter to return with their meals.

"Be happy to take care of that, Ace. You know that. How has your shopping gone thus far?"

"Better than I expected. Got some great stuff. Picked up some very handsome paintings, sculptures, native drums, cloth, a whole bunch of stuff."

"So, you're satisfied, not disappointed?"

"Not a bit. And I do think this trip was what I needed, in more ways than one."

Omar looked up from his meal. Each had ordered braised chicken with gravy, peas, rice, and candied yams. Each man had a tall glass of local beer as well. They ate silently, then Omar spoke.

"So now, my good friend, you will tell me what really brought you here. I know it was more than a shopping trip."

Ace shrugged his shoulders, picked up his glass of beer and took a swallow. He pushed his empty dinner plate to one side. Rubbing his forehead as if his fingers could soothe away the anxiety he was feeling, he explained his dilemma.

"Omar," he began slowly, "I've been through a rough time these past few weeks. I just had to get away from Boston."

"I had a feeling that something or someone had upset you. You were not the Ace Brimmer that I knew. Anything I can help you with?"

"A friendly ear and a non-judgmental attitude would be good right about now."

"Let's hear it, see if we can sort it out," Omar encouraged.

"To begin with, I fell in love with the most beautiful, smartest, most unusual woman . . ."

"Congrats!"

"No, congratulations are not in order."

"No? Why not?"

"She won't have me."

"Because?" Omar's eyebrows were raised in twin question marks as he stared at his friend.

"Because she has been married before. Her husband was killed in Iraq."

"Oh, that's very sad. Awful, really."

Ace agreed, saying, "It is, but, and this you won't believe, before he left for the war, he deposited sperm to be frozen. Six months after his death, their lawyer, under the husband's wishes, gave her the information . . . a letter her husband left for her."

His voice faltered then.

"So now she expects to have the baby in the spring," he continued in a sober tone of voice.

Omar's eyes widened in disbelief.

Finally, after an awful, numbing silence, Omar responded, thunderstruck by what Ace had just said.

"Wow! No wonder you were floored."

"Omar, how do I compete with something like this?"

"You do, that's all! If you love this woman, then you do everything in your power to win her love. It's as simple as that. There's nothing else you can do but woo her with tenderness and love."

"But . . ." Ace started to say.

"No buts. Her husband is dead. You are not. You are a real man, flesh and blood, that she can see and touch. Don't let a past situation stop you from getting what you want. Think realistically, face what is real, tangible."

"Man, you're right, of course. Why didn't I think . . ."

"Because you were not prepared for it," Omar continued. "Now you go back to the States. I'll take care of shipping your goods to you, and in return the next thing you can do for me is to send me an invitation to your wedding!"

The next day on his flight home, Omar's words echoed in Ace's mind. He had pointed out that Elyse's husband was dead. And that it was very likely that as she reared their child, memories of him would fade among the activities of daily living. She could very well turn to him, Ace, a real person, for comfort and support. A memory was just that, something that had occurred in the past. Life was meant to be lived, not remembered.

"Can you see what I mean, Ace?" Omar had asked.

Ace had agreed with him, adding, "There must have been something that made me need to distance myself from the situation and seek advice from someone like you, Omar."

———— ✺ ————

"Everything went fine," Stanley Benjamin told Ace the first morning after Ace's return. "Did you have a good trip? You look rested."

"I did have a good trip, Stan. Have lots of stuff I've brought back. I think you'll be pleased when you see what I bought. My friend Omar is shipping even more art pieces that I was able to buy. It was a nice change of pace for me, and I'm pleased with the trip all around."

He thought about his tenuous relationship with Elyse and how he needed to form a plan of action.

Getting back to his temporary employee, he knew he had to get on with his regular work routine.

"So," he prompted Stan.

"Oh, well, we do have some customers anxious to see what you've brought back, and I did keep a list of all the telephone calls from folks who want to get in touch with you. It's right here. Some e-mails, too, from out of town."

He handed Ace a clipboard with several sheets of paper attached.

"Good work, Stan. Thanks."

"No problem."

"You've done a good job. Think you'd consider staying on . . . helping me out? I'd like to extend my hours now that I have new merchandise and if I'm branching out of town . . ."

"I'd like that, Ace, but I have to tell you that as soon as I graduate I'm leaving Boston."

"How so? Boston is not for you?"

He was twenty-six, a slender young man whose dark brown eyes seemed to miss very little. Ace had been aware that he was finishing his last year of law school, so he was not totally surprised when Stanley gave his reason for leaving.

"I'm from Texas, you know, and my plan is to start a law practice there. So when I get home, I hope to pass the bar and get started in my law career."

Ace said, "Sounds like a good plan."

"And also," Stanley hesitated for a moment.

"And?"

"My fiancée is waiting."

"Aha! *That's* the reason you're leaving Beantown."

Stanley said yes, but that he would stay with Ace as long as he remained here.

Later that day Ace reviewed the accumulation of mail and messages he had received while away. Most of it could be dispatched with a check or a brief handwritten reply. Then he turned his attention to the phone messages.

Most were from customers who were seeking artwork for their homes, especially Mrs. Hallett, a self-proclaimed expert on African art. She had commissioned Ace to provide her with African fabrics so that she could be attired with authentic African garb at any of Boston's social functions.

Emerald Stokes. The name leaped off the page. So Emerald had called, but Elyse had not. He did not find her name on the list. He wondered if she was doing all right. When would he see her? Did he need to explain his absence to her? Or did it matter to her?

CHAPTER 20

Elyse went shopping at Baby Aboard, Inc., a maternity shop at the mall. She purchased a pair of maternity jeans with an expandable waistline, two maternity tops and a long floral print skirt. She also bought a pair of maternity slacks, a pair of low-heeled shoes and a pair of leather sandals. She had gained about twelve pounds so far in her pregnancy and had become accustomed to the flutters and stirrings within her basketball-sized abdomen. She thought as she left the shop with her purchases, *I have part of Barry with me, right now.*

She decided to stop at the food court in the center of the mall. It seemed to her that she became incredibly hungry without warning. Maybe her blood sugar was low, or something like that. She'd ask Dr. K about it. But so far she did feel fine.

Ace was delighted when he saw Elyse at the January meeting of the local Business and Professional Group of Greater Boston. When he spotted her, she was chatting with some young people. She was wearing a gold pleated silk top that hung loosely from her shoulders, black velvet slacks and black sandals. Her large gold hoop earrings accented her soft, curly halo-like haircut.

He watched her turn in his direction, scanning the crowd, but she did not see him at first.

He stood mesmerized by her regal, stunning beauty. Her eyes shone with good health, and to Ace she looked radiant. He waited for her to glance in his direction. He held his breath when finally she saw him. Her face lit up in a wide smile when she recognized him, and they moved toward one another through the crowd.

"Elyse, you look beautiful!" He wondered if she could see the happiness on his face.

She smiled at him. "Ace, I'm glad to see you! How are you, and how was your African safari?"

"Oh, I'm just fine, but how are *you*?"

"I'm doing quite well, thank you."

She patted her abdomen. "Past the halfway mark. Only three more months to go."

"And then?"

"Then I'll meet my daughter. Ace, I can hardly believe it. But every once in a while she lets me know she's there."

"Active little one, eh?"

"Oh my, yes. It's so exciting. I can hardly believe I'm having a baby. It's really a miracle."

"It's plain to see that you are happy, and I'm very glad about that. So, how is Emerald, and are things going well at the store?"

"Em is fine, and so far all is well at the store. We did well this Christmas season."

He led her to the side of the room to a quiet area with some empty chairs. He wanted to be certain that Elyse was comfortable. He studied her face, her movements, as she walked beside him.

"Your trip?" she looked up at him as he helped her to a comfortable chair. "It was successful?"

"Right. I'm happy with what I was able to pick up. Can't wait to show you and Emerald some of my finds."

Elyse was interested in what Ace had to tell her about the trip, and she had to admit to herself that she had missed him. She'd missed his kindness to her and Em, his enthusiasm for his work, especially his deep interest and respect for African art.

Tonight his eagerness to talk to her became apparent, and she found that indeed she was looking forward to hearing what he had to say.

She noticed his changed appearance since she had last seen him. His skin seemed smoother and browner as a result of his time in the African sun. He had shaved off his mustache, which made his face look younger. His eyes were bright, and it appeared to her that his interest in her was warm and sincere. She did not sense an overly romantic edge to this encounter, despite Em's pronouncements.

But she did remember how shocked he had been when he learned about her pregnancy. However, that was his problem. Her focus was on her child, hers and Barry's. Ace would have to understand that.

"Elyse, I want to tell you how sorry I was that I left for Africa so quickly, but you know, I had never been so stunned in my life. I had to get away, but I want you to know that I respect you for doing what you and your husband wanted. A love like the pair of you shared is truly remarkable. I want you to believe that I respect and appreciate your decision. But I also want you to know," he reached for her hand, "if there is ever anything that I can do for you, I want you to let me know. Anything, at any time. I want you to believe that."

"Thanks, Ace. Thanks for saying that."

"You are most welcome. And, Elyse, I have to say it. You have never looked so happy or more beautiful."

Emerald was pleased when she saw Holly's paper on Chaucer.

"Way to go, miss! An 'A'," she said.

"Thanks to you, Ms. Stokes. Couldn't have done it without you."

"Of course you could have. I gave you a push in the right direction, but you did the work. Don't sell yourself short, Holly. You are smart and talented, young lady."

"I had to show it to you. I'm proud of what I've been able to do. I feel like I'm making some headway."

"Keep it up, you'll make it," Emerald encouraged. "Need anything today?"

"Not for myself, but Mr. Harkins, my former patient, is becoming quite a reader. Now he wants books by African-American writers. Guess he's outgrown *Ebony* and *Jet*."

"Have a whole section of African-American authors, right over here." Emerald showed Holly the section. "You're sure to find something here to interest him."

With her right hand Holly touched off a snappy salute to her mentor. "Yes, ma'am!" she said as she started her search.

Emerald thought, *Looks like something I've seen someone else do.* A phantom face flicked in her mind, but was gone quickly and she could not identify the image. This memory thing was driving her crazy. Why was it that she thought she knew this girl, or someone who looked like her? She decided she'd have to ask a few questions and see what came up. She would not rest until she figured it out.

Two weeks after returning from Africa, Ace got the idea to design an African diorama for Elyse's storefront window. He did not want to be too invasive, but following his own mind, and heeding Omar's advice, he hoped to continue some type of relationship with her.

When he broached the idea to Elyse and Emerald, they both approved, but Elyse insisted that she would not agree unless she could pay him for the work. He tried to discourage her from that idea, but in the end agreed to accept a fee agreeable to them both.

His hope was to create a diorama featuring native musical instruments, drums, cymbals, thumb piano, gourds, rattles, banjos and other native stringed instruments. In the background a cassette of African music would play.

Within two weeks the display was ready. Emerald designed flyers announcing the event and her nephew distributed them. Both Elyse and Emerald were delighted with the response from the community.

Ace had arranged for a caterer to serve finger sandwiches and coffee. He assumed the expense for the food and service requirements, much to Elyse's dismay.

"You should not have gone to that extra expense, Ace," she told him.

"It was my pleasure," he said. "Case closed."

CHAPTER 21

Ace's diorama was such a success that he decided to keep it on view for a month. Elyse and Emerald couldn't thank him enough for the increased business the exhibit brought to the store.

A month later he changed the exhibit. This time he featured paintings, costumes of animal skins and feathers used in native ceremonies and dances. Again, he had indigenous music playing in the background.

Since the store was open until nine and since many customers came in during the evening hours, both Elyse and Emerald were usually there. Sometimes Ace came in as well, bringing Chinese food, pizza or some of the Colonel's fried chicken. Emerald would put on a pot of coffee or supply cold drinks. This made for a warm, friendly atmosphere that each of them enjoyed, especially Elyse, who found welcome support from them in her advancing pregnancy. Emerald was Elyse's self-appointed coach for the birthing classes. Ace listened as the two reported on her progress. Elyse said she was lucky to have caring people like them to help her.

"Dr. Kellogg says that I should be walking each day, that it will help in my delivery," she told the pair when they asked how she was feeling.

"I can help you with that, Elyse," Ace volunteered. "The weather is getting better, spring is on the way, days are longer . . . be good exercise for me, too."

They agreed to drive to Jamaica Way, walk around the pond, and if Elyse tired, find a park bench and rest.

They started the routine the first week in March.

"I've another six weeks to go," Elyse explained to Ace that evening when he picked her up.

"Are you feeling good?"

"Yes, Ace, I do feel good. Much better than I expected to feel at this date."

"Good, I'm glad you're doing so well."

He helped her into the car, secured the seatbelt below her bulging abdomen. "Is that comfortable for you? Not too tight?"

"It's fine."

"Okay, on to our walk!" He smiled at her, happy to have her beside him, and happy that he was helping her.

The weather was cooperative. It was a mild, calm evening with walkers, joggers and others on bicycles taking advantage of a welcome spring evening. The delicate yellow forsythia, green leafing of the trees and the cheerful faces of crocus and pansies in beds around some trees foretold of warm days ahead.

Elyse sighed deeply, breathing in the warm air.

Instantly alert, Ace asked, "Are you feeling okay?"

"Ace, I do have one little worry that's been nagging at me."

"Anything I can help you with? You only need to ask, you know."

"Yes, I know." She turned to face him on the park bench. "It's Sebastian, my cat."

"What's wrong with him?"

"Nothing, really. It's just that I'm worried how he's going to get along with the baby. I've heard that pets can be jealous if their owner's attention is focused on a baby. You know what I mean?"

"I've heard that."

"He's been real good company for me, but I don't want to take any chances."

Ace spoke quickly. "I'll take him and you can come visit him. After the baby comes, you can bring the two of them together gradually. See how it works out."

"Ace, you're a genius!" She reached over and squeezed his hand. "Seb is really Barry's cat, and I'd hate to get rid of him."

"You won't have to, I'll see to that. Don't worry." He clasped her hand in both of his, aware of his deepening concern for her.

She withdrew her hand slowly and looked over the quiet pond before them, then spoke softly. "Barry would be so excited about the baby. You know, Ace, I have always felt that I am a better person for having loved and been loved by a man like Barry. He helped me become a better woman."

"Oh, no, he worshipped you, my dear. How could he not? If he were here, I know that's what he would say. You're special, and don't ever forget that."

She surprised him with her next question.

"How come you've never married, Ace?"

"Came pretty close a couple of times, but decided each time I didn't want to spend my life with that person. Simple as that." Then he added, "Not until I met you."

She frowned, "Wish you wouldn't talk like that, Ace. There can never be more than friendship between us. I value your friendship, but I'm committed to Barry and our child. You know that. And besides, as soon as I'm able I want to start building our dream house that we planned."

"Never say never, Elyse. None of us knows what the future holds," he said, wondering as he did so if he would ever have the chance to be important in her life. Would just "being there" be the most effective way to do so? He had every intention to be available to her, to watch over and support her whenever he could. With those thoughts foremost in his mind, he asked, "Elyse, are you still driving? I mean, are you still comfortable behind the wheel? What does your doctor say?"

"Oh, my, yes. So far I'm comfortable."

"I'm only asking because I would be more than happy to chauffer you wherever you need to go. I'm my own boss, so it would not be a problem."

She shook her head in denial. "So far I'm okay. Dr. Kellogg hasn't said I can't drive, not yet, anyway."

"I don't want you to be in jeopardy. I don't mean to worry you, but you have to think . . ."

"I know . . . the baby," she conceded.

There was a quiet peace between them, Elyse noted, as she rested beside Ace on the park bench. They were almost like an old married couple, each one almost able to anticipate the other's response.

Unexpectedly the baby moved, and Elyse reacted with a slight grunt.

Instantly aware of her apparent discomfort, he asked, "Are you all right?"

She saw the anxious look on his face and tried to reassure him.

"The baby's been moving a lot this week and she just kicked me in my ribs, that's all."

"Can she do that?"

"Sure, does it all the time. Especially when I'm trying to rest. Want to feel her foot?"

"Can I? It won't . . . hurt anything?"

"No, not a bit. Here," she took his hand, pulled her light wool jacket to one side and guided his fingers to a slightly rounded area beneath her lower right rib.

"Feel that?" she watched his face, saw his look of wonderment.

"God, yes, I do! Awesome! It feels like a round marble."

"That's her heel. Dr. Kellogg said that quite often the baby will turn around completely. Like floating from the bottom to the top, sometimes head down, then will bob up like a cork with its feet down. He says that sometimes they sneeze, cough, suck their thumbs . . ."

"Gosh, can they do that? Doesn't seem possible."

"Bro, they let you know they're there, believe me!"

The thought crossed Elyse's mind that her husband should be with her, sharing this phenomenal experience. She knew how thrilled and excited he would have been. *Way to go, babe,* he would have said.

However, she was grateful for Ace. He did show reverence, awe and excitement, which made things easier to bear.

She was not alone. Even though her parents had decided sometime ago to take a long-awaited cruise to Australia and New Zealand, Ace had made himself available whenever she needed him, as he had promised. She could not ignore his steadfast support. She had *expected* Emerald to be supportive. They had been friends since high school and were in business together. But the way Ace always seemed to come through for her strengthened her. She would never forget him.

Back at the store Elyse greeted Emerald when she returned from her dental appointment.

"I finally met your young friend," she told Emerald.

"You mean Holly Francis?"

"Yes, and I can see why you like her so much. She's so personable, and she really is fond of you. Very much so . . . says you've been a great help to her."

Emerald shrugged off her raincoat, shook her damp hair and, with a deep sigh, plopped down into her desk chair.

"So, tell me, Leese, did she remind you of anyone you know?"

"Not really, but I know what you mean. She's very friendly, easy to talk with. It's as if I've known her before."

"That's the same feeling I get when she comes in."

Elyse hefted her burgeoning body out of her chair and waddled slowly to the small kitchen.

"I'm having a cup of tea. Would you like a cup?"

"Sure would. It's nasty weather out there."

Then, noticing Elyse's ungainly walk, Emerald jumped up from her chair. "You sit down, Leese, I'll get it."

"Oh no, that's fine. I need the exercise."

A few minutes later Elyse returned with a tray with two mugs of hot tea, sugar substitute packets, creamers and a sleeve of crackers.

Emerald reached for the tray and put it on the coffee table. They both settled themselves on the couch. Emerald took a sip of her tea after she had poured some of the creamer into it and sighed deeply. "Just what I needed. So, what else did Holly tell you?"

"Oh, that she was in college, loved it, and how she and her boyfriend, Branch, were getting on. Said she had no parents, had been raised by her mother and grandmother, now both dead. Said she never knew her father, but she was cheerful and upbeat despite her sad situation."

"She told you a lot, didn't she?"

"Maybe because she saw I was pregnant."

Then Elyse added thoughtfully, "I hope my daughter will be like that. You know, thoughtful, polite . . . and the girl has pluck and determination. That I do admire."

"Still think I've seen her before or . . . someone who looks like her," Emerald said.

"Em, it'll probably come to you when you least expect it."

CHAPTER 22

By the end of March, Emerald had moved into Elyse's condo.

"You've got to have someone near, in case you go into labor." Elyse agreed, and Emerald slept on Elyse's queen-sized pull-out sofa, quite comfortably, she reported.

One morning shortly afterwards, Elyse came out of the bathroom and announced to her longtime friend, "I've gained forty-five pounds, and when I stand up I can hardly see my feet!"

"It's mostly water, I think. Your weight gain, that is," Emerald told her. "But I do think, Leese, that you should be wearing shoes that will give you more support. Those leather sandals just don't cut it. You need sturdier shoes."

"With these swollen ankles, girl, it's a good thing I can put my feet into anything!"

But it was Emerald who tripped over a rug and sprained her right ankle so badly that, after the X-rays were taken, she was placed on crutches.

Dismayed by her sudden disability, she warned Elyse, "Don't you dare have this baby until I get off these crutches!"

"Look, honey," Elyse told her, "if and when this baby 'starts turning for the world,' as my West Indian grammy would say, you better be able to hobble to my bedside one way or the other. Remember, you *promised* to be there."

"Oh, I'll be there, even if I have to be in a wheelchair."

"Yeah, right. Like they need someone in a wheelchair coaching an expectant mother."

Ace picked up Sebastian about a week later and soon reported to Elyse just how well he adjusted to his new home.

"He has discovered the kiln," he told her. "He knows not to go near it when it's hot, but as soon as it cools down he loves to curl up on top and go to sleep."

With all of her focus on having her baby, Elyse was glad that she did not have to worry about the cat. She had been having minor contractions, but had still been able to continue her work routine at the store.

"Both you and Ms. Stokes have been so good to me," Holly explained to Elyse the next time she went into the bookstore. "I know you're expecting your baby soon, and if there's anything I can do, all you have to do is let me know. Sometimes I have free time between classes. At least for now, anyway. In April I'll be doing a rotation in medical nursing at the Suffolk General Hospital."

"Really? That's where I'm going to have my baby," Elyse interrupted her.

"I was born there, you know."

"No! What a coincidence. It will be something if you're there when I deliver."

Holly agreed, saying, "Why don't I give you my address and phone number so we can keep in touch."

Holly Francis had lied about not knowing the identity of her father. She had known since she was nine years old. In her fourth grade class the teacher had announced a father-daughter outing. Holly had wondered at the time why the woman made such a ridiculous proposal. Didn't she know that many of her students didn't have fathers, were being raised by single mothers? That was the day her grandmother, Theodora Francis, sat her down in her bedroom to "explain some things."

"Girl," she said, "let me tell you 'bout the day you was born!"

Her grandmother was not a large woman, about five feet, five inches tall, and perhaps one hundred twenty pounds, but to Holly she seemed to be made of steel. Her silky white hair, thin in spots, was worn with twin braids crossed over, pinned to her scalp with steel hairpins. Her face was a smooth buttery brown, unlined, and her eyes were a dark brown, almost black, so that if she fixed them on a person they could cause the most stalwart foe to falter. She had a steel-like grip in her hands that came from milking cows twice a day on her father's farm in Virginia.

From her bedroom closet she retrieved an old cigar box, removed some papers and began to talk. Wide-eyed, Holly listened.

"This grandmother of yours was *not* going to let *anybody* tell me what was goin' to happen to my grandbaby! I knew that your momma, at sixteen, was not of legal age, that I was her guardian, and yours, too! When she told me that folks at the hospital had decided that you should be adopted, I pitched a fit! I said, 'Over my dead body!' I told those people they didn't know who they was trifling with. I had done some housework for a lawyer friend and when I mentioned *his* name, they couldn't move fast enough to give me the papers I demanded! Your birth certificate and the piece of paper your daddy had signed agreeing to your adoption were handed over to me right quick! I know he was only eighteen, didn't know any better. Guess he couldn't face the responsibility of raising a child, being a child himself.

"So I saved these papers because I figured someday you might need them . . . this."

She handed Holly a folded piece of paper. When Holly opened it the first thing she saw was the seal of the City of Boston. It was her birth certificate, the scent of tobacco still on the formal paper.

"And you need this, too." She handed her granddaughter another document.

This one, Holly read, stated that the undersigned had "released all responsibilities and rights of said above mentioned child, Baby Girl Marshall." It had been signed with the name Barry Edward Marshall.

All of a sudden, Holly could hardly catch her breath. The bedroom seemed very quiet and still, as if she had been placed in a vacuum chamber. Her heart quickened in her chest. She looked at her grandmother, saw only love and concern.

"He didn't want me . . . not much of a father," she said.

Her grandmother understood. She rose up from the floor in front of the open closet door and made a "make room" gesture.

"Scoot over," she said as she moved to sit beside Holly. She put her arm around her.

"Listen, child, you came into this world because God wanted you to be here! I know this is hard for you, but you gotta be practical and deal with the hand that was dealt you."

"Why should I?" Holly sniffed, eyes filled with tears. "Why should I care 'bout someone who didn't care . . ."

Her grandmother took both of Holly's hands in hers.

"Don't cry, baby. Like I said, God intended for you to be here. And I know for a fact that your folks loved each other. They just came up on something they couldn't handle." She closed her eyes for a moment, took a deep breath, then continued to speak.

"Maybe I should take the blame for not schoolin' your mother more about . . . well, nohow should you hate your father. He was only eighteen, your ma, sixteen. Babies themselves," she added. Then she said something that Holly had not expected to hear.

"Don't hate him, child. You look just like him."

For a long time it had bothered Holly, the fact that her own father didn't want her, could not be bothered with her. So she began to deny his existence. It was the only way she could live with her feeling of worthlessness. She determined that if he had not wanted her, not wanted to be the father of a helpless newborn, she did not need to identify him as a father. That bitter seed grew like a hard kernel in her mind and motivated her to validate herself and elevate her self-esteem.

One Friday night after a week of classes, Branch and Holly followed their usual custom of having dinner at one of their favorite seafood restaurants. Branch looked at Holly, who had been quiet since they had ordered their food. He knew that she had something on her mind.

"So?" he asked.

She rubbed her forehead for a moment as if trying to sort out her thoughts. With a deep sigh as a preface, she told him.

"When I was nine years old I found out who my father was. I have lied about not knowing since the day I found out about him."

"How did you find out?"

"My gram told me when I was nine that he had surrendered any rights to me, signed papers that I could be put up for adoption. I always felt that meant he didn't care about me. So I didn't need to care, either."

"Are you going to try to find him?"

"No, not now. It's too late."

"What do you mean, *too late*?"

"You know the woman who owns The Kwanzaa Book Shop?"

"I've never met her, but I've heard you speak of her, how nice she and her partner have been to you."

"Her name is Elyse Marshall. Sometime ago, when I was picking up books for Mr. Hawkins, her partner, Emerald, told me she's about to have his baby."

"But, but, you said it's too late to meet him. Why can't you meet him?"

"He was killed in Iraq."

"He's *dead*? But you said . . ."

"Before he left to go overseas, he deposited sperm to be frozen. He wanted his wife to have their child by in vitro fertilization."

Branch stared, open-mouthed, at Holly, emitted a low whistle, then said, "I'll be damned."

Then he questioned her, concern evident in his voice.

"Are you planning to tell her who you are?"

"No, Branch, I don't intend to. Both my mother and grandmother are gone. You are the only living person who knows, and I'd like to keep it like that. The man was never real to me."

"I'll respect your wishes, Holly. You know that without asking. Wouldn't help his widow now, anyway."

"I know. She's got enough to contend with, being a single mother and all."

"But, Holly, have you considered the baby? Now you will have a sibling, family . . . a half-sister."

Holly's eyes widened as the possibility entered her mind.

"Oh, my God, no! And . . . Branch, I've already offered to babysit!"

CHAPTER 23

Dr. Kellogg informed Elyse that her baby's head was descending into the birth canal, and because of that he wanted to see her every week. Her next appointment with him was on April twentieth, at three in the afternoon.

Emerald was still dependent on her crutches to get about, but her orthopedist had suggested that she might be free of them in another week or so, depending on her X-rays. But Elyse's baby had other plans.

One week before her due date, Elyse was having a light lunch before her weekly doctor's appointment. As she ate, she was leafing through the latest copy of her favorite fashion magazine, *Marie Claire*.

Boy, she thought as she rubbed her stomach, *I'll be glad when I can wear regular clothes again.* Then it hit! A pain so searing, so excruciating, she thought she was being ripped apart. It took her breath away. She gasped, reached for her cell phone on the table.

"Em, Em, I . . . I, ooh, I think I'm in labor! Can you come . . . need to go . . . need . . ." Her pain made her breath come in short gasps. "Please hurry," she moaned as another spasm rose in a painful crescendo across her lower back.

It was only ten minutes, but seemed an hour, when she heard her front door being opened.

"Em! I'm in here, the kitchen! Thank God you're here!"

"It's me, Ace. Em got me on my cell phone. Where's your bag? Let's get you to the hospital." He moved towards her bedroom. "The bag?"

"On the closet floor," Elyse gasped as another pain struck.

"Got it." Ace emerged from her bedroom, the overnight bag held aloft in his hand.

"We're on our way." He grabbed her sweater from the back of her chair and draped it over her shoulders.

"Come on," he urged. "Let's get you to the hospital," he repeated. "Quick!"

He helped her into the car, fastened the seatbelt around her lower abdomen, asked. "Are you all right?" She nodded and he hurried to get in, fasten his own seatbelt and start the car.

"I'm okay, just get there . . . please."

"Hang in there, Leese. I've already made some trial runs to the hospital. It's exactly twenty minutes from your condo, and I've found out the best way to get there. We'll be there before you know it. Just hold on!"

"Thanks, Ace. I'm so glad you're with me. Em called you, did she?'

"Yep. We planned it . . ."

"That you'd take me?"

He grinned at her. "Ah, yup, we planned it."

"God," she said, shaking her head, "what would I do without you guys?"

"Not to worry, Leese. We're with you all the way. Doctor knows you're coming?"

"I called him while I was waiting, right after I called Em. Had a three o'clock appointment anyway, but he said to come right to the hospital."

It was then that she grimaced and clutched the dashboard with both hands as she tried to ride out the searing pain that seemed to envelope her whole body. Ace swerved to pass a slow-moving car ahead.

"Hang on, Leese, we're almost there." He wanted so desperately to help ease the pain of the woman he loved. He realized that the pain she was experiencing was because she loved another man, a man seemingly able to reach her from the grave. But Ace knew his love for her was real, was alive, palpable and tangible. All he could do was love and support her the best way he knew. Would she, could she, ever love him . . . that way?

He swung the car into the hospital's admissions area, came to a halt, jumped out, raced to Elyse's side and helped her get out of the car. She was doubled over with pain, almost unable to walk. Ace breathed a sigh of relief when he saw a hospital aide approaching them with a wheelchair.

"Thank you, thank you," he said as the two of them helped a grateful Elyse sit in the chair.

"Dr. Kellogg is expecting her. This is Mrs. Elyse Marshall," he told the attendant.

"Yes, sir, right this way. We go to the triage area first."

He wheeled Elyse to an area, Ace following with her bag and purse.

After a brief exchange of information and document signing, Elyse was wheeled to the third floor of the maternity wing, Ace following close behind. When they were about to get into the elevator, another contraction caused Elyse to scream, "Ace, Ace! Where are you?"

Quickly, Ace moved to her side. "I'm right here," he said calmly. "Everything is going to be just fine."

Before he knew what was happening, the hospital staff, acutely aware that immediate action was necessary, wheeled Elyse behind a pair of swinging doors that closed silently behind her. All Ace saw was the back of her head and the marking *No Admittance*.

"You may wait in here." A middle-aged nurse escorted him to a room obviously set up for expectant fathers and other anxious relatives. Ace spotted the usual dog-eared magazines. A man who was watching a wall-mounted TV exchanged nods with him.

The nurse pointed out a credenza holding a coffee machine, plastic cups and stirrers, packs of instant coffee and sweeteners. The small refrigerator contained individual creamers, Ace thought.

"Help yourself. Someone will be with you shortly to let you know whatever progress your wife is making."

"Mrs. Marshall is not my wife, ma'am. She's a friend," Ace explained.

The woman's face flushed slightly, but without acknowledging her false assumption she continued with her terse instructions.

"You're to wait here until instructed to do otherwise."

Ace was beginning to be upset by the cavalier attitude of the nurse whose name tag identified her as Miss Beaumont, R.N. He felt that he had to erase from her mind the untoward category that she had already assigned to Elyse. He *had* to defend her reputation. The nurse had misjudged her.

"Mrs. Marshall is a widow. Her husband was killed in Iraq and she is having their baby by in vitro fertilization. Possibly you're not aware of that," he said, watching her face pale as she heard the admonishment in his voice.

"No, I was not aware, but we'll take good care of her." She looked at her watch. "Excuse me, I must get back. We'll keep you informed."

After she left, he took a seat across the room, away from the television set. The other man in the room asked, "First one?"

Ace said, "Yes." The man smiled ruefully, raised four fingers. *Old timer*, Ace thought, wondering how such a thing could happen.

He heard thumping sounds coming from the hall and looked up to see Emerald, her face flushed, trying to negotiate the door with her crutches.

"Oh, Em, wait a minute! Let me help you!" He jumped up from his seat to help her.

"What's happenin'? How's she doin'?"

"Don't know yet. They just took her into the delivery room, I think."

"I should let them know I'm here. I'm her labor coach."

"Is there someone here for Mrs. Marshall? An Emerald or Ace?" The nurse dressed in operating room scrubs asked from the visitor's room door.

"I'm here, I'm Em," Emerald said, trying to stand on her crutches.

"Can you stand alone?"

"No, ma'am."

The nurse shook her head.

"I'm sorry, there's no way you can come into the delivery room with crutches."

"Can I help?" Ace asked.

"Yes, I think so. Mrs. Marshall did ask for you. Come with me."

He turned to Emerald as if she could immediately impart information to him. He opened his arms wide in a helpless gesture. "Em, I've never seen a child being born before. What'll I do?"

"Me, neither, Ace. Just do what they tell you, and keep your cool."

"Girl," he pleaded, "wish me well. Don't want to mess up."

"You'll do fine. Remember, you're doing it for her."

And for myself, too, Ace thought as he followed the nurse through the swinging doors. *She's the woman I love, and I must help her. Any way I can.*

CHAPTER 24

Standing at the scrub sink, Lisa Hamlin tried to give Ace a crash course in what would be expected of him as a birthing coach.

"Remember, this is a natural event," she said. "Happens all the time, all over the world. Your job is to encourage the mother to work in the most efficient way possible. That is, she should follow our instructions, breathe properly to insure that her baby gets oxygen. Help her to count down and to bear down hard when we tell her to. Try to reassure her that she's doing a super job and that everything is going well. Dr. Kellogg has briefed us all on her history and we want it to be an awesome experience for her. She *deserves* it."

"I agree with that," Ace said. He dried his hands on a sterile towel that the young nurse had handed him and put on the sterile paper gown and cap.

"We back into the room. Be careful not to touch anything," she instructed as she showed him how.

"Can I touch Elyse?" Ace wanted to know.

"By all means, hold her hands, wipe her brow. She's laboring, you know, to do the best job she can."

When he walked into the brightly lit room he was almost immobilized by his overwhelming anxiety. He was truly ambivalent about what he was about to do. He desperately wanted to be at Elyse's side, to show her how much he loved and cared for her. But on the other hand he was scared to death, not only of what he might see, but of how he might react. *God help me*, he prayed silently.

It was cool in the room. Steel cabinets lined the walls and steel tables held shiny, lethal-looking instruments lined up with rigid precision. There was the overpowering smell of an antiseptic and a huge lamp above the O.R. table spread a blazing bright light over everything and everyone.

His eyes went to Elyse lying on the delivery table. He willed himself to focus on her, although he was so frightened he wanted to flee from the scene.

She turned her head, saw him come close to her, reached out her hand. Her face was wet with perspiration. She was pale and appeared worn and weary.

"Ace." Her voice was raspy and harsh. "Ace, help me, please. I can't do this, I can't!"

He bent over to kiss her forehead.

"Oh, yes you can! We're going to help you. Believe me, you *can* do this. I'm sure of it. We're all here to help, no turning back now."

He acknowledged Dr. Kellogg, who was standing at the foot of the table.

"She's a trouper. She's doing well, and I expect some real action within the next few minutes," the doctor told him.

Suddenly, as he watched, Elyse's face took on a strange look. Ace saw her begin to strain and groan. With her left hand she grabbed Ace's hand as she struggled to bear down and push her baby into the world. The nurse, Lisa, had begun to count, and as she reached "ten," told Elyse to take a deep breath and prepare for the next contraction. Then the nurse spoke.

"You're doing very well, Elyse. Would you like a sip of water?" She pointed to the table beside Ace. Immediately he picked up the paper cup of water, adjusted the straw so that Elyse could take a sip through her parched lips.

She did so, then dropped her head back on the pillow with a deep sigh. No sooner had she done that than a fresh contraction assailed her body, and again she strained mightily.

Dr. Kellogg spoke quietly to his patient.

"You are doing very well, my dear. The head is coming down nicely, and when I tell you to 'go for it,' just give us all you've got. Okay?"

Elyse nodded weakly, whimpered a weak "Okay."

"Ace, please help me, help me-e-e!" she almost shouted as the pain attacked her.

"Push! Elyse, push!" Ace said to her, trying to will her to persevere. Sweat was forming on his forehead and his green eyes widened in awe as he saw the baby's head, covered with dark hair, emerge from Elyse's body.

He saw the head rotate. The doctor pulled down and one shoulder emerged. He pulled up and the lower shoulder showed, followed a second later by the baby's body.

The doctor made the announcement, "It's a girl!" and quickly suctioned out the baby's nose and mouth. When the child's cry pierced the room, Ace could not help himself. Tears streaming down his face, he bent over and kissed Elyse's forehead. "You did it! You did it! Elyse, you did it!"

Lisa brought the wrapped baby to Ace, who placed her in Elyse's arms. To the tearful, weary mother, he whispered, "Meet your daughter."

Ace had never before witnessed or been part of such an emotional event. He felt drained, weak at the knees, but he knew he would have done anything for Elyse.

With tears in her eyes, she looked at him, cradling her newborn in her arms.

"Thank you, Ace. I couldn't have done it without you."

Shaken, disbelieving, awestruck by what he just witnessed, Ace stumbled from the delivery room. Both mother and baby were fine, but Ace was emotionally and physically drained. He gave Emerald the good news.

"It's a beautiful baby girl, Em!" His green eyes filled with tears as they hugged each other. "Six pounds, four ounces, with a full head of black hair. She's a beauty and, Em, her eyes were wide open when she looked at me! Can you believe it?"

"Oh, Ace, that's wonderful!" Her eyes filled with tears, she asked, "Elyse okay?"

"Oh God, yes! Right as rain . . . and happy! She has every right to be, and I'm so proud of her! Em, it took my breath away. It was awesome, no other word for it. What a privilege for me to see a brand new life come into the world. It was like a hidden jewel emerging into the light! I can't tell you how. How can I explain it? Made me feel like it was a spiritual event. I've never had such a moment in my life before."

"I envy you, Ace. I really wanted to be there. I feel cheated that I couldn't be."

Ace helped Emerald to stand up with her crutches and they took the elevator to the second floor to Elyse's room, where they found a beaming new mother. Her baby lay in a bassinet beside her bed.

Emerald hugged Elyse. "Congrats, girl, I knew you could do it!"

Then she peered over the bassinet at the baby.

"Her name is Margaret Joyce," Elyse told them. "My grandmother's name. My gram was one strong woman, you know, and I wouldn't be half of who I am without her. And, of course, Joyce is my maiden name and I want her to have that."

"Have you called your folks, honey?" Emerald asked.

"They're due back Saturday. Em, would you call and leave a message?"

"Sure thing, kid. Anything else?"

"Yes, there is something else I'd like you to do for me."

"Yes?' Emerald's eyebrows went up in question marks.

"Please find a gold medal to pin on my friend Ace here, who went way beyond the call of duty."

Ace lowered his head, smiled and shook his head in a modest gesture. "Aw, ma'am, t'weren't nuthin'."

"Yeah, right," Elyse mocked with an impish grin.

Suddenly, without warning, tears filled her eyes.

"What's wrong?" Ace asked.

Elyse reached for his hand. Her voice shook; she was overcome by the life-changing experience she had just gone through. She tried to explain.

"Ace, I, I, well, I will never forget what you did for me. You, you . . ." here her voice broke but she flung away the tears, shaking her head as if she couldn't get her words out of her mouth.

"I'll never forget how you supported me all through this. I don't know how I would have made it, especially right there . . . at the end."

Ace bent over, kissed her forehead.

"Elyse, I wouldn't have had it any other way, believe me."

CHAPTER 25

Ace dropped Emerald off at Elyse's condo. She had come to the hospital by taxi.

"You know, Ace, Elyse will be coming home tomorrow. You'll pick her up, won't you?"

"By all means."

"You have to come to the condo to get the car seat for the baby first."

Everything was in order and all went well when Ace took mother and daughter home.

After leaving the new mother and her baby in Emerald's care, Ace returned to his own apartment. Sebastian seemed happy to see him, and Ace told him all about the great event.

"You're going to love her, old man," he said to the cat, who purred loudly, seemingly in agreement.

After he fed the cat and filled his water bowl, he made a chicken sandwich for himself and took a bottle of beer from the fridge. Suddenly he felt weary, bone tired, and it seemed to him that he had been holding his breath for hours. The accumulated tension of the event had drained him. He exhaled slowly and bit into his sandwich. What was going to be his role, if indeed there was to be one, in this new baby's life?

He was an only child and both of his parents were dead. His mother, from a heart attack when he was in college, and his dad a few years later from a cerebral hemorrhage. He was just a few years out of grad school, trying to find his place in the world, when that happened. That was when he joined the Peace Corps. Ace always felt that experience saved his life. The new country, new culture, made him feel more able to deal with life's twists and turns. The people he'd met in Cameroon had shown him how to accept life as it presented itself and still display a willingness to seek new, wider, more fulfilling experiences. He hoped he'd become a better man, better able to deal with the challenges that he faced. Today he wondered as he chewed his food, would this baby become an impediment in his relationship with her mother?

He took a deep swallow of his beer and he wondered how to win the woman he loved.

Emerald was sitting in Elyse's bedroom, watching her feed the baby, when the doorbell rang. When she answered the door, a young man said, "For Mrs. Marshall."

"Special delivery for Mrs. Elyse Marshall," Emerald announced.

She placed the box of flowers beside Elyse and moved the sleeping baby to her bassinet.

"Here's the card that came with them."

"To the most beautiful new mother in the world," Elyse read aloud. "It's from Ace. He's signed it, 'With my love and admiration.'"

"Well, open it."

"A dozen roses! How thoughtful of Ace."

"That's Ace, all right, one thoughtful young man," Emerald said.

"He wanted me to feel special . . ." Elyse hesitated. "He knew there was no one else to do this for me. Something Barry . . ." Her eyes were moist, shiny with unshed tears.

Emerald spoke up quickly, as if anxious to deter any negative thoughts Elyse might have.

"He *didn't* do this because Barry might have done it. He did it because he *cares* about you! Leese, you've got to stop thinking about Barry. You've accomplished what he wanted. You have given birth to his child, which means that part of him lives on, but now you *must* think about her and your future. You do have a future, you know. Now, put Barry to rest, you hear me?"

Elyse blinked away the tears, nodded, "Yes, Em, I hear."

Elyse's parents were delighted on their return from their vacation to learn that they had become grandparents for the first time.

Elyse's mother insisted that they provide a "live-in" nanny for the baby. Elyse insisted back that a nanny was not needed, but her mother told her, "Girl, you do need help, at least until the baby sleeps all night. And besides," she said, looking at Emerald, "I know Emerald will be glad to get off that sofa bed."

Emerald responded with a brisk high five in Mrs. Joyce's direction.

Elyse realized that Emerald had made sacrifices for her and that it was very selfish of her to impose upon her friend longer than necessary, so she relented.

"Until the baby sleeps through the night, then, Mother. Thanks."

"Margaret Joyce is surely Barry's daughter," Emerald observed, watching Elyse bathe the baby. "There's no doubt in my mind. It's like she was cloned. She's got his smooth chocolate brown skin and that same broad fore-head, curly black hair and deep, dark brown eyes. Don't know where you come in, kiddo, but you've got to be somewhere."

"Oh, Miss Margaret Joyce has got my family's stamp on her. Just look at those long fingers and toes, then look at mine!"

She shucked off her slipper and waggled her toes at Emerald.

"But you know, Em, I'm delighted that Margaret Joyce Marshall looks so much like her dad. It validates all I went through to get her here."

As soon as the baby was bathed, clothed and fed, she was placed in her bassinet and went right to sleep.

"She's a good baby. Leese, you're very lucky."

"Em, don't I know it."

"When do you plan on coming back to the store? Not that we're not doing okay."

They were having a mid-morning coffee break. Elyse broke off a piece of her favorite pistachio muffin before she answered.

"Soon, I believe, Em. The nanny is working out well, thanks to my folks. I've got to set up some kind of routine with her, but right now things are good. I'm to see Dr. Kellogg in a few weeks and then I'll have an idea of when I can come back. I miss the place."

"I know. Well, take your time, don't rush. We can hold the fort a while longer."

On a bright spring day in May, Branch drove to Suffolk General Hospital to pick up Holly, who had completed her medical-surgical rotation. It was an unexpectedly warm day and Branch opened the sun roof. He relished the benevolent rays of sunshine that soothed him. He noticed the welcome yellow of forsythia bushes that flourished along the green lawns of the hillside area where one of the oldest charity hospitals in the country had been established. Suffolk General, or SGM as it was generally called, was still in operation after more than a hundred years. Started as a hospital ship in Boston Harbor for the patients with infectious diseases, now years later, it took care of some of the city's most ill, most needy citizens. Medical students from three of Boston's most prominent medical schools received much of their medical and surgical experiences there.

Holly had told Branch more than once how privileged she felt to be able to enhance her experiences there. She said, "What you don't see at SGH is not worth talking about."

His response was, "Honest?"

"No, I'm not kidding," she said to him. "Boston is a seaport town with seamen and people coming here from all over the world. I understand sometime back a sailor with a case of leprosy came in."

"Oh, my God! No!"

"Yep. But they shipped him right off to the leprosarium in Louisiana."

"What's next?" Branch wanted to know.

"Well, I'm due back at Prime Care for my work semester. You know, Branch, I'm lucky that Summit University offered a work study cooperative plan. It helps me out a lot, both educationally and financially. I consider myself very fortunate that Ms. Dagleish agreed to let me do it."

"Well, I think she's made an investment in you and your abilities."

"Think so?"

"Like me, she thinks you're special," he teased. "What's your next rotation? You know what it will be?"

"I will be going to a psych facility at a hospital in a place out on Route 2, about twenty-five miles from Boston."

"I'll be sure to visit you out there. That's not a problem." He smiled at her, patted her hand. "You're not getting away from me, kid."

Holly grinned back at him. She realized that Branch Adkins was becoming an important person in her life. In fact, she could not imagine her life without Branch being a part of it. How much a part, for the moment, she was not certain. *Perhaps,* she thought, *I should play it cool until after I finish school.*

Today he did look particularly handsome in his camel hair sport jacket, gray flannel trousers and a blazingly white shirt open at the neck. He was wearing black tasseled loafers. She caught the scent of his aftershave cologne, a clean, citrus-like odor that made her think of summer, white sand beaches and pounding, roaring waves of a Caribbean island. She noted his hands on the steering wheel were strong and well cared for. She understood how important his hands were in the operating room. She felt a sudden quiver in her stomach as she fantasized about those warm brown hands on her body.

And despite the warning of her friend Leola that she'd better latch onto Branch before "some conniving hussy" nabbed him, Holly truly believed that if Branch was to be important in her life, he would be. She was happy with the warm relationship they already shared, and if that was to become something more, then it would. Her grandmother would have said, "What's to be will be." Holly believed that.

Branch took her bag and quickly had her settled in his car. He was glad her next assignment was her work detail at Prime Care. She would be much closer to him there.

"Thanks for picking me up, Branch."

"No problem, m'dear. Glad to be of service."

"And I do appreciate it, really I do."

She said nothing more, watched as Branch put the car in gear and headed toward Holly's loft apartment.

Branch noted how quiet and introspective Holly was, not her usual talkative self. But he knew he'd be wise not to probe. He had the feeling that the news of her father, his marriage to Elyse and the impending birth of their child was on her mind. And he was right.

Staring out of the car window as Branch drove carefully through the crowded streets, she wondered what part she would have in the child's life, or whether Elyse Marshall would allow any relationship to take place.

She thought, too, about Elyse having her dead husband's child. *What motivated her to do such a thing? Was it because she loved him that strongly? Why would she opt to be a single mother? Was she trying to prove something . . . to herself, or to whom?*

Thinking about the approaching dilemma she might possibly find herself in, Holly emitted a soft, long sigh that alerted Branch.

He turned his head quickly.

"You okay?"

"Yep, just thinking about something."

"Your dad?"

"Uh huh."

"Care to share?"

"Not right now, Branch. Perhaps . . . maybe later."

"Anytime." He patted her hand. "You know that."

"I do, Branch, I do. Thanks."

CHAPTER 26

When Holly returned to her part-time job at Prime Care, one of the first patients she wanted to see was Mr. Harkins. She went to his unit, anxious to see her old friend, only to be told by a staff member, "Mr. Harkins? Oh, no, he's been transferred to the unit for independent living. He's too 'with it' for this unit," she was informed.

When she found him in the lounge area, clean shaven, wearing a shirt and tie, brown slacks and shoes, with a navy cardigan, she could hardly believe her eyes.

"Well, look at you," she said to him, and was rewarded with a big smile. "I just turn my back for awhile, next thing I know you'll be steppin' out of here."

He looked up at her. "Didn't think *you* were the only somebody who could make changes, did you? Bringing me those books made me start to sit up and take notice. Knew I had to make a change. Besides, couldn't take much more of old man Grabel snoring like a freight train every night! Had to make some *moves*! Know what I mean?"

He smiled at her, the wrinkles in his worn brown skin smoothing out his pleasure at seeing his young friend.

"Well," he demanded, "don't just stand there! Tell me what you've been up to. No good, I 'spect, knowing you as I do."

So she told him about her course of studies, a little of her medical experience at Suffolk General, and how pleased she was to be able to do her co-op work at Prime Care, even though now she was assigned to the rehabilitation department.

His eyes open wide, he listened intently, nodded in agreement when she brought him up to date about her exciting new life.

"Sounds good to me. You just stop by an' see how *I'm* doin'. Might be surprised."

"Oh, Mr. Harkins, I'll be back every chance I get. You can count on that. Is there anything I can do for you? Any new books you want?"

He thought for a moment.

"Yes, there is. You know that young African fella, the one who spoke at the convention? What's his name?"

"Yes, I know who you mean. He's a senator from Illinois."

"Tha's the one! What *is* his name?"

"Barack Obama."

"Right! I'd like to read his book."

"Okay, first chance I get I'll go by The Kwanzaa Book Shop. I'm sure they'll have it, or can order it from the publisher."

"Good. Now," he said firmly, "you let me know how much it costs and I'll give you . . ."

"You don't need to give me any money."

There was no mistaking the surge of independence Holly saw in his eyes when he insisted, "I know I don't need to pay you, but I have to pay you or I can't take the book. That's all there is to it, young lady! You hear me?"

His bony forefinger was pointed directly at her and she knew he meant what he had said. A retiree of the Transit Authority of Boston, she understood that he had a pension, but Prime Care was not inexpensive. The cost could be as much as several hundred dollars a day, and she knew costs might have risen even more during the few years she had been employed there.

Ace was pleased with the mobile he'd made for Elyse's baby. It was to be hung over the baby's crib.

Made of clay, the individual pieces had been shaped, fired and painted with appropriate colors. He used nursery figures like Little Miss Muffett, Cinderella, Humpty-Dumpty and Jack and Jill, to hang from the flat, dinner-plate-sized header. Each figure was secured with varying lengths of strong plastic coated fiber. The small figures danced and swayed as air currents swirled around them.

He used a flexible strip of balsa wood to anchor the mobile and metal clamp to attach it to the baby's crib. The tinkling sound of the mobile was pleasant to the ear and Ace smiled with satisfaction when he heard the cheerful sounds it made as it swayed in delicate circles.

He had talked to Elyse on the phone but had not visited her, believing that she was busy setting up a new schedule for her life. From their conversations, he knew that things were going well. Margaret Joyce, "Emjay," as Elyse called her, was a serene, relaxed infant.

"She's a real good baby, Ace. I'm so lucky to have such a treasure. Can't imagine my life without her. Sometimes I can't believe that I did this, that I'm somebody's mother!"

"Oh, you certainly are, my dear. I can attest to that! An experience I'll *never* forget."

CHAPTER 27

Ace made it a habit to call Elyse several times a week.

"Do you need anything from the store? I'd be happy to pick up anything for you or the baby."

"Ace, no, we're doing fine, thanks."

"In any case, may I come by to see you girls?"

She laughed over the phone. "At any time. You are welcome."

Whenever he did visit, he was surprised by the changes the baby made week to week.

"She's growing nicely, Elyse, isn't she?"

"Doing great. So well I plan to get back to the store. I have a playpen so she'll be safe."

Later, when he went by the store, he was delighted to see the baby was comfortable. Elyse was content to be back at work.

He went over to the playpen. The baby gave him a crooked smile.

Stirred by a sudden feeling of wanting to hold her, he asked Elyse, "Can I pick her up, hold her for a minute?"

"Of course you may. I've just changed her. She's nice and dry. I was about to get her bottle."

He bent over, scooping the infant into his arms. The baby never took her eyes from his face.

"My goodness, how much does she weigh?"

"Almost fifteen pounds. Not bad for three months old. She's almost tripled her birth weight."

Ace talked to the baby, telling her how beautiful she was and how proud he was of her. He was rewarded with smiles and cooing sounds as if she was talking back to him. Elyse was amazed at the instant bonding between Ace and her daughter.

"She likes you, Ace. I believe she's flirting with you."

"Well, my dear, we do have a history, you know. We go way, way back."

At that moment Emerald came into the back room and noticed the domestic scene that Ace, the baby and Elyse made. She thought how natural they looked together, but kept it to herself and instead announced her reason for entering.

"Elyse, remember Holly, the young student that offered to babysit for you? She's here with a friend of hers. I told her you were here with the baby and she'd like to see her. Can they come in?"

"Of course, by all means."

What an attractive couple, Ace thought when he saw Holly and Branch.

The girl was wearing a navy wool, military-looking jacket with a white turtleneck blouse and red plaid pleated skirt. The young man looked as if he could be a linebacker for the New England Patriots. They both looked like college students.

Emerald made introductions and Ace was impressed by the firm, manly handshake he shared with Branch as he held the baby protectively close to his chest.

He handed the baby to Elyse, who showed her to Holly.

"Mrs. Marshall, she's just beautiful! May I hold her?" She sat down on the sofa and reached for the child.

Emerald returned to the room with a tray of cold lemonade and potato chips and placed the tray on the coffee table. When she raised her eyes, she stared at the pair. *My God*, she thought, *those two look just alike!* They could be sisters! Then it struck her. Holly resembled Barry Marshall, Elyse's dead husband. But how could that be?

Holly's hair, soft brown, framed her smooth brown sugar face with soft tendrils. Margaret Joyce shared the same silken curly hair. But it was the broad forehead and dark brown eyes that she remembered as part of Barry's handsome face. These two had the same eyes, the same broad forehead. Then Emerald noted something else.

The baby was responding to Holly, had clamped her tiny hand around Holly's fingers. Emerald noticed they both had distinctive wide, stubby fingernails—just like Barry.

No one in the room seemed to take notice, but Elyse had been staring at the pair sitting on the couch in her office, the young girl and the baby . . . *her* baby. The truth had hit her like a paramedic's fist pounding on her chest to resuscitate her.

She looked around the room to see if others were watching her. Both Ace and Branch were conversing with each other; Emerald was busy playing hostess. No one seemed to know that *she* was being assailed by a shocking, life-altering moment. What earthshaking truth had thrust itself into her life?

The girl Holly looked very much like Barry. Why hadn't she seen this before? And then, when she had handed his baby to Holly, she'd noticed the oddly-shaped fingernails that she and her husband had laughed at so many times. His fingers were well defined, but his nails were short and stubby.

"Guess they are a throwback to some Cro-Magnon ancestor," he'd said when she teased him about his unusually shaped nails.

She remembered another time when she asked him a more serious question. The memory hit her tonight like a thunderbolt, unexpected and frightening.

"Have you ever had a really serious relationship before, Barry?" she'd asked him.

He admitted, "Once, when I was eighteen." His voice was quiet and she thought at the time that he was reluctant to give her an answer, but he did try to explain.

"Like I said, I was eighteen, barely knew up from down, and she was sixteen. We thought we were in love, but soon reality set in and we realized we were too young. She was still in high school and I was just a college freshman. But don't worry, Leese, you're the only woman I've ever loved, or ever will."

Tonight Elyse wondered, who *is* Holly Francis? Could she be the result of that relationship?

The two men talked about their careers. Branch was deeply impressed when he learned of Ace's Peace Corps experience.

"You spent two years in Africa? Man, that's awesome. I'd like to hear more about that."

"Sure. Sometime we'll get together. Think Holly would be interested?" Ace asked. "Maybe Elyse could come along, too. I do have many slides of my time in Cameroon, and she's often said she wanted to see them."

"Sounds very good to me," Branch said. "Why don't I give you my cell phone number and we can set something up. I'll have to check with Holly. Work it around her school hours."

"She's in school?"

"Yes. We both are. I'm trying to become a physician's assistant and Holly is working towards a B.S. degree in nursing with a specialty in geriatrics."

Elyse had walked over to where the two men were standing and she heard the last part of their conversation.

"I just heard about your schooling, Branch. I think that is so commendable. It's great to meet ambitious young people. Getting an education means an opportunity to move into a better lifestyle. I hope and pray that my little daughter will be able to have a good education."

Ace nodded in agreement. "I don't see why not. I know you'll give her every advantage."

"I aim to do my best," Elyse said.

Holly looked over towards Elyse and the men. She noticed the firm slant to Elyse's mouth as she spoke with them. That made her think that Mrs. Marshall was a woman who knew what she wanted and how to get it. Holly filed that notion in the back of her mind, realizing that it was perhaps the woman's unique focus on her goals that had aided her in deciding to take on single motherhood. It was not an action she'd had to take. She *had* wanted to do so.

Then Holly's thoughts turned elsewhere. What kind of man had Barry Marshall been? It seemed that even from his grave he had been able to persuade his wife to have their child. Evidently she loved him enough to honor his wish. Holly was not sure she understood that kind of love. She looked down at the baby in her arms . . . her sister. She thought, *In a way he, their father, abandoned both of us. Neither of us will ever know him.*

She felt a jolt of sympathy strike her for the infant. She recalled feeling so valueless as a young child growing up without a father. Would Margaret Joyce feel the same way? Have the same feelings she had endured?

Ace asked Branch, "How long have you known Holly?"

"A few years now. We met at MT, Medical Technical School . . . it prepares people for entry-level jobs in the medical field."

"Well, it sounds to me as if you two are moving up the ladder. *And*," he grinned at Branch, "I take it she is very important to you. Am I right?"

"You bet you are!" They both looked over at Holly interacting with the baby, who was responding with coos, smiles and gurgling babbles.

Ace noticed the loving exchange between the pair, then was taken aback when, with his artist's eyes, he saw a resemblance between them. *How could such a thing be possible?* He watched as Elyse took her daughter from Holly. It was then that he saw that Margaret Joyce looked more like Holly than she did her mother.

"She looks just like her father," Elyse had told him one time. Looking at the pair now, he wondered. *Naw*, he said to himself, *it couldn't be!* But he wondered all the same.

After Elyse settled the baby on the soft blankets in the playpen, Ace brought out the large Christmas gift bag.

He announced, "I made this for Missy."

"Missy?" Elyse asked.

Ace opened the bag, removed the tissue-wrapped bundle.

"That's the way I think of her. A beautiful, precious little Miss. Missy."

There was total silence in the room as Elyse, Emerald, Holly and Branch watched him carefully peel the paper back, trying not to tangle the figures hanging from the thin cords.

There was complete silence in the room as Ace slowly revealed his work.

"Ace! How beautiful!" Elyse said as she realized what she was looking at.

"A mobile for the baby!"

"You *made* this?" Branch asked.

"Yep. Wanted Missy to have something to look at."

He straightened the strings and everyone admired the delicate colorful figures that hung suspended from the plate with the painted blue moon and gold stars.

Emerald said, "Look, there's Humpty Dumpty and Little Miss Muffet!"

Elyse chimed in, "I like Sleeping Beauty. She's so delicate." She touched the small figurine and laughed when she heard the tinkling sounds as the figures swayed and touched each other.

Ace and Branch clamped the mobile to the head of the playpen and Missy looked up intently at the slowly revolving figures.

"Ace, I can't thank you enough for making this."

"My pleasure, Elyse."

Branch and Holly left soon afterwards, saying something about studying, but both promised to keep in touch.

Ace gathered up the crumpled sheets of tissue paper as well as the Christmas bag.

"By the way, Elyse, I've been meaning to tell you that Sebastian is doing very well."

"That's great, Ace. I'll come by someday and introduce him to Missy. See how they get along."

"Come by anytime, we'll be there."

She thanked him again for the baby's gift. He said goodnight to her and to Emerald, and as he walked through the now empty store he glanced at the display window, wondering if he should work up a new display, something new. At the moment, however, he had no new ideas at all.

He got into his car and sat in the dark a moment before putting the key in the ignition. He had seen the photograph of Barry Marshall on Elyse's desk in her office. There was a strong resemblance to the two girls he'd seen that night.

One was about three months old, and the other about twenty-two years old. Was there any connection between Holly and the man in the photo, with his tennis racket in hand, seemingly ready for a serious tennis game?

As Ace drove home that night, the disturbing photo on his mind, he wondered, *Should I be concerned by what I saw?*

CHAPTER 28

"Branch, I have to tell you something. Before she died, my grandmother gave me those documents that prove that I am Barry Marshall's daughter."

"Oh, my God, are you kidding me?"

"I am not. I really don't know what I should do about . . ."

"Don't make any decision in a hurry."

"That's why I'm asking you what you think."

"Somehow, Holly, I think she has to be told."

"Probably so," she sighed.

Branch suggested to Holly that perhaps she should make copies of all the documents that she had so that she could keep the originals and still have copies to give to Elyse Marshall.

"She might want to talk this over with her lawyer, you know," he said. "It wouldn't surprise me if she did. Seek legal counsel, that is."

Holly agreed with a nod, but then she asked him, "After I make the copies, what then?"

They had cleared away the leftover food, washed the dishes and tidied up the kitchen. They were seated on a loveseat, the only furniture in Holly's small living room besides an occasional chair and a small television set. Her coffee table was a pair of crates on top of which she had placed a large metal tray.

"What do you mean?"

"Should I mail them to her? Take them to her? Call her on the phone? Branch, I . . . I don't know what to do!"

Her voice quavered and Branch saw fear and consternation flicker in her eyes. His heart ached for her.

"Oh, Holly, honey." He grabbed her, held her close as her tears ran down her cheeks. "You don't have to do this *alone*. I'm not going to let you try to handle this by yourself, no way!"

Despite her tears, Branch thought she had never been more appealing, more beautiful. He continued to hold her, his only thought being, *How can I help her . . . I have to, she has no one else.*

Emerald walked to the front of the store. Ace had already started to work on his next window display.

"Ace," she called out.

"Yo!" Ace answered back, his voice muffled as he struggled to drape a large black cloth over the display shelving that he had created.

"Got time for a fresh coffee break?"

"You bet!"

He reached for a nearby chair, turned it around, straddled the seat and crossed his arms over the back. He accepted the cup of hot coffee and took a gratifying sip.

"Ah, Em, this tastes good. What's on your mind?"

"Elyse is not coming in until later. The baby is teething and I gather from what Elyse said, neither of them slept much last night."

"Baby goin' to be okay?"

"Oh, I think so. A little cranky, that's all."

"Good."

"Ace, can I ask you something?"

"Sure, shoot."

"I need to ask you if you noticed any resemblance between Holly and little Missy the other night?"

He took another sip of his coffee before he answered. Nodding his head, he looked directly at Emerald before he spoke.

"You know, I did. Didn't understand at first what I was seeing, but suddenly it struck me how much the baby looked like Holly. Then, as I was leaving, I noticed Barry's picture on Elyse's desk and I was struck by the facial similarities."

"Ace, I've been racking my brain ever since I met Holly, trying to figure out who she reminded me of . . . someone I knew, but all this time I couldn't put my finger on it. I'd get a fleeting, ghostly image in my mind, then it would vanish. Now I believe there's only one person who could be responsible for two individuals who look so much alike. They could be sisters."

"You mean Barry Marshall?"

"Who else? We *know* he's Missy's father. But why is it that she and Holly have the same brown-sugar skin coloring, the same dark, silky hair and the same shaped mouth? And I've noticed another thing. They both have the wide, oddly shaped fingernails that Barry had. Elyse and I used to tease him about them. The only prominent feature the baby has that's different is her mother Elyse's slightly slanted eyes. And as Leese pointed out to me, the long slender toes that run in her family, the Joyce family."

"Do you think Leese noticed anything?"

"Not that she's mentioned. Course I haven't *said* anything."

"Could be she's in denial."

"Ace, I don't know." A worried frown crept over her face as she continued. "What if, say, Holly is Barry's daughter. How will this affect Elyse? I've never heard of Barry having a previous dalliance, but then I'm not privy to everything in Leese's life, although we've been friends since high school."

"You two have known each other for a long time."

"We have. She went to college here in Boston and I went south to a historically black college, Fisk."

"Then you got back together?"

"Right. I majored in library science and she had her MBA from Harvard, so we pooled our resources and started The Kwanzaa Book and Gift Shop. And, Ace, Barry was always a good guy. He and Elyse were quite a pair and very happy. He was always straight-up with me and he worshipped Elyse."

"So I've heard," Ace remarked dryly.

Emerald, sensing his dismay, spoke up quickly. "Oh, Ace, I'm not a stupid woman. I know how much you love Leese. However, there may be trying times ahead. Think about it."

Ace drained his coffee cup, placed the empty cup on the floor beside his chair. He looked directly at Emerald. His voice was firm, and with determination apparent to Emerald, he told her, "Emerald, I've been halfway 'round the world in my lifetime. I love Elyse with all that I am, or will ever be. I will do anything and everything to see that she is happy. You can bet on that!"

"I know, Ace, I know, and I will do whatever I can. We're in this together, right?"

"Right!"

Ace did not feel quite as positive as he sounded, but, with the information Emerald had shared with him, he knew full well that he should begin his own search for the truth.

Emerald started to walk towards the small kitchen in back to return the empty cups, then turned to face him.

"Ace, I'm going to sound Holly out the next time she comes in. Somehow I think she may know something. Wouldn't hurt to ask. What do you think?"

"Could be a start. Tell you what. I've invited Holly and Branch over to my place. They want to see my studio and my shop. You know I've been able to add living quarters. I want you and Elyse to see what I've done. I have Branch's cell number, and I'll let you know that night."

"Sounds good. This has been such a puzzle to me. Know what I mean?"

He nodded and returned to his work. He thought how life could sometimes be complicated. His relationship with Elyse had presented so many obstacles, but he had *no* choice. He could not give up his pursuit of the woman he loved. No way . . . unless she rejected him and turned away.

"Jerome, we're late! I promised Elyse that we would pick the baby up by eleven! It's ten-thirty now."

Her husband's voice came from upstairs. "We have plenty of time, it's only a ten-minute ride to Leese's place."

"Don't want to be late. Besides, she might want to give us instructions."

Her husband appeared at the top of the stairs. "What instructions?" he asked as shrugged on a navy blue sweater. "God, Frances, you've had two children of your own, how come you need instructions?"

"Well, this is my first grandbaby, that's why. I'm not the mother this time. And knowing our daughter as I do, she *will* have instructions!"

"You two women are more alike than you know," Jerome Joyce said as he led his wife out to the car.

Elyse had asked her parents if they would mind keeping Missy overnight.

"Are you kidding?" her mother had said. "Of course we'd be delighted! Our first grandbaby! We've got a crib, an' a baby-bouncer swing all set up for her. Everything! I'm looking forward to having Missy all to ourselves. You know, Leesy, being a grandparent means that God is giving us a second chance around, and I for one intend to make the most of this blessing. It's our pleasure to help you with this precious child."

"Thanks, Dad. Thanks, Mom."

She couldn't help noticing how her mother was accepting the baby as if all along it had been with her one hundred percent approval. She wondered how her mother would react when she learned of her daughter's next obstacle.

She left her condo soon after her parents had headed to their home in Milton. It was the first time she had been separated from her child. She felt sad, but she had urgent business to attend to. She called Emerald on her cell phone.

"Yes, Em, it's me. Look, I've some business I have to take care of today. Are you very busy?"

"No."

"Good. I'll be in as soon as I can. See you in a few."

There was one person who might be able to help her, Elyse thought. Her next call was to him.

"Jay, how are you?"

"Good," he said and asked about her.

"I'm fine, and my daughter is doing well, thank you. Jay, would you be able to see me for a minute or so? You could? I'll be there in ten minutes."

Jay Collins was not only their lawyer, but he and Barry had been fraternity brothers in college and had continued to be close friends. If Barry had indeed had a previous relationship, Jay should know.

When she arrived at Jay's law office, his eyes lit up at the sight of the vibrant young mother.

"Elyse! Girl, you are looking good! How are you, and how is your daughter?"

They exchanged hugs and cheek touching.

"Here, have a seat. It's really good to see you."

"Thanks, Jay, for letting me come by like this. I know how busy you must be."

"Not today. No court appearances, and not too many appointments. And you know, Elyse, I'll always find time for you."

"I appreciate that, Jay."

She reached into her handbag and handed him a small photo of the baby. He looked at it for a minute and when he spoke, his voice was soft with emotion as if he were looking at a past memory.

"God, she's the spitting image of Barry, isn't she?"

Elyse's tone of voice was equally as emotional as Jay's.

"Yes, Jay, she is, and I'm very happy that she does look so much like her father. That's why I've come to you. I hope you can help me."

"What is it? Elyse, what's wrong?"

"You're the only person I could think of to help me, Jay. Barry was an only child and both of his parents are dead, so you are the only person I could think of to help me."

"I'll do anything I can."

"A few months before I had my baby, a young girl, a customer, came into the book shop looking for some reference material. Emerald told me that she thought the girl reminded her of someone but couldn't figure out who it was. Finally I met the girl, a very pretty, nice young lady, but unlike Em, she didn't look like anyone *I* knew. The girl came in last week with her boyfriend. They are both in college, and she asked if she could see the baby. And Jay, that's when I noticed how much she resembled Barry!"

"The girl? What are you talking about?"

"Her name is Holly Francis. I think she is twenty or twenty-one years old. What happened, Jay, was that I handed her the baby. She was sitting on the couch, I went to the back of the room to get a baby blanket, and when I turned around it hit me like a ton of bricks! They looked like sisters! I have to ask, was Barry seriously involved with anyone? Once he told me he thought he was in love with a girl, but that they both felt to young to continue the relationship. You know anything about that?"

He shook his head. "I know he was dating a high school student for a while, but it seems to me, as I remember, they quit seeing each other. I do remember Barry saying something about being 'too young.' But never anything about a baby."

"Jay, I do remember one thing. Before I had my baby, Holly, the young girl, told me that she had been born at Suffolk General and I told her that was where I planned to go for delivery. Seems she was doing a student rotation there."

Jay had been taking notes on a yellow legal pad. He looked at Elyse, gave her a warm smile.

"Let me do a little research, see what I can uncover."

"I would appreciate any help you can give me. If this girl turns out to be Barry's daughter, it means she's my child's half-sister. If so, do I have any responsibility towards her?" Elyse worried.

"Now, let's cross that bridge when we come to it. Then we'll figure out what's best for all concerned."

When she left Jay's office, Elyse felt a little better about her situation. Having his promise to help her sort out Holly's true identity eased her mind a little.

She returned to the bookshop at about twelve-thirty, having stopped at Wendy's to pick up two chicken Caesar salads for Emerald and herself. She was looking forward to a cup of hot tea, which she hoped would help calm her nerves.

Emerald greeted her with a broad smile when she saw the salads.

"Glad you brought lunch, Leese. I love Wendy's salads."

"I know you do, and I do, too." She placed the salads on her desk. "I think I'll put the 'Back in Thirty Minutes' sign on the front door. Sound about right?"

"Sure does."

As Elyse went into the small lavatory to wash her hands, Emerald started getting the tea ready in the kitchen. As she washed and dried her hands, Elyse looked at her reflection. What she saw was a woman with a worried look. What was coming next in her life? Would she ever find the ultimate happiness she once had with Barry? This man that she had loved so desperately but who was now dead was able to turn her life upside down. If Holly was his child, why hadn't he told her? Was it shame, guilt, or did he even *know* about the child?

She dried her hands, went into the kitchen, took a box of crackers from the shelf.

"All set," Emerald announced as she set the steaming teapot, cups and sweeteners down on her desk.

They each sat at her desk and began to eat in companionable silence.

"Um-m, good," Emerald said after a few minutes. Then, after several sips of tea, she asked, "By the way, did your folks pick up Missy?"

"Yes, they did. Happy as two kids. You'd think I had given them a million dollars."

"Well, you did."

"Dad said grandchildren are God's way of giving parents a second chance."

"Probably why they tend to spoil 'em so much."

"I guess so. Never thought my mother would be so nutty over Missy, certainly not the way she acted when I told her that I wanted to have Barry's child."

"Goes to show you. You never know how people are going to react in any situation."

"Sure don't."

Then Emerald remembered.

"Ace called this morning."

"He did?"

"Uh huh. Said that Branch and Holly were stopping by his place tonight to see his art store, wondered if you and I would like to come by. Said he has about finished the redecorating he has been doing."

"What time? Did he say?"

"About eight."

"I need to call my folks later on, see how Missy is doing. If she's fussy or crying, I might have to bring her back home, although they want to keep her overnight."

"Okay. Then we'll let Ace know."

Elyse dialed her parents' home at six, before leaving the store.

Her mother's voice was happy and cheerful.

"Oh, honey, we're doing just fine! Your dad took Missy out in the stroller. She loved it. She's been fed and now she's napping. Elyse, she's such a *good* baby!"

"So it's all right for her to stay overnight?"

"You betcha!"

"Good. So you'll bring her home about nine tomorrow?"

"Will do. See you in the morning."

Elyse put down the receiver and turned to Emerald.

"Boy, my mother sure has done a turn over the baby. You'd think my having Missy was entirely *her* idea!"

"Leesy, Leesy, she just wants you to be happy."

"I guess, but she sure was hard on me at first."

"Don't dwell on the past, hon. It's the present and the future that you should be concerned about. Your life with little Missy."

"That's what I'm worrying about now."

Hearing the sober tone in Elyse's voice, Emerald snapped her head around to stare at her friend.

"What? What on earth are you talking about, girl?"

"Talking 'bout what you've been talkin' 'bout these past few months."

"What? What?"

"You know right well, Emerald Stokes, what you've been nagging me about. That Holly Francis looks like someone you know."

Stunned, realizing that Elyse might be facing a life-changing truth, Emerald stared open-mouthed at her friend. She waited for Elyse to continue.

"It was the other night, Em! It was like being slapped in the face. It just struck me!"

"What struck you? Did you see what I've been noticing, a resemblance?"

"Yes, when Holly was holding Missy I saw how much alike they were . . . they looked like sisters! And I knew if that were true, that meant they had the same father . . . my husband Barry."

"Oh, Leese, how can that be?"

"To me it means that my husband must have had a relationship with the girl's mother. He did tell me once that he had been serious about someone, but they broke it off. Said they were both too young. Whether they had a baby or not, I don't know."

Emerald asked, "Have you any idea how you can find out the truth?"

"Went to see Jay Collins, said he would try to help. He and Barry go way, way back. Frat brothers and all."

"Did he know anything?"

"No more than what I knew, but he did say he would see what he could find out."

Emerald was quiet for a moment, then faced Elyse.

"You know, Leese, you're not the only one who saw a resemblance between Holly and the baby."

"Who else noticed?"

"Ace."

Elyse's face flushed deep red with consternation. She glared at Em.

"You mean you discussed this with *Ace*? How *could* you?"

"Hey, hey! Don't go getting all defensive on me! Girl, you know I would never do anything to hurt you, and neither would Ace. You know that. Deep in your heart you do!"

"But . . ."

"But nothing! I merely asked him if he had noticed any resemblance between Missy and Holly, and he said he had. Said it was when Holly was holding the baby. He said he was amazed when he saw how alike they were, same skin coloring, wide, smooth forehead, the dark brown eyes."

So like Barry's, Elyse thought as Emerald ticked off Ace's observations.

"Said they both had the same brown, silky hair. But then he told me that as he was leaving that night he happened to notice the photo of Barry on your desk. Made him wonder, he said."

There was bitter irony in Elyse's voice. She spoke through clenched teeth, her anger evident to her friend. "I can't believe you two. My supposedly good friends get together, behind my back, to talk about me."

"Now you listen to me! I only asked Ace what he had noticed. He told me just what I told you, and that made me feel validated. I wasn't the only one. You said that you never saw anything at all!"

She took a deep breath, waited for Elyse's anger to subside.

They had been sitting side by side at their twin desks. Elyse swung around, her elbows on her desk. "Now what are you two cookin' up? Like I haven't been through enough . . . losing my husband, having our child and now this. I don't know if I can handle many more twists an' turns in my life." She sighed deeply.

Emerald sprang from her chair, eager to comfort Elyse. She put her arms around her.

"Oh honey, you're stronger than you think. You will get through this!"

"I'm trying to think, Em. How am I going to react if Holly does turn out to be Barry's daughter?"

Without waiting for an answer, she gave Emerald a one-sided grin.

"You know, Emerald, I do have to confess that I'm impressed with what I've seen of her so far. She seems focused, ambitious, and if she is Barry's daughter, he would be proud of her. And I do admire her because it's obvious she's had a difficult life."

"You have to give credit where credit is due, as the wise man said."

"Agreed."

"You do know that both Holly and Branch will be at Ace's place tonight. You okay with that?" Em asked her.

"I'll be fine. Right now I want to know the truth. Then I'll go from there."

"Whatever you decide . . ."

"I know ultimately it's my decision. My first responsibility is to my baby."

⁂

Elyse decided she needed to go home to change before going to Ace's place. She had been in her suit all day. Emerald would close up and pick her up and they would ride together.

Driving to her condo, Elyse's mind tumbled with thoughts of her situation.

Why didn't you tell me? she said in her silent conversation with her dead husband.

I didn't want you to know how imperfect I was, she could imagine him saying. *You were always so special to me, and I didn't want any imperfection to come into our lives.*

But you should have told me. We were supposed to share our lives, she thought.

She drove into her parking space and went into a dark empty apartment. She felt so alone. There was no Sebastian to greet her, and the baby's crib was empty. Then she saw the blinking light on her telephone. Quickly she punched the play button. *Don't let it be my baby, please!*

It was Jay. His voice boomed over the phone.

"Haven't been able to get a copy of Holly's birth certificate. It's sealed because her parents were not married when she was born. But, Elyse, we can do a DNA test which will help identify her father. Call me tomorrow. The whole procedure should not take long.

205

Holly will be checked as well. She should be informed of that possibility."

When Elyse got into Emerald's car it was apparent that something had happened since she left the store.

"What gives? You look like someone just handed you a million dollars!"

Breathlessly, Elyse explained.

"Jay Collins left me a message on my answering machine. Seems there was no marriage between Barry and the girl's mother, and he said we can have a DNA test done."

"Not a blood test?"

"No, Em. A blood test that matches blood types like A, B, or AB will only denote who the father is *not*. But now with DNA testing the characteristics of the genome can produce a positive match."

"That means you have something that can prove paternity."

"Right. I'm going to call first thing in the morning."

"Good idea."

"Em, I feel so relieved, and I've decided that I'm not going to fret over this until I know the truth . . . if Holly is Barry's child. He was only eighteen, after all, and a college student, and if he made an error in judgment, he's not the first person to do so."

"I agree." Then she added, "Boy, you're looking mighty sharp tonight."

"You don't look so shabby yourself," Elyse answered back, noting the black and white geometric print caftan-type dress Emerald was wearing, possibly to hide a slightly stocky figure. She was also wearing several gold bracelets and large hoops in her ears. Elyse thought she looked like an African princess.

"It's a warm night, but I threw a jacket in the back-seat in case it turns chilly," Emerald explained.

Each of them was aware of the lighter mood between them, and they were happy to have their brief animosity at an end.

"Everything's goin' to work out fine, you'll see," Emerald said as she drove from Mattapan Square, down Blue Hill Avenue toward Melnea Cass Boulevard, named for a well-loved activist in Boston. She turned into the area that would take them to Ace's store near the Christian Scientist Mother Church. Luckily, they spotted a rare parking space and Emerald pulled into it with no difficulty.

Ace greeted them at the front door, welcomed each with a kiss on the cheek.

"Come on in," he welcomed them. "it's great to see you both."

Elyse thought he looked quite handsome in black slacks and a crisp white oxford shirt opened at the neck. He ushered them into his gallery where Holly and Branch were seated on the low bench in front of a wall painting. Greetings were exchanged, with Branch rising to his feet when the women entered.

Elyse remarked to Ace, "I can't believe what you've done to this place! It's awesome, doesn't look a bit like it did when I first came in and bought that beautiful vase. This room is something else! I like it. I like it very much."

CHAPTER 29

The steel gray painted walls of Ace's gallery provided a serene backdrop to the vibrant colors and textures of his artwork.

High gloss African oil paintings formed a distinct flavor of the exotic native culture of the African nation Ace had served for two years.

Some of his original lacquered vases were displayed on simple black wooden tables about the room. Two walls opposite each other were decorated with pieces of cloth with unusual patterns.

The lighting in the room was from recessed lights in the stark-white ceiling, which was accented by white crown molding.

Several native instruments, such as drums made of animal hides, sitars made from teak wood or gourds and other pieces handcrafted by Cameroon artisans, were placed on the floor about the room.

Ace had also placed a low red leather bench in front of the wall of paintings so that viewers could sit and examine them more comfortably.

There was a glass counter containing some smaller items, such as ceramics, vases, figurines, small African carved heads, jewelry, a thumb piano and reed pipes, all displayed on glass shelves.

In the front of the room a bay window faced the street. Cream colored heavy drapes fell ceiling to floor, softening the starkness of the gray walls. Two small black leather chairs flanked a low round table, also black, on which rested a shiny brass bowl filled with a mixture of colorful coral and seashells.

Elyse walked over to Branch and Holly. "It's nice to see you both. How are you doing, and how's school?"

"Great," both said in unison. Then Holly asked about the baby.

"She's doing great, too," Elyse laughed. "Tonight she's with my parents, her first sleepover."

The tense moment was over and everyone laughed. Branch excused himself, saying that Ace was about to show him his workspace in the basement.

Standing with Ace, Emerald linked arms with the two men, leaving Holly and Elyse alone.

Elyse sat down on the bench, patted the area beside her, indicating that Holly join her. She looked at the painting in front of them, a painting of Jacob Lawrence, one of several on the wall . . . It was call The Migration of the Negro, a casein tempera work with both vibrant and somber colors depicting a group of heavily burdened slaves fleeing an area. Dark birds flew over their heads, indicating their own migratory flight pattern.

"We've come a long way from that," Elyse said, nodding at the painting.

"Yes we have, thank God," Holly said.

Elyse was acutely aware of the tension she was feeling and sensed that her companion was feeling it, too. She turned to face her.

"Holly, I feel that you and I should talk. Don't you?"

"Please," Holly said in a self-effacing manner.

"I don't want to be a concern or a bother to you, don't want to upset you or your family, but, Holly, I have already decided that you are my husband's first daughter."

She was not prepared for the glistening tears she saw. Deeply touched by the sight of them, she took a deep breath, then continued.

"It was my friend, Emerald, who told me that the minute she first saw you she had a feeling that you resembled someone, but didn't know who. However, I didn't see anything. Maybe it was denial, I don't know, but the other night when I saw you holding my baby I could see your father."

"Really?"

"Yes, I could. It shocked me because even though a long time back Barry had confessed to me that he had loved a girl and had almost married her, he *never* mentioned a child."

"He didn't want me," Holly blurted out, her face stormy with her deep-seated anger.

"Knowing the man I loved, I believe he did. But at eighteen he knew he couldn't care for you. Holly, may I see your hands?"

Silently, with wonder in her eyes, Holly held out both hands, palms up.

Elyse took them in both of her hands, turned them over to examine the nails.

"These are your father's hands," she said softly.

Holly stared open-mouthed.

"Are you sure?"

"No one else has these wide, stubby fingernails except your father, Missy and you."

"Oh, my God!"

"Holly," Elyse continued, "what else can you tell me about your birth?"

Holly opened her handbag and handed Elyse a white business-sized envelope.

"My gram showed me this when I was nine years old."

Elyse took the envelope and opened it slowly, aware that this moment could very well change her future. She sensed, too, the anxiety Holly was feeling as she watched her read the document in her hands.

The only sound in the room came from the muffled voices of the three people in the basement workroom.

Elyse read a copy of Holly's birth certificate. The father's name at the bottom jumped out at her. *Father's name: Barry Edward Marshall, Age: 18, Occupation: student.* There it was. Her breath caught in her throat and quickly she read the other information about Baby Girl Francis. *Mother's name: Tiomara Francis, Age 16, Occupation: student.*

"Your parents were not married." It was more a statement than a question.

"No," Holly said, matter-of-factly, "they were not. My *father* knew what to do!" Holly said. There was no mistaking the hostility in her voice towards the man she never knew. She handed Elyse a second white envelope.

"What's this?"

"It's what my father decided to do with me!"

When she read the second document, in which Barry had given up rights and agreed that Baby Girl Francis be put up for adoption, Elyse understood the intense disappointment and pain that the girl had lived with all her life.

She leaned forward to take Holly's hand, aware of the hurt, the shame, the girl had endured.

"Holly, you have to believe me, the man your father became, the man I married was not the boy who signed for your adoption. I know that with all my heart. If he could have provided for you, he would have. I could not have loved him the way I did if he had been otherwise. Holly, you've got to believe that!"

CHAPTER 30

"May I keep these papers?"

"Yes. Branch suggested I make copies in case you wanted them. To tell you the truth, Mrs. Marshall . . ."

"Please call me Elyse. Now, I don't want you to worry, but my lawyer has suggested a DNA test should be done to be certain that you and Missy have the same father. I believe you do. You may not know it, Holly, but you are very much like your father in your personality. You have the same ambitious drive that he had. It's amazing to me, but the more I am with you, the more I see Barry. You're in the medical field. Did you know he was a pharmacist? Joined the National Guard so he could go to medical school. Oh, Holly, there's so much about your father that I want you to know. So, will you take the DNA test?"

Holly smiled for the first time.

"Yes, ma'am . . . ah, Elyse."

"Good."

Then they heard the footsteps of the trio coming up the stairs.

"Shall we tell them what we've decided?" she asked.

"Don't see why not," Holly said.

"Oh, my God, I've heard Barry use that expression *so* many times! Holly, it's so surprising to me that you are so much like a man you never knew. Must be in the genes!"

They both laughed.

When Ace, Branch and Emerald re-entered the art gallery, they saw two smiling women standing side by side, facing them.

Ever the observant one, Emerald spoke first. "So, what's with you? What's goin' on?"

"Holly and I have had a marvelous conversation. She's agreed to a DNA test, but I want you all to know that I'm sure she's Barry's daughter. *My* stepdaughter!"

"Hear, hear!" Ace said. "This calls for a celebration. Believe I've got some champagne around here just for such a momentous occasion!"

He hugged Elyse, Branch and, with a wide grin, Holly. Then Emerald hugged both women.

‿◊⌒

As soon as Elyse was able to call Jay Collins, he told her he had already scheduled an appointment for the DNA testing to be done at a laboratory in Cambridge. "I do hope that two weeks from today will be convenient for you both," he said to her.

"Oh, Jay, of course it will be. I'll let Holly know. We'll go together. Thank you so much."

"No problem. I understand it might be six to eight weeks, perhaps longer, before you have the results."

Elyse did not respond at once. Jay said, "You still there, Elyse? Can you hear me?"

"Oh yes, I can hear you, but, well, I was thinking. I am almost 100 percent sure that Holly Francis is Barry's daughter. But, Jay, would you mind, you being one of Barry's closest friends, if I brought her around? I'd like you to meet her."

"Anytime, feel free."

"You know, Jay, just as I'm going to tell Missy about her dad, I intend to do the same for his other daughter."

"Holly, this is Elyse. I'd like to pick you up at the hospital so we can go to the lab for the DNA testing together."

Elyse thought Holly's answer came over the phone rather quickly.

"Oh, you don't have to do that! I've already asked my student advisor for the day off and she has agreed, as long as I make up the day. Branch plans to come for me. We'll meet you at the lab."

"Fine. You have the address?"

"I do. See you there."

Elyse said goodbye and hung up the phone. She was disappointed because she had planned that the drive to Cambridge would give them some quality time, an opportunity to get to know one another, to bond, as it were.

Then a small voice in the back of her mind said, *How do you know that's what she wants? Have you thought that perhaps she doesn't wish to have a relationship with you? Why should she? You are a stranger. She has no past history with you. She had none with her father. Put yourself in her shoes. Would you want a stranger to lay claim to you? Change your life?*

Elyse sat at her desk, thinking about the call. *Maybe I have come on too strong. I should try to understand her point of view. How would I feel in similar circumstances?*

❧

"Ace?" He looked up from his coffee, hearing the worry in Elyse's voice.

"Yes, what's on your mind?"

They were having a coffee break at her store. Ace had just happened to come by.

"Holly."

"What about Holly?" he questioned.

"You know, I called her before the tests, suggesting that I pick her up so that we could go to the DNA testing lab together."

"And."

"Well, I got the idea, from her tone of voice and what she said, that perhaps I've been coming on too strong. What do you think? Have I?"

"I know you mean well, honey, but just think of it. You *are* a stranger to her, someone who unexpectedly entered into her life. She is probably as bewildered as you are about this sudden change."

"I thought my motives were clear. I just wanted to talk about her father . . ."

"I understand that, Leese, because you loved him and you want her, somehow, to care for him as well."

"I feel it's my responsibility to let her know what a wonderful man her father was," Elyse persisted, her eyes moist. "I want her to see him as I saw him," she added. A sudden revelation flooded her mind as she spoke to him. Clearly, she was beginning to depend on Ace.

She realized that somehow, since Ace had come into her life, there had been unmistakable changes. When and how had that happened? Was it when Ace held her in his arms that morning, comforting her, assuring her that it would get better? Or was it his artistic talent that had brought the attractive ambiance to her bookshop? Could it be the strength with which he supported her during her pregnancy and birth of her dead husband's child? Whatever it was, Ace Calhoun Brimmer was an important part of her life.

She sensed, too, that somehow it was Ace who had been able to help her feel more confident about the way she was coping with the unusual, unexpected circumstances her life had imposed upon her. Her self-esteem was soaring. She felt more comfortable with the life decisions she had made. A huge part of that was due to the qualities Ace saw in *her*. And there was the warm, secure, serene feeling she felt whenever he was around. He seemed to belong in her life. Did she love him? She shook her head as she tossed the idea around in her mind.

"So, Ace, how *do* you suggest I handle this situation with Holly? I'm not at all sure *how* to act."

He had a habit of drumming the fingers of his left hand on a table as he thought. She waited, realizing how much his response would mean to her.

Ever patient with her, he answered in a quiet voice, "Look, honey, I know your heart is in the right place, your intentions are noble, but right now, my advice would be to give her time. The way I see it, she'll begin to bond with you in her own good time."

Elyse nodded, seeing the sense in what Ace was saying.

"Sounds like good advice. Guess I should pull back, then let her set her own pace. That would perhaps be better all around. Then I'll really know how she feels about the whole situation. Thanks, Ace."

"No problem, my dear. I'm so proud of you. Your acceptance of Holly as Barry's daughter proves that you are a strong, well-grounded woman, secure in her own value system and a secure knowledge of who *you* are. Not many women would do what you have done. You are one in a million, my dear. At least that's what I believe."

CHAPTER 31

A few nights later they were having dinner at The Persimmon House, one of Ace's favorite restaurants in Boston. He had wanted to have time alone with her.

"For your birthday, Elyse," he explained, "I wanted someplace special. I'm so glad Em could baby sit Missy."

"Me, too," she said, looking around the room, a well-appointed, well-decorated room that spoke of wealth and opulence. Rich velvet draperies hung all over the windows, their gold color reflected in the crystal chandeliers overhead.

There was a working fireplace near where Elyse and Ace were seated. Soft candlelight and the seductive sounds of a trio's music in the background gave Ace hope for the marriage proposal he planned.

They had finished their entrees, the waiter had cleared the table and they were waiting for their dessert, strawberry shortcake and coffee.

"You know, Elyse, how much I love you," he said, reaching across the table for her hand. "Ever since you came into my shop to buy my first vase, I've loved you. I went all the way to Africa to try to forget you, but I could not."

He squeezed her fingers and she responded with pressure from her own fingers.

"I know your life has changed in so many ways, unexpectedly to be sure, but I'm real proud of the way you've met every challenge."

"It's been because of you, Ace, that I've been able to do so. You are one of the best friends I've ever had. And it's been your support that has helped me. I couldn't, really couldn't, have done it without you."

To his eyes she had never looked lovelier. Her face glowed with serenity and good health. Her black hair once again fell straight to her shoulders, framing her face. Her dark, slightly slanted eyes looked at him from beneath her gently curved eyebrows. Ace knew that someday he would want to paint her.

"It has been my privilege and pleasure to help you in any way I could."

He placed his right hand over her left hand, then clasped it between his own hands. Instinctively, she sensed he had reached a serious moment.

"Marry me, Leese. Come live with me and share my life. Please. I love you so much."

Elyse was not surprised by Ace's request and knew she had to clear the air between them.

"I have to tell you something, Ace. I must confess—" she started to say.

He interrupted her, shaking his forefinger at her. "No confessions needed, my dear."

"But," she continued, "I have to tell you how it is with me, Ace. Without my even being aware of it, you *have* become a part of my life. And for a long time my life has been at sixes and sevens, so confused I hardly knew where to turn."

"You don't have to explain," he said.

"But I do," she insisted. "I've had to come to terms with my relationship with Barry. I had not recognized what I now see as his stubborn selfishness, his determination to have everything *his* way. I had seen those traits as his self-confidence, his self-awareness, perhaps a bit of strong ego. All of which I admired, and I will never know if it was abandoning his first child that made him make arrangements for me to have *our* child. And, like I said before, I'm happy that I did because I did love my husband . . . despite . . ."

Ace interrupted her, seeing the glint of unshed tears in her eyes.

"I understand, Leese. Don't torment yourself."

"Oh Ace, please give me a little time. I have . . . been . . . so much has happened . . ." her voice faltered.

He interrupted. "If you have to have time, Elyse, I understand. But you've got to know this. I will always love you, always want you in my life. Call me whenever you need me, and I'll be by your side. But I will *never, ever* again ask you to marry me. I love you with my whole heart, but I cannot accept anything less than a full commitment from you. I want us to be a family, a true family. That means me, you, Missy, and maybe Holly. A whole family. Nothing less. It will have to be your decision, and I hope you can understand what that will mean to me."

"I do, Ace, and I appreciate your honesty. And I'm . . . I'm deeply humbled by all that you have done for me and

. . . my baby. I can never tell you how much you have meant to me."

"Then marry me."

She shook her head as the tears flicked across her face.

She was stunned by Ace's proposal and ultimatum and, as she put her key in the lock to go into her condominium, she could hear Ace's last words to her as he kissed her goodnight on her cheek. *Don't play with me, Elyse. I won't accept anything less than* all *you have to give.*

She set the alarm, went to check the baby sleeping in her crib in her room and tiptoed past the living room where Emerald slept on the fold-out couch.

She slipped into the bathroom, illuminated only by a nightlight, brushed her teeth, washed her face and returned to her bedroom. There was only a nightlight there as well. She undressed by its light, put on her nightgown and slid into bed. She wondered if she would be able to sleep.

She tried to bring Barry's face into focus in her mind, but found that she was unable to do so. Instead, it was Ace's. She kept hearing his words, *I'll not ask you again.*

She lay there in the darkness, hearing her daughter's soft sleeping noises. She remembered Ace being such a strong supporter during the baby's birth and knew that a bond had been forged between them. She thought of Holly born to Barry before she herself had ever known him. Ace was willing to love Holly and Missy both, be a father to them. But was that *what* she wanted?

Barry was gone, but existed in the two daughters he had given her. But what about her life? Could she live without love? The answer came back to her. "As long as you're alive, you need love," Ace had once said.

How about Ace? He always made her feel valued, made her feel special, as if he had placed her on a pedestal. There was an undeniable warmth and passion to his personality and, moreover, she felt the magic of life when she was with him. She knew he needed her to be a complete man and wondered about her own feelings.

God, please help me. Tell me what to do, she prayed silently.

She slept . . . and she dreamed.

He was waiting for her at the doorway of his gallery. She started to walk toward him but somehow, trying as hard as she could, she could not get near him. He stood quite still, his eyes steadily focused on hers. Her legs felt like rubber, barely holding her erect.

"Ace," she whispered, "I need you . . . so that I can live. I came to tell you that."

"I know. Come to me now. You can do it. I know you can."

She pleaded with him, "But I can't . . . I can't . . . I can't cross over the doorway. The threshold is too high."

"No, Elyse, it's not too high. You can do it, believe me. You can if you want to, that is."

She looked around, but there was no other entry. She saw the wall of paintings swaying towards her, beckoning for her to step forward. The African objects all around the room were enticing her to step inside.

She looked at Ace, again imploring him to help her.

"What if I fall?" she asked.

"I'll save you just like I always have. I will catch you, I promise."

With her eyes fixed on his, and with her arms outstretched towards him, she leapt across the doorway into the room as if the space were a deep, forbidding chasm. She fell into his arms like a bereft, wounded starveling. Her heart was beating against her chest wall so irregularly she thought she would faint. Ace closed his arms around her and his whispered words comforted her.

"You're safe now, right here in my arms where you belong, where you've always belonged."

She started to cry then as if her heart was breaking. He held her even closer, realizing that, now that she had put her past behind her, she was struggling to accept the future, whatever it might turn out to be.

He led her from the gallery to his bedroom between the gallery and his tiny kitchen, picked her up, gently laid her down on the bed and pulled a soft down comforter up around her shoulders. Wide-eyed, she stared at him in the room lit only by moonlight.

Ace saw the confusion in her face and spoke softly. "It's all right, Leese. You are here, and that's all that matters. I love you, and I know you love me or you would not be here."

He leaned over and kissed her and she felt her body begin to relax. She knew then that she was safe, was cared for and was loved by this wonderful man who had come into her life.

Then he knelt on the floor beside the bed.

"Leese," he said, "I knew you would come to me, because I love you."

"I love you, too, Ace. I always have since the day I asked you to hold me, but I didn't know it then. I know it now."

Then, weary from the intense emotion she was feeling, she closed her eyes. She could hear him quietly moving about as he shed his clothing. When he slid into bed beside her, she turned to face him. He took her face in his hands, whispered in the dark, "At last you're here with me, my beautiful Elyse."

She reached around to the back of his head to draw his face closer. Their kiss was sweet and tender. Then he pulled her nightgown down her shoulders, gasping as her full, rounded breasts sprang into view.

"My God, you're so beautiful, so beautiful," he murmured as his lips traced kisses along her neck and the deep cleft between her breasts. She felt her body begin to melt. She began to strain to reach the experience that she knew she needed or she would never again be whole, would always be wanting, unsatisfied, never alive if she couldn't share what she yearned for with this man. He was her only hope for complete fulfillment. She knew that now with her whole heart.

The moon continued to spin silver rays into the room as Ace's gentle hands moved expertly over her smooth, soft skin, searching for sensitive areas to love. Her breath came in quiet gasps as her nerves responded to the feather-like sensations that almost drove her mad. She twisted her head wildly as her hungry body reacted to Ace's touches. Then their bodies fused into a single unit and the world dissolved and faded away.

He kissed her again and she held on to him for dear life as if she were drowning.

"Ace, Ace," she whimpered, her whole body convulsing.

There was no answer, no response from him.

She woke up then, her body drenched with perspiration, a quickening in her inner core that frightened her with its fierce intensity. She was alone. The dream had been so real, her whole body still quivered.

She got out of bed at six-thirty. Missy was still sleeping soundly as she slipped into the bathroom. After a quick shower she dressed in sweats and sneakers, went into her kitchen, put on a pot of coffee and then went to the living room to find Emerald stirring about, half-awake.

"Good morning. Have a nice birthday?"

"Good morning, Em. Yes, I had a wonderful birthday, wonderful. Look, Em, I left something over at Ace's place. Do you mind? The baby's still asleep, but I set her bottle out right beside the warmer if she should wake up before I get back. Be right back."

"Sure, no problem."

"Thanks, Em. I owe you, big time."

"No problem. See you when you get back."

When she got into her car she checked her face in the mirror. *Well,* she thought, *he'll have to take me as I am or else.* Then she thought of Missy's birth. *So he's already seen me at my worst.*

She dialed Ace's number on her cell phone. It rang only once before she heard his sleepy response, "Ace here."

"Ace, it's me. I have to see you right now . . ."

"Elyse, what's wrong? Is the baby, is the baby all right?" he stammered.

"Oh no, she's fine. I'll be there in a few minutes."

He was waiting at the door when she drove up and parked the car, a worried look across his face. A dark stubble of beard shadowed over his chin. But to her he had never looked more handsome, so strong, so manly. This was the man who cared for her, that she knew would continue to care for her all the days of her life. She knew, too, that with him in her life she would be a complete woman.

She ran to him and he held her close, pulling her forward and gently closing the door behind them.

"You're here," he murmured as he kissed the top of her head. "You're here."

"Ace, I had to come. You . . . you said you wouldn't ask me again . . . that I," she could hardly get the words out, "that I would have to come to you. So I'm here, Ace." She swallowed, then began to cry, her tears flowing freely down her cheeks. "Look, I . . . I don't know what's ahead for me, but whatever it is I can't face it without you. I love you, Ace. I guess I began to love you the first day I met you and asked you to hold me. I so needed you then, but I need you now more than ever."

The pleading look she gave him almost broke his heart. He looked at the lovely face of the young, beautiful woman who had already lived a lifetime of events that would have destroyed a lesser woman. She had prevailed and wanted him in her life. He smiled at her, teasing her with his next words.

"So, my dear, you have something you wanted to ask me?"

She nodded wordlessly, looked down at the floor for a moment, then raised her eyes to his.

"Ace," she said in a soft voice, "will you marry me?"

Still in a playful, teasing mood, he placed his fingertips on his mouth, looked up at the ceiling as if pondering an answer. Then he bowed gallantly like a knight of old.

"It would be my pleasure and my distinct honor to do so, Miss Elyse." He grinned at her, continuing, "Thought you'd never ask. Come with me. Let's start off right. Got a pot of fresh coffee waiting."

Responding to his jocular mood, she linked arms with him as they walked back to his kitchen to start their new life.

She prepared his favorite meal for their dinner that night, one that Ace had really begun to anticipate. He had come to her condo apartment to continue with their wedding plans.

"Food's ready," she told him.

"It smells great, Leesy, and I'm ready."

Elyse had cooked beef carbonnade, a stew-like dish of beef pot roast cooked with beer. She sliced the beef, placed a generous portion on Ace's dinner plate and added a mound of steamy white rice and a serving of baked butternut squash seasoned with brown sugar, butter and cinnamon.

She placed the filled plate in front of Ace, who rubbed his hands together, ready to eat. She put a silver gravy boat filled with hot gravy near his right hand.

"Help yourself, Ace. I have to get the salad from the fridge."

He took her advice and ladled a good serving of gravy over his rice and meat. He looked up at her and grinned. "Woman," he teased, "please get your plate ready and sit down! I can't wait much longer to get at this food!"

"I'm coming right now," she said, and joined him with her own plate of food. She couldn't wait until Ace saw the dessert she had made. Homemade cream puffs filled with vanilla ice cream and topped with fresh sliced strawberries. She knew that Ace enjoyed her cooking. He never failed to tell her so.

"There's one thing I know for a fact," he'd once said. "You are a genius in the kitchen."

That night, after eating, he asked, "How did you learn to cook like this?"

"My Aunt Ginny has a small eatery on the Vineyard. I worked summers for her and she taught me. Everybody loves Aunt Ginny's . . . that's what she called her eatery. It's one of the places the *brothas* and *sistahs* meet, greet, and eat."

"She still owns it?"

"Sure does. We'll have to visit this summer. She's one of my dearest relatives. Could always count on her."

"I do look forward to meeting her." Suddenly he had a thought. "Look, Leese," he took her hand, "why don't we do everything on the Vineyard?"

Elyse's eyes opened wide and said, "What a great idea! My folks have a cottage there and they will be able to take care of Missy while we do a little honeymooning."

"Think we can work it out from here?" he asked.

"Piece of cake," Elyse said. "You do know that I want a small, intimate wedding with close friends and family, Ace?"

"Whatever you want is fine with me, you know that."

When Ace and Elyse finally settled on June twenty-second as their wedding day, Ace said quietly, "That's a very lucky day."

"How come?" Elyse wanted to know.

"It's my birthday! You didn't know? What a birthday *this one* is going to be!" He reached for her. They were in Elyse's living room, seated beside one another on the couch. With his arms around her shoulders, he pulled her close to him.

"I can't believe how well our plans seem to be coming together."

"Why shouldn't they?" she said. "We are special people, and we deserve to have the best, wouldn't you say?"

When he kissed her in answer to her query, his touch only reaffirmed to her just how much she loved this man. She had survived horrendous ordeals because of the steadfast practicality he brought into her life. His ability to face problems dead on, with none of the flamboyant optimism of her late husband, had anchored and steadied her.

The love she shared with this man was the love she needed to sustain her life. "It's the present," he'd said to her. "The past robs one of life, can hold you back, even drag you deep into despair. Life is to be lived, and living means the 'here and now.'"

As she felt the secure warmth of his mouth against hers, she realized that Ace was right. It was the *moment* that mattered, and she was fortunate to share it with Ace Brimmer.

She trembled in his arms; the warm breath of his whispers in her ear chased away any lingering doubts she might have had. His words were a song of love.

"My darling, tell me it is real to you, what you truly want in your life. I love you and always will, now and forever."

"I love you, too, Ace. You are all I'll ever need in my life."

She wiped her eyes with the back of her hands. "Got no more time for emotions, dear sir. Still have more work to do."

"Don't you worry. Everything's going to be fine, you'll see," Ace responded in a firm voice. "I won't have it any other way."

The Rev. Talbot Brimmer, Ace's great-uncle, his grandfather's younger brother, had agreed to come out of retirement as an Episcopal priest to preside over the wedding.

A tall, dignified-looking figure, his snow-white hair formed a stark contrast to his tobacco-tan skin.

"As your only living relative, it would be my honor and pleasure to preside at your nuptial," he said when Ace asked him to preside. He told Ace, too, that though it was a bit unusual, he had no objections to their writing their own vows, "within limits," he'd said with a warm smile.

The music school located near Ace's art store was able to recommend some senior students who regularly hired out as musicians for local gigs, weddings, parties, dances and the like. Ace asked for a cellist, violinist, saxophonist and drummer. He met with them, all males, and was pleased when they performed for him. After their audition, he gave them a list of the music he'd like to be played but also told them that requests from the guests would be okay, especially for dancing after the luncheon. His only request was to have Beethoven's "Für Elise" played as the bride came down the aisle.

There was one bit of business that Elyse knew she had to face. Finally the DNA results had arrived, proving that Holly was Barry's daughter. She wondered about inviting the girl to her wedding. She wondered, too, if knowing she was Barry's child, Holly might want to become involved with a new family.

Elyse sat down at her desk. Someone, she suspected it was Emerald, had moved Barry's picture. *That chapter of my life is over,* she thought.

She reached into her desk drawer for a sheet of her personal writing paper, then began to write. She would take Ace's suggestion and send the invitation. It would be Holly's decision, might even offer a hint of their future relationship. Indeed, Elyse thought, *if there is to be one.*

Dear Holly, she wrote.

When Holly finished her psychiatric rotation at Western New England Hospital, Branch drove out to the facility to return her to her apartment.

He had four months left to complete his program as a physician's assistant and he was already putting out feelers for a job, perhaps with one of the surgeons he knew. Holly had less time in school than he had. She would complete her work in a little over two months. Then she planned on studying for her board certification to become a registered nurse.

They had worked hard, each of them, he thought, and God willing, they would have a happy future together. As he drove along the road, passing open fields, dairy farms, truck farms that sold produce at roadside stands and chicken farms, he noticed a sign indicating that Andes Llamas were raised at that farm and clothing such as sweaters, scarves, hats and mittens could be purchased there. He even spotted a few of the exotic animals lined up against a fence, peering out at the cars speeding by.

He had passed Fort Devens, now closed, the post that had served as an induction center for many young men entering the military during World War II.

Branch's dad had been one of them, had been born and raised in Haverhill, Massachusetts, and many of his classmates, especially in high school, were sons of immigrant parents, mainly French-Canadians or Italians. They had played football, basketball and baseball in high school, so it was a given that upon graduating from school they would all join the army, "be buddies for life," they had agreed.

As he drove past the army base, Branch thought about his father, who had advised him, "Do whatever you can to make a decent life for yourself and the family you will have someday." He had never forgotten that advice. Branch hoped that by becoming professionals in the medical field both he and Holly could have a decent future.

Summer stretched ahead of them and Branch could hardly wait to spend time with Holly at the beach, or take short trips in his old car. Maybe after his course of studies was complete, he'd buy a used SUV. He smiled to himself wondering what Holly would think of that idea.

She seemed to be enjoying her life so much more than before. She was very enthusiastic about her classes, seemed more hopeful about her future. He wanted to give her a ring, a "friendship" ring, he told her, but she'd said no, she didn't need a ring. He was her friend, he knew that, but she had added, "Let's see how we stand after we finish up. Then maybe . . ."

A few weeks back, Holly had said, "You know, Branch, my psych rotation is nearly over and I have to tell you I have learned a lot."

"Honest?"

"Yes, honest. At first I didn't like it at all. I couldn't understand the patients' illnesses . . . how a patient's caregiver has to appreciate the small, baby-like steps many patients have to take towards recovery."

"That must have been hard for you."

"It was, but then I decided that if I was going to be an effective nurse . . . a patient advocate, I needed to care for the individual, no matter what illness the patient had, be it in his mind, his heart, his belly . . . if he was ailing *anywhere* in his body, his life, that alone would have to be my paramount concern, to help him heal. After I made that decision, everything began to fall into place."

"That must have made things easier for you," he said to her.

"You could say that, I guess. Seems to me, from what I've learned, the choices we make give us our experiences and shape our lives."

Branch returned his thoughts to the present as he reached the hospital. He followed the road signs pointing to the administration building and visitors' parking.

Holly was waiting in the lobby. She had one suitcase, a duffle bag and a briefcase.

"Hi, Holly!" He pecked her cheek and then bent down to pick up the suitcase and duffle bag. "This is it? All you have?"

"Yes, Branch. I shipped some stuff to my apartment last week, books 'n stuff, you know. My landlady is holding them until I get home. How are you doing? Thanks so much for coming to get me."

"My pleasure, wouldn't have it any other way."

He led her to his car, stowed her bags and her briefcase in the trunk, opened the passenger side door for her, then got into the driver's seat.

"Seatbelt fastened?"

"Yes, it is, but would you mind, Branch? You're not in a hurry, are you?"

"Why, no, not at all. What's up?"

She reached into her handbag and pulled out a white business-sized envelope.

"This came two days ago, but I wanted to have you with me when I opened it."

"What is it?"

Then he saw the return address in the upper left-hand corner indicating it was from the lab. *The DNA results*, he thought. He waited for her to open it.

Holly placed her handbag on the floor between her feet. She ran her left thumb beneath the flap and took out a folded sheet of paper. Before she read the contents, she looked over at Branch. He was moved when he saw the glistening moisture of tears in her dark eyes.

"Oh, honey." He reached for her, loosening his seat-belt as he did so. "You will always be special to *me*! I don't care whose daughter you are! King Tut's, Attila the Hun's, or Barry Marshall's! You are the woman I love and want to spend my life with *you*, Holly Francis! That piece of paper doesn't mean *squat* to us. Not a thing! Do you hear me? Understand?"

Holly nodded wordlessly. The tears plopped down her cheeks and she sniffed as she read the letter.

"Well, what does it say?" Branch asked.

"It's . . . it's a match. I'm Barry Marshall's biological daughter," she whispered in a slow, husky voice as if she didn't really believe her eyes.

"May I see?"

He took the piece of paper from her shaking hands and silently read its contents.

"Babe, how do you feel now that you know the truth?"

"Don't know . . . how to feel."

"If you could, what would you ask him?"

"Why? Just . . . why?"

Her eyes misted over again. She tried to explain.

"It wasn't that he was not there for school plays, class outings, father-daughter things, to sign my report card. It wasn't just that! He wasn't there at all, not one single day of my life! And I don't want anyone, including his widow, telling me how wonderful he was! He wasn't wonderful at all! He denied me . . . wanted nothing, *nothing* to do with me!"

Branch took Holly's hand, drew her close to his chest, rested his chin on the top of her head. He spoke softly and slowly.

"Holly, he was only eighteen. He loved your mother, and you were born, thank God, out of that love. At eighteen, he was bewildered and confused by the heavy responsibility he knew he could not handle. You have to forgive him. He was only doing his best. He gave you life. He loved you."

Branch pointed out that that letter from Cambridge Laboratory stated a copy of the DNA test results had been sent to Elyse Marshall.

Branch helped Holly collect her stored belongings from the landlady. Now that school was over, she was moving back into her third floor loft apartment.

Holly said, "Branch, I'm too frazzled to go out and eat, and there's nothing to eat here. Would you mind if we ordered something. Pizza, maybe?"

"I understand, hon. Why don't I go to the store and pick up dinner? Maybe fried chicken, rice pilaf, broccoli and some dessert. Would you like iced tea as well?"

"Oh, Branch, sounds mighty good to me!"

"Be back in a jiffy!"

While Branch was out, Holly decided to go through her mail. There was the usual plethora of junk mail, grocery store flyers announcing their usual weekend sales, advertisements for windows, floors, siding for the home, assorted bills she had to pay—she'd look at them later—and she noticed, too, a few letters from credit card companies offering her large, unthinkable lines of credit. She knew very well what she would do with them.

Then she spotted a cream-colored envelope. The sender's name in the corner was *Elyse J. Marshall. What does she want?* Holly thought as she tore open the thick envelope. Inside she found a folded handwritten note.

Dear Holly, she read. *First of all, I want to let you know that I have received the information from the Cambridge lab. I assume you have been notified as well. I wanted to call you, but thought I should give you some time. I want you to know that I am happy with the news, and I hope for a bright future for all of us as a family, if that would please you.*

Ace and I are going to be married on June twenty-second, at Oak Bluffs on Martha's Vineyard. We both want you and Branch to come. Will you call me so that I can give you information about the ferry schedule and accommodations? We will be able to put you both up for the weekend. I do hope you can come. Always, Elyse. P.S. Missy is standing up now.

Holly held the note in her hand, wondering how Elyse really felt, learning that her husband had fathered a child before he married her, and had kept that information from her. And why had he prevailed upon her to have *his* child, after his death? And why had she done so? Holly thought it must have been a stunning blow to Elyse to find out the truth of Holly's existence. Elyse must have felt that she really knew the man she had loved and married, Holly decided.

How would I feel under circumstances like those that she has been through? She thought back to the look she had seen on Elyse's face the night she saw the resemblance between Missy and her. It was a look of bewilderment, disbelief and shock. Holly knew she would never forget that moment. Lives were altered, never to be the same for any of them. The dynamics of an action that began twenty-two years before spun with extraordinary force to affect changes in the lives of Holly, Branch, Elyse, Ace, Missy . . . even Emerald and Elyse's parents. And Holly knew, too, that the act, like a stone dropped into a body of water, caused unknown ripples far afield. Even as she interacted with her patients in years to come, Holly knew her own personal past history would somehow be reflected in her interactions with them.

When Branch returned home from the store, Holly handed him the letter.

"What's this?" he asked.

"Read it," she said and she began to set the kitchen table and place the cartons of hot food on the counter. She got serving utensils from the counter drawer and she poured the iced tea into glasses which she set at their places. Then she looked over at Branch.

"So, what do you think? Should we go to the wedding?"

Branch pursed his lips and was silent for a moment before answering.

"You know, hon, it's your decision, but you are asking me what I think. And I say go. None of these things that have happened have anything to do with you. But since the facts show that you are a member of this family, you have every right to be part of it, however much you choose to be. But I wouldn't just close the door entirely. So, I say go and 'play it as it lays,' as the gambler said."

Holly was standing at the kitchen counter. She had opened the various containers of food so that she and Branch could serve themselves. Steam, fragrant from the enticing odors of the chicken, rose up in the small room.

Branch saw the uncertainty in her face as she listened to his reasoning. Her dark, curly hair framed her lovely face. He wanted so much for her to be happy and he hoped these moments would somehow ease her unsettled mind.

"Look," he continued, "I know you have a lot on your plate right now, school, your job at the nursing home, even though it's part-time, and you are trying to study for your nationals, but you have to look forward to a life of your own."

He put Elyse's letter on top of the stack of mail that Holly had set on top of her briefcase on the counter. Standing beside her, he accepted the plate she offered and began to make his selections. He was hungry, hadn't eaten since early morning. He picked out a chicken thigh and drumstick, a helping of hot rice, some buttered stalks of broccoli and a buttered roll. Then he sat at the table and waited for her.

When she joined him, he reached for her hand, wanting more than anything to take her in his arms . . . to love her, comfort her and do everything in his power to see to her every need.

"You know, don't you, Holly, how much I love you? Since the day we met at school, I have thought of nothing but your happiness. I know life has not been easy for you, but I admire the way you've made it on your own . . ."

"Well, Branch," she smiled shyly, "you've helped me. Couldn't have made it at all without you."

"Only trying to help," he interrupted. "And I still say let's go to the wedding. You've been invited, which means you're wanted."

"Maybe you're right, Branch." She took a sip of her tea, picked up her fork and began to eat.

Branch joined her, thinking as he took a forkful of the steaming rice, *God help me, help her.*

"How are you doing, Mr. Harkins? Behaving yourself?" Holly greeted her patient the next morning.

"Now why would I do anything like behavin'? Girl, this old man got lots of tricks up his sleeve!" he teased, delighted to see her.

And she was equally pleased to see him. His all-over health seemed to have improved, his copper-hued skin was shiny and clear, even his walking had improved. He no longer needed his walker, but used only his cane to help him walk.

Holly had begun to see this elderly man as a dear friend, someone who cared about her and someone she had someone to care for.

She decided to confide in him.

"Would you like to go into the sitting room?" she suggested. "I'm off duty now and Branch is going to pick me up later, so we can be comfortable in there."

"Don't see why not," the old man agreed. "You still seein' that young fella from the operatin' room?"

"We're kinda close, you might say." She smiled as she helped him stand and gave him his cane. They headed down the hall to the all-purpose sitting room of Prime Care.

Holly found two comfortable chairs in a quiet corner.

Prime Care's visitors' sitting room contained several vending machines. Holly selected a Coke for Mr. Harkins and a ginger ale for herself.

"I know you remember my gramma, Theodora Francis," she began.

"Sure do," he murmured. "One fine woman."

"Yes, she was. She and my momma raised me. Never knew my father."

"That so?"

"Yes, and that really bothered me for a long time. Still does, in a way."

"I can understand that. Everybody wants to belong to somebody."

"That's exactly how I felt, Mr. Harkins. I knew that my mother and grandmother loved me, but what about the man who should have been part of my life?"

"You do know, child," Mr. Harkins said quietly, "you're not the *first* somebody who didn't know their daddy . . ."

"I know that, but when I was about nine my gramma told me that she had prevented my father from giving me away, I really became angry and bitter. I believe that's when I decided I would show him and everybody else that I was *somebody*, not some nobody to be thrown aside!"

Mr. Harkins, wise in years, wanted to help Holly. He realized that her venting of what she perceived to be a stumbling block in her life was really the catalyst that had transformed her into a strong young woman. Stronger than even she recognized. But he did. He watched the ripple of emotions cross over her youthful but sober face and he listened.

She told him then about finding out about her father.

"He was killed in Iraq?" he asked.

"Yes, he was."

"So you never got to meet him?"

"I finally met his widow. She runs . . . owns the bookstore where I've been able to get some of your reading material."

"That so? What do you think of her?"

"She's nice and all, but . . . well, she's had a baby by her dead husband. Seems he left frozen sperm."

"Great day in the morning! You mean she had a live baby from a dead man's seed?" The elderly man's eyes were wide with disbelief.

The old man threw his head back against the chair and began to shake it side to side in disbelief.

"That's not all, Mr. Harkins. The baby, a little girl, and I have been tested and the results prove that we have the same father. So I have a half-sister."

"Girl, you sure have told me something tonight! Can't believe . . . a dead man making a baby! What's next!"

"Elyse, that's my . . . I guess you'd call her my step-mother . . . she's been trying to tell me what a wonderful man Barry Marshall was, but somehow that doesn't register with me." Holly took a sip of her soda, recapped the bottle. She continued to explain.

"I don't hate the woman, but I don't feel close to her. Now she is going to get married again. I like the man she's going to marry. He is a wonderful person, and I can see how much he cares for her. Branch and I are invited to the wedding. It will be at Oak Bluffs, on the Vineyard. Branch says we should go, but . . . I don't know."

"Branch is right." Mr. Harkins took Holly's hand, rubbed his fingers across her knuckles. She was surprised at the smooth, warm softness of his touch.

"Listen to me, child. You are a fine young woman that anyone would be proud to have as a daughter or granddaughter. I know I would. Now you have a bright future ahead of you. I'm as proud as a peacock that you've come into my life. You don't know, will never know, what was in your father's mind when you were born. You said he was eighteen and your mother sixteen?"

Holly nodded, unable to speak, her eyes brimming with tears.

"Honey, I know what you have to do, and it's *all* you have to do."

"What, Mr. Harkins?"

"Forgive them, both of them. They didn't know what else to do. You have a good life ahead of you. I know that young man loves you very much, so I'm sayin' all you have is your life to live. Live it without resentment or pain. Don't turn your back on the future that's ahead of you. Forgive and go forward to a happy life. Go to Martha's Vineyard. God bless you, little girl. You are going to be all right. *I* know what *I'm* talking 'bout." He patted her hand.

"Thanks, Mr. Harkins. Mr. Harkins?"

"Yes, child, what is it?"

"I think as soon as Branch and I finish our schooling and get jobs, we might get married. Would you please be the man who gives the bride away?"

"Honey," he grinned at her, happiness flooding over his face, "as long as you don't mind walking down the aisle with me *and* my cane, can't think of anything I'd rather do! It will please this old man, very much."

As she walked him back to his room, Holly felt a lightness in her hear. She was free to live and love. She could hardly wait for Branch to pick her up that night. Mr. Harkins was right, "Forget and live." That was what she planned to do.

CHAPTER 32

Their wedding was to take place in the garden in back of Elyse's parents' summer cottage. Her father had hired a carpenter to build a trellis at the far end of the garden, and the local florist planned to decorate it with roses, ivy, bridal wreath and white lilacs.

A tent would be set up for the reception, which would include a sit-down luncheon, since the wedding was scheduled for one in the afternoon. There would be champagne for the toast and wine to be served with the luncheon of lobster salad, tiny croissants, stuffed mushrooms and individual strawberry jello molds on a bed of crisp lettuce. Elyse's Aunt Ginny insisted on preparing the food for the fifty guests and the bridal party. Emerald would be Elyse's maid of honor and Omar Ace's best man.

Emerald had confided in Elyse that never in all her born days had she seen a more handsome man than Omar Eugendidi looked to be in his picture.

"Do you think I've got a chance?" Em wondered.

Elyse laughed, "You're so excited and you haven't even met the man! Sure you're going to be able to walk down the aisle?"

"Huh? With a chance to walk with the brotha and sit next to him at the bridal table, you betcha!"

~~∿⌒

Omar arrived at Logan Airport early on June first. Ace met him and they headed to Ace's place, stopping first at Dunkin' Donuts to pick up breakfast.

"Good flight?" Ace asked as they drove out of the airport.

"First rate, my friend. I slept most of the way from London. Made the change there after the flight from Cameroon." He looked out the car window as Ace headed the car to the tunnel beneath Boston Harbor.

"So," he said in his clipped, pedantic sounding voice, "this is Boston, eh?"

Ace chuckled, "It is." Then he recited the familiar lyric.

" *This is Boston, the home of the bean and the cod.*
Where the Cabots speak only to the Lodges, and
The Lodges speak only to God."

Omar laughed. "I hope I get to see some of this city . . . I've heard so much about it."

"Elyse and I have an itinerary planned for you. We want you to enjoy your stay."

"Can't wait to meet your bride, Ace."

"Nor she to meet you, my friend. It was your level-headedness that gave me the impetus to persist in wooing her. You know I was with her when her daughter was born. And I believe that might have been when Elyse realized the depth of the love I have for her. We've had our differences, but I have to say we've come through with flying colors. And in three weeks, God willing, we'll start our new life together."

Omar grinned widely, his dark brown face reflecting the happiness he felt for his friend.

As they exited the tunnel, Ace began to point out various landmarks.

"This is Haymarket Square. See all the vegetable and fruit stalls?"

"Nothing like our markets," Omar observed. "Don't see many women, all men . . ."

"That's the way this market runs, mainly male vendors. Outside the city, in small towns, you may see family-owned farms. There you'll see women selling farm produce."

"Very interesting," Omar said.

"Now," Ace told him, "we're heading toward the South End, and soon you'll see folks that might remind you of home."

As Ace was driving along Columbus Avenue Omar quickly spotted two men of color chatting in front of a barbershop.

"Aha, I see what you mean, old chap," he said, excited by what he saw: women pushing baby strollers; teenagers with their low-slung jeans; joggers whose muscular legs glistened with perspiration; pedestrians of all ages, skin hues and hair styles.

Omar could hardly believe his eyes. He just stared, trying to take it all in.

"As soon as we get to my place, Omar, we'll have some breakfast." He glanced at his watch. "It's only eight-thirty. Then I suggest you shower and try to get some sleep, help you get over your jetlag. We are going to have dinner tonight at Elyse's home. You'll get a chance to meet some folks. They can't wait to meet you."

Omar sighed, "Hope they won't be disappointed."

"Believe me, they will not be disappointed, not at all."

Elyse found the menu she wanted to serve that night in the catering department of a local food store. Dinner was scheduled for seven, and she requested the food to be delivered at five o'clock. That would give her time to take care of Missy and prepare for her guests, six in all: her parents, Emerald, Ace, Omar and herself.

She chose a cheese and fresh fruit platter for an appetizer, to be served with crackers and a light wine, followed by chicken marsala, maple glazed baby carrots, fresh green beans and rice pilaf. Dessert was to be chocolate fudge torte or ice cream.

Ace and Omar were the first to arrive. Ace could hardly contain himself, he was so anxious for the pair to meet.

Elyse welcomed them when they came. She was wearing a pair of beige silk slacks with a simple white silk long-sleeved blouse. Tiny gold studs flashed on her ears, and the only ring she wore was her diamond engagement ring.

Ace was delighted when he saw that she was wearing her hair in a sleek, sophisticated manner that gave her an exotic look. To him, she had never been more beautiful.

He gave her a gentle kiss and then turned to Omar. "Omar, this is Elyse."

"Welcome, Omar. I'm delighted that you are here."

Emerald and Elyse's parents arrived a few moments later. Introductions all around were made by Ace, and a lively conversation took place with Omar talking about his native Cameroon. He invited them all to visit at anytime.

"I would love to visit Africa," Emerald said. "I've always wanted to see the motherland."

"You'd be most welcome," Omar said with a bright smile. "I'd be pleased to have you, any of you," he waved his hand in an all-encompassing gesture, "and you must consider this an open invitation."

Jerome Joyce, Elyse's father, turned to his wife. "Frances, would you like to make such a trip?"

Looking at Omar, she responded in a flirtatious voice, "With such a handsome host, why not?"

Emerald wanted to kick the older woman under the table, but instead she rose from the table to remove the cheese and fruit platter. She took them into the kitchen and proceeded to help Elyse serve the dinner. She whispered into Elyse's ear, "Your mama better lay off Omar. I got first dibs on him, you know. She's already got a man."

"Oh, Em, don't mind Mama. Lately, it seems, she loves to play the flirting game. She's harmless."

She handed two dinner plates filled with food to Emerald.

"For Mother and Dad, okay?"

Emerald raised her eyebrows as she accepted the plates.

"Sure I won't drop food on yo mama?" she teased.

"Go on, girlfriend, behave!"

Elyse followed Emerald with servings for Ace and Omar. Then she and Emerald joined the others with their own servings.

Ace poured the wine according to each one's preference, and Mr. Joyce made a toast.

"It is my great pleasure to welcome Ace into our family. It is also my wish that he and our daughter have many, many years of happiness. Now I would be remiss if I did not welcome Omar to our hearth and home. Welcome, Omar!"

Glasses were raised, clinked together and voices echoed, "Hear, hear!"

Elyse invited everyone to eat, saying, "Help yourselves, eat hearty. There's plenty more for seconds."

Omar looked at her, and she noticed that he was eating in the European style with his fork in his left hand and his knife in his right.

He asked, "Did you prepare all this delicious food?"

Elyse laughed. "Not hardly. I picked out what I wanted, the caterers delivered it as I requested, and all I had to do was serve it."

"Well, it is certainly delicious, I must say."

"I'm glad you're enjoying it."

Ace broke in, anxious to make his point.

"But, Omar, I want you to know that my intended can cook with the best! I'm sure you'll see before you leave. Right, hon?" he said to Elyse.

"Oh, I agree. It will be my pleasure to introduce Omar to some American cuisine." She ticked off on her fingers, "Boston baked beans, Fenway franks, Maine lobster and clam chowder."

"Really sounds interesting, but I don't want you to trouble yourself on my account."

"No trouble for me, Omar. Not at all."

Then Emerald asked a question. "Omar, can you tell us about your country? It's really exciting to meet someone from Africa." She gave him a bright smile.

He turned to give her his full attention.

"I'd be happy to. We are a republic with over twelve million population. We are mainly Christians and Muslims. Our Cameroon encompasses about two hundred thousand square miles on the West Coast of Africa."

Emerald listened intently. "Could perhaps be the ancestral home of some of my family," she mused.

"Could be," Omar said. "Welcome aboard."

Everyone laughed. There was a comfortable silence at the table, which pleased Ace.

CHAPTER 33

June twenty-second proved to be a delightful day. It was a bright blue-sky day with temperatures in the middle seventies. There was not a single cloud hovering overhead. When Elyse got up that morning, the first thing she did was take her daughter to the balcony outside her bedroom, the room she had as a child every summer. Since she was being married from her parents' home, and they would be caring for Missy while she and Ace were taking a few days' honeymoon, it made sense to be staying there.

"Look, baby, see the pretty garden where Mommy is going to be married? Someday, my child, I hope you will find a wonderful man to love. It's what I wish for you with all my heart."

She went downstairs with the baby in her arms. She could smell the invigorating odor of freshly brewed coffee.

"Oh, honey, what a beautiful day for you and Ace!" her mother greeted her. "Here, let me take the baby. I'll put her in her high chair and feed her. Want some coffee?"

"Thanks, Mom. Smells great."

She filled a ceramic mug.

"Now," her mother said in her "take charge" voice, "don't worry about a thing! I'm going to take care of

Missy," she said as she prepared a dish of warm cereal for the baby.

As she returned to her room upstairs, Elyse reflected that in another four hours or so she would be Mrs. Austin Calhoun Brimmer. A brand new life, a new beginning, a fresh start. As she sat in her room, sipping the hot coffee, she could hardly wait for the day to be over. Her thoughts turned to Holly.

Elyse still didn't know how she felt about her relationship with Barry's daughter, but she had felt comfortable in sending the invitation.

In the end, Holly had called to inquire about getting to the island, finally saying that she and Branch would come for the day, taking the four o'clock ferry back to Woods Hole.

She finished her coffee, sighed deeply and went to the bathroom to prepare for her wedding. As she walked down the hall to the bathroom, she could hear voices from the floor below.

Emerald, her mother and father were evidently enjoying a hearty breakfast. She could hear the clatter of dishes, smell the sweet aroma of the blueberry pancakes her mother always made for breakfast on Sundays and special days. She was too nervous to eat breakfast.

After her shower she returned to her bedroom, made up her bed, then completed her packing for their brief honeymoon. They had agreed that it would not be wise to go too far away from Missy, so they'd decided to take a quick two-day trip to Nantucket. Ace wanted to visit the Folger Museum and other historical sites such as the African Meeting House.

Emerald has assured them that she would entertain Omar with sightseeing trips. They need not worry about his welfare, she said.

The decision had been made between the two store owners to close their stores for the week. *On vacation. Reopen on June 30*, the notices had read.

She thought about their discussion of where they would live.

"I'd like to buy a house that would be close to our businesses and to your parents," Ace had told her.

She'd agreed and the realtor they'd met worked very nicely with them and found a lovely raised ranch with three bedrooms, two baths and a fenced-in backyard not far from the Blue Hills in Canton. It was move-in ready, but the best part came as a surprise.

When they told Em about their plans, she quickly made an offer.

"Leese, can I buy your condo? I'm in an apartment and would love to have a place of my own. Name your price."

So it was settled, and they were to pass papers on July first.

Elyse was happy because Em was walking on air with her pride of ownership of her new home.

Satisfied that she had packed what she needed for the trip to Nantucket, she decided to give herself a quick manicure. Then she polished her nails, pleased with the warm softness the translucent pink lent to her hands. She heard footsteps outside her bedroom door and recognized them as her father's. When he tapped on her door she invited him in.

"Come on in, Dad," she said. "It's all right, I'm decent."

"Just wanted to have a few minutes with my baby doll," her father said as he sat down in a wooden rocker that had been in her room at the summer cottage since she was a child.

"How're you feeling, little girl? Big day for you, right?"

Partially dressed for the wedding, her father was wearing black trousers and a crisp white shirt. His shirt cuffs were fastened with silver cufflinks that she had given him one Christmas. The crisp odor of his cologne made her smile as she kissed his cheek. She remembered hugging him in the morning when he would leave for work, his citrus-like cologne swirling about them. On this, her wedding day, as always, he was her loving dad, her hero.

"Well, m'dear, just wanted to have us a private minute. You do know how proud I am of you? I know it has not been easy for you . . . your relationship with your mother was not always smooth, always a competitive edge . . ."

Elyse raised her hand as if to stop his flow of words, but he smiled at her and continued.

"Hear me out, hon. Many child psychologists have said that it is often true that there is likely to be a rivalry between a child and the same-sex parent. You always wanted to prove *something* to your mother, almost as if fighting for her love and affection. I've told you about her scarred childhood, and I'm not excusing her for her emotional shortcomings because I know she has always loved you in her own way. Now that you have a daughter of your own, you will find the real lessons that your mother taught you will support you in your relationship with Missy. And I want to tell you one more thing." He rose from the rocker, reached for her hands. She stood up, nearly as tall as he was, and stepped into his embrace.

"To do what you did . . ." he murmured into her dark hair.

She raised her face to his. "You mean to have my baby, in vitro? By myself?"

"It was one of the most courageous things I have ever witnessed. You defied convention, found out who you really were, and both your mother and I wish you and Ace all the happiness in the world. You both deserve it."

"Thanks, Dad." She kissed his cheek.

"All right, then! See you at the wedding. Don't be late!" he teased.

Fifty wedding guests were seated in white chairs in a semi-circle in front of the flower-decked wooden trellis. The musicians were seated to the left of the site where the couple would repeat their vows. The path down which Elyse and her attendant would walk had pots of pink and white roses. This made a lovely path across the lawn to the marriage site.

Jack Joyce, Elyse's brother, and Stanley Benjamin, Ace's assistant, were ushers. The news that Jack's wife Marcella was at last pregnant with the Joyces' second grandchild precluded her from being an active participant in the wedding, but she proved to be quite helpful in other ways, such as maintaining the guest book and directing the guests who needed to find the bathroom.

Ace told Elyse much later that when he saw her coming toward him his knees turned to jelly and he would have dropped except for Omar's firm hand on his shoulder and his strong, deep voice reassuring him, "Steady, old chap, steady."

"I'd never seen a more beautiful bride, and you were going to be mine, my wife," Ace had added.

As Elyse walked toward Ace that day, accompanied by her father, she thought how fortunate she was to have the love and support of the handsome man who waited for her.

She wore an ivory silk sheath with an ivory chiffon redingote. The cuffs and notched collar of the coat were bound in ivory satin. Her pumps were ivory satin. She wore diamond and pearl earrings and carried a simple bouquet of tiny pink roses.

Emerald wore a jacket dress of hand-painted silk. The soft lavender floral-printed sheath showed delicate stems, leaves and flowers all over the sleeveless sheath. The jacket itself, with its notched collar, was the same. She carried tiny white roses. Her heart bumped wildly for a minute when she searched for and found Omar's smile.

In consideration of Rev. Brimmer's age, a lapel microphone had been attached to his jacket, and his voice came out strong and vibrant as he began the ceremony. He started by asking God's blessing on the assembled guests, and particularly on the wedding pair. Then he turned to Ace.

"Please take your bride's hand and recite your vow to her," he said.

Ace was able to smile at Elyse as he took her hand. His voice shook a bit at first, but he managed to recite his vow.

"I, Austin, take you, Elyse, to be my lifelong partner. I pledge to do all in my power to provide for you, honor you, comfort you and love only you until my life on earth is no more."

Rev. Brimmer than turned to Elyse.

"Please take your groom's hand and make your vow to him," he told her.

Her voice was quiet but firm. "I, Elyse, take you, Austin, to be my husband. I will always rely on the safety of your loving arms in my life. I will love you, honor you and support you. This I promise this day until my life is over."

Elyse and Ace clutched each other's hands as they knelt for the final blessing. When they rose Rev. Brimmer wrapped their hands together with his stole, gave the blessing, pronounced them husband and wife. Then, in a booming voice, he said, "It is my pleasure to present to you Mr. and Mrs. Austin Calhoun Brimmer." Then he kissed Elyse and shook hands with Ace.

"You may kiss your bride," he told Ace.

Pumping his fist in the air, Ace complied with loud applause from the guests.

While Aunt Ginny and her staff were completing the setup for the luncheon, the bridal party were having their photographs taken.

Ace insisted that Missy be included in a photo of himself and Elyse. The baby was wearing a pink cotton sundress with pink socks and shiny white Mary Jane shoes and seemed delighted with all the attention she received.

After three quarters of an hour, the photo session was completed. Elyse and Ace returned to the tent. Marcella offered to take Missy inside for a bite to eat and a nap.

"I don't think the three of us need to be in a crowd," she said to Elyse and Ace, patting her large abdomen. "I'll take care of her. Enjoy your reception." Then she kissed both of them and slowly waddled her way into the cottage.

"I don't think she has much longer to go before she delivers," Elyse observed.

Ace agreed, saying, "Hope she has a safe delivery."

"Maybe you should give my brother some tips on being a labor and delivery coach, seeing as how you've had experience," she teased.

Before they entered the tent, he stopped her. "Honey, I wouldn't give up that experience for all the tea in China . . . no, in the *world*, Mrs. Brimmer." Then he kissed her.

"Shall we face the music?"

"With you by my side, I can face anything!"

As they stepped into the open doorway, the lead musician spoke into the microphone. "Ladies and gentlemen, may I present to you Mr. and Mrs. Austin Calhoun Brimmer."

After they had taken their seats at the bridal table, Rev. Brimmer said grace and the meal was served. Omar requested that everyone raise their glass for the toast, and the dancing began with Ace leading Elyse onto the dance floor.

"You are Mrs. Brimmer?" he teased as he led her in a waltz.

"Indeed I am, sir."

"Are you happy?"

"You had to ask? Look at my face!"

Other couples joined them on the floor, and Jerome Joyce claimed his daughter for the father-daughter dance.

"I'm so happy to know that you are happy with Ace in your life," he said as he moved in slow dance steps. "You've been through a lot and deserve all the happiness there is . . . love you, baby." He kissed the top of his daughter's head.

"Thanks, Daddy. Love you, too."

After the meal was over and the wedding cake cut and distributed, the couple moved from table to table, thanking friends and family for their support and good wishes.

As they moved toward the rear of the tent, Elyse said, "Ace, there are Holly and Branch, right over there!"

As they neared the couple, Branch stood to shake Ace's hand.

"Congratulation, my man!" he said, giving Ace a hearty handshake. Then he turned to Elyse.

"I wish you much happiness." He kissed her cheek.

"I'm so glad you could come, both of you!" She hugged Holly, surprised by the glint of moisture in the girl's eyes.

"Thanks for the invitation. It was a beautiful wedding." Then she asked about Missy.

"Oh, Holly, she's growing up so fast. She can stand alone now, is trying to walk . . . and talk! She's in the house with my sister-in-law, down for a nap. Can you and Branch come by sometime to see her? We'll be back home in another week. Call and come by. And Holly . . ."

"Yes?"

"You look so beautiful, and thanks so very much for coming to our wedding."

"It was our pleasure, Elyse."

For her traveling outfit Elyse wore a fully lined light jacket of beige, white and a soft rose. Beneath was a sleeveless knit shell of silk and cotton with a square neckline. The skirt that ended just below her knees rippled lightly as she walked. She still had her diamond and pearl earrings, carried a smart patent leather purse and wore a corsage Ace had given her of orchids and baby's breath.

The ferry dock was crowded with well-wishers to see the happy couple off. Ace and Elyse stood together on the top deck as the ferry slowly backed away from the pier, waving at their friends until they were no longer in sight.

They went below to the lounge where they were able to find an empty table. Ace placed his camera on the table.

"Would you like something to eat or drink?"

"I'm not hungry right now, but I am a little thirsty."

What may I get for you? Coke, soft drink, fruit juice?"

"A bottle of spring water would be perfect."

"No problem, my dear. Be right back."

He hurried to the refreshment bar located in the center of the lounge. Elyse watched him as he strode in a confident manner to complete his errand. *It seems like only yesterday that I met this wonderful, vibrant man, and on that first meeting asked him, a perfect stranger, to hold me in his arms,* she thought.

Now she was legally bound to him for the rest of her life. Never had she thought after Barry's death that her poor heart would be filled with the love she felt for Ace.

She spoke up when he returned with her bottle of water, a paper cup and a bottle of light beer for himself.

"Ace, have I ever told you how handsome you are?"

He smiled at her. "No, ma'am, don't think you have. I'm all ears."

"Well, you are one handsome man, husband mine. And when I saw you standing under the trellis, looking like a movie star in your gray suit and gray silk tie, I said to myself, 'You can thank your lucky stars that Ace Brimmer came into your life.'"

"You just wait, kid," he said. "Good things happen to good people and . . . we're some of the best."

He opened the bottle, poured some of the water into the cup and handed it to her. Then he tapped it with his bottle of beer.

"Here's to us, my darling."

It seemed that already eager passengers were beginning to gather up their belongings and head towards the gangway.

"I've got a surprise for you."

"You have?"

"Yep. You remember our plans were to reserve a room at the hotel?"

"Yes, we did discuss doing that. What's changed?"

"You remember I told you about one of my customers who always wants to keep up with everything African? Well, she has always been one of my best customers and has insisted that we stay in her condo on Nantucket for as long as we like. She gave me the key. She also gave me the key to her Mercedes. I'm leaving my car in the parking lot. Let's look for her car."

"My God, Ace, are you for real?"

"See?" He dangled the keys in front of her face.

"Ace, I can't believe it! Are we the lucky ones or not!"

"Believe it. We *are* the lucky ones!"

They found the beige Mercedes parked in the designated parking lot. Ace stored their luggage into the trunk and they started off, moving slowly to avoid the heavy pedestrian traffic. It seemed as if there were even fewer cars than on the Vineyard.

They looked at the substantial sea captains' homes with their widows' walks on top of Victorian mansions, the narrow cobblestone streets and sidewalks. It was a scene from the opulent past.

The condo was situated not too far from the shoreline. It was a handsome townhouse with a large living room and a working wood fireplace.

Elyse drew in a deep breath as she admired what she saw.

"Ace, this is lovely, and I can't believe we have it all to ourselves. Look at this dining room, and that chandelier!"

"Here's the kitchen," he said. Looking out the back door, he added, "Look, here's a nice sundeck!"

When they went upstairs they found two large bedrooms, one with a queen-sized bed and a full bath.

He put his arms around her.

"Welcome to your new life, my love."

"Thanks, Ace. I love you more than you know. Today I am a happy woman."

"Waited a long time to hear those words."

His kiss told her just how much he meant it.

They returned to the living room.

"Be right back," Ace said. "I'm going to get our luggage from the car."

He took their bags up to the master bedroom, and as he descended the stairs, he said, "Have you thought about dinner? Would you like to try one of the local restaurants, order in . . . what's your pleasure?"

"Why don't we go out, pick up some seafood, bring it back here?"

So that was what they did. But instead of returning to the condo, they found a lovely spot overlooking the ocean and, spreading a blanket, enjoyed fried clams, French fries and iced tea.

It was a beautiful night and they watched the full moon rise over the horizon. Ace finished his drink, gathered up their empty cartons and deposited them in a nearby rubbish bin.

"Ready for home, Mrs. B?" he asked when he returned to the car.

Elyse nodded wordlessly.

As she looked at her husband, she wanted him with such an ache that she thought she might lose her breath.

She reached for him, her face awash in tears. She knew with certainty that without this man she would not survive. She held on to him as he kissed the hot tears from her eyes and cheeks, her tumbling heart quieted by his loving touch.

"Hold me. Don't ever leave me."

His words were an affirmation of his love for her. "Never, never, in this world, or the next. I love you and will never leave you."

<hr />

That night in Nantucket, Ace insisted on carrying his wife up the stairs to the bedroom that would become their sanctuary. So much had gone on in their lives, but they could finally share this moment of complete fulfillment.

The trials, setbacks, misunderstandings and priorities that had hindered them now seemed to have been washed away to reveal a clean, unblemished slate. Through the open bedroom window, the boisterous waters of Nantucket Sound roared up to tease the shoreline, then receded with pulsating vigor.

From the bed Elyse watched Ace come to her. She breathed deeply, aware of the moment, and opened her arms to receive him.

"Honey, I'm home. Leese, baby, I'm home." His voice was soft, deep with passion as he lay down beside her, his head on her bosom. His breath came in uneven gasps as she took his face in both of her soft hands and kissed him gently. He responded with an exploratory search with his tongue as if to garner the sweetness of her mouth. Then it was her turn to moan, and as she did so, Ace trailed seductive kisses along her face, her neck, the lobes of her ears, finally reaching the glorious crests of her breasts. She thought her body was going to explode because of the tension and anxiety she was feeling. But she closed her eyes and held on tightly to her husband as if she might float away without his anchoring love. Then she felt his touch, so tender, so smooth, so deft, as if he were molding her body to his own personal desires.

She gasped from the exquisite sensations that assailed her body.

"Love me, please, love me," she begged. Then it happened. Their bodies flamed with heat like a glowing torch, forging a steel bond of love, and each knew there was no turning back as the ocean continued its relentless pulsations and the moon passed through the dark sky, a man and his wife slept in each other's arms.

CHAPTER 34

Once Branch and Holly got their degrees, they made plans to marry. Elyse was thrilled that their plans called for the wedding to include her family and occur at their house.

"You know, Ace, Aunt Ginny could go into planning weddings," Elyse said. "She's managed almost every detail for Holly and Branch. And I know they both love her for what she's doing for them. Makes me happy, too, to see that Holly seems to be accepting us as her family."

Ace nodded, agreeing with his wife.

"Branch is a fine young man and I see nothing less than a bright future for them."

A knock on their bedroom door interrupted their private conversation. Elyse's second pregnancy was progressing nicely, but Ace watched over her very carefully, insisting that she rest frequently.

He went to the door. Aunt Ginny came in, asking about her niece's condition.

"We're doin' okay. How about you? Everything goin' all right? Need any help?"

The older woman beamed as she made her report to the pair.

"Not a bit! My staff have set up the family room for the ceremony. Flowers have already been delivered. My cook and wait staff have turned your dining room and living room into an elegant reception area. Wait 'til you see it! And Ace, you sure did a bang-up job, turned those rooms into a beautiful chapel."

"Aw, t'weren't nuthin'," Ace drawled with downhome modesty. Both women laughed at him.

"You're a talented artist, and you know it," Elyse chided him.

Her aunt agreed. "He knows, Elyse, he knows."

She headed for the door.

"Better get downstairs. You'll be down before five, Elyse?"

"I will. Plan to rest for awhile, but wild horses couldn't keep me away."

"Atta girl! See ya!"

"You have an amazing aunt, Elyse."

"Don't I know it. She's always been my favorite . . . could tell Aunt Ginny anything. She'd always come up with good advice, and I truly love her. God's been good to me."

"To us, my dear."

"Branch, can I ask you something?"

"Nothing serious, I hope, Holly."

"No, not *really* serious. But it's something I'd like to do and I want to hear what you think."

"Fire away. What's on your mind?"

They were on their way to the south shore to check on their house being built on the land Elyse had deeded to them as a wedding gift. She'd insisted it was what Barry would have wanted. The Cape Cod style house was nearly completed, and the couple hoped to move in right after their August wedding.

"Branch, I've been thinking. Now that we both have our degrees, and you already have a job at Mass General and I hope to find a nursing job, I'd like to visit Jane Dagleish, thank her for starting me on this path. I'd still be working at Prime Care, working my tail off, if she hadn't given me a chance. What do you think? I don't want to seem like I'm pandering or groveling, but . . ."

"I say go ahead. She was the one who saw the potential in you. I see no reason why you shouldn't let her know how much her interest in you means. I say go ahead."

"I will. Thanks for your advice."

"Anytime, anytime, sweetheart."

Jane Dagleish was pleased to see Holly come into her office. Quickly rising from her desk, she offered her protégé a firm handshake.

"Holly! How wonderful to see you! You look well. How have you been?"

"I'm doing well, thanks."

Her mentor waved her to a chair and returned to her seat behind the desk.

"Holly, I'm so glad to see you. You seem to be more mature, more grown-up than the fearful young aide that I called into my office a few years back."

"A lot has gone on in my life since then. A whole lot," Holly said, not intending to reveal all that had happened.

"But," she continued, "I wanted to tell you how grateful I am to you for giving me a chance. And I wanted you to know that I have my degree in Geriatric Nursing."

Jane Dagleish's face lit up. "Holly, how wonderful!" she clapped her hands together and leaned forward towards Holly. "Would you believe it? The gods must have sent you!"

With raised eyebrows, Holly gave the excited woman a questioning look. What was she *talking* about?

"Would you believe that Prime Care has opened a special unit here for geriatric patients? They have started the units in some of the other centers in the country and it's worked out well. How would you like to be the nurse manager at our unit here?"

"I . . . I really don't know . . . haven't thought that far ahead. I'm getting married next month."

"Holly, congratulations! I'm so happy for you."

"Thank you. Branch and I are planning a small wedding at my stepmother's home. Since I have no living relatives, we're planning a simple ceremony with perhaps a justice of the peace."

Holly stopped talking, upset by the tears that glistened in her mentor's eyes. Now what had she said?

Jane Dagleish's voice was so somber, so quiet that Holly instinctively steeled herself, fearing she might hear some untoward comment.

"Before I went into nursing, I worked as a secretary in a law office. I became a notary public as well as a justice of the peace. Would you and your fiancé allow me to participate in your wedding? It would be my deepest honor."

Stunned, almost speechless, Holly swallowed hard.

"I'll . . . I'll have to ask Branch," she stuttered.

"Three years old, Missy is really excited about being a flower girl in her sister's wedding," Elyse said to her husband. "Wouldn't surprise me if she steals the show."

Her husband nodded his head in agreement.

"She's a little actress, that one! But to me, she's a perfect little sweetheart, just works her way into your heart. You are lucky to have such a lovely child, Leese." Then he amended his statement, "No, *we* are both lucky that she's in our lives."

"I know, Ace, and I love her more and more each day and I thank God for her. She's such a delight."

"She's a manifestation of the love that you and her father shared. You were one brave, determined young woman to do what you did . . . bringing that love to life."

She lay against him and he rubbed her back in circles to ease some of the strain of her large abdomen. Their son was due almost any day.

She twisted her head, looked into his concerned face.

"Ace, I *had* to have that baby! I was proud of the fact that at least Barry had really wanted *me* to have our child . . . and I knew, too, that no one else on this earth could give life and meaning to our love except *me*! And you know, in some way, Ace, I was so proud that I could do it, even though everyone thought I was delusional!"

She laughed, then turned over to face him. They had been resting on their king-sized bed.

"You know something, husband mine?"

"No, what?"

"If I had not had Missy, we might not be together on this glorious day," she said, smiling at him.

"Oh, sweetheart, I believe Fate has a way of directing our lives. I will always remember that day when you came into my store. I saw a beautiful, elegantly dressed young woman who almost made my heart turn over in my chest. I could hardly breathe, and I knew at that moment that you were meant to be in my life, just knew it."

"Guess I sensed something too, Ace. It wasn't long after that when you came to the bookstore, shortly after Barry had died, that I was bold enough to ask you to hold me. Talk about being brazen!"

"You weren't brazen at all, honey. You just needed to be comforted, and I'm extremely happy that I was able to provide you with what you needed at that time in your life."

He caressed her extended abdomen and was rewarded by a sharp thrust against his hand. He pulled it away and said, "Leese, did you see that?"

"Not only saw your son kick you, I felt it, too!"

"He can't wait to get here."

"And his mother can't wait, either."

Moved by the reality of the life within her, Ace kissed her.

"I do hope that this will be an easy delivery for you, honey."

"Oh, it will be, as long as you are by my side. That's all I want."

He reassured her. "Nothing will keep me away! By the way, how do you think Missy is going to react to her brother?"

"I think she's going to be okay. She knows he's coming, and I expect she'll be as possessive of him as she is of Holly. She dotes on her 'big sister,' as she calls her. I hope they will always be close, despite the age difference."

She lay quietly for a moment, slowly rubbing her abdomen as if to soothe the baby. When she spoke, Ace heard a reflective tone in her voice.

"Don't you think it's amazing, Ace, how much alike those two are? Both resemble Barry. Anyone can see that, although I certainly didn't at first, but their personalities, ideas, thought processes are alike. Never ceases to amaze me."

"It's something to think about, that's for sure."

Elyse went on, "Just the other day, Ace, I was telling Missy that she had to be more gentle and patient with Sebastian. The poor old fellow is lowing down. I told her that she couldn't play rough with him anymore. Know what she did?"

'What did she do?"

"Looked at me, as solemn as a judge, snapped off a salute to me and said, 'Yes, ma'am, understood, ma'am.'

I was so shocked I didn't know what to say. You know I've seen Holly make that gesture, and God knows how many times their father would respond to me that way!"

"They are his daughters, and carry some of his genes. It's the only explanation there is."

"You're probably right." She turned over on the bed. "What's the time?" she asked.

He checked his watch.

"We've got plenty of time. It's one now and the wedding is not until five this afternoon. I'm glad that Holly and Branch decided to have their wedding here in our home, that there's a bond between us. Your Aunt Ginny said that she will be here at three to set things up in the living room. You need to rest yourself, honey."

"But . . ."

"No buts. You will have enough to do, being the hostess. You stay calm and collected. Can I get you anything?"

"No, thanks, hon, I'm fine. Glad that my folks are taking charge of Missy. I expect they will be here at three, too, along with my aunt."

Ace got up from the bed. Although he and Elyse had been married for almost three years, still Ace wondered about her past history with her late husband. He walked slowly down the stairs into the kitchen at the rear of the house which looked over the backyard. He saw the sandbox, the toys, the jungle gym he had erected for his stepdaughter. His thoughts tumbled back to the unforgettable morning that Elyse came to him. He had slept poorly the night before, rebuffed by her hesitancy in accepting his proposal of marriage. Had he been too blunt with her, telling her he wanted a total commitment from her? Had he made a mistake, pushed her into a corner with his harsh promise never to propose to her again? His thoughts turned to that eventful early morning that changed his life.

When Elyse had called, his heart almost skipped a beat and he feared that perhaps something had happened to Missy.

He had been at the door to greet her when she came to the shop. Breathless, pale, she seemed bone-weary, as if she had just completed a marathon race. She almost fell into his arms.

"I *had* to come, Ace, had to," she sobbed.

He had wanted to reach out, hold her close, but because he had challenged her the night before with his ultimatum, he needed to be sure she was truly committed. When she blurted out, "Ace, I . . . know. Oh, Ace, will you marry me, please?"

He remembered that he remained silent, wanting to hold her, looking for any sign of reluctance in her face. He had to be sure.

"Barry?" he dared to ask. He saw the tears in her eyes and she shook her head at him. She'd answered, "I will always honor his memory, and love the child he gave me. He will always, always have a place in my heart because he was the anchor in my life. But now, now," she spoke softly, "that world has changed. My life has changed, and Ace, it's you I need to be in my life . . . to be the man I trust, rely on. That's why I came back this morning. Ace, I cannot go on in this life without you. I love you."

As he stood in his kitchen, preparing the tea, placing crackers on a small plate, and setting two mugs on a tray, the past three years now appeared like the turnings of a kaleidoscope of events, changing, meshing, evolving to bring him to where he was standing at the moment. He was in his own home, his own kitchen, his own beloved wife resting upstairs, the birth of their child imminent.

Today his mind was at ease. Barry Marshall was at rest. Elyse had chosen to follow her heart, filled with love for Ace and the family they were about to become.

He took the tray up to her.

"If you have this cup of tea I brought to you, you'll have plenty of time to empty your bladder before the wedding. I know you don't want to have to be rushing to the bathroom."

She looked up at him.

"My dear husband, I think you know me better than I know myself. This is a great idea."

She pushed herself back against the headboard. Her husband helped her by placing two pillows behind her shoulders.

"How's that?"

"Perfect, Ace, couldn't be better."

They drank their tea in companionable silence. Finally Ace spoke his voice thoughtful and solemn as if he had something weighing on his mind.

Elyse heard the tension in his voice.

"I'm very proud of you, honey, the way you've handled everything, deeding the land on the south shore to

Holly and Branch. What a generous gesture on your part. What a wonderful wedding gift to them."

"Well, Ace, they both deserve it. Both of them have worked hard, finished their education, and I know it's what Holly's father would have wanted for her. He would have been proud of her. You know, when he was killed in Iraq, I truly believed my life was over. But then you came, and from that first day when you held me in your arms, the tiny hope that you put in my heart, well, you gave me my life back."

"Couldn't do anything else. I love you, and always will."

"And I'm happier than I have any right to be, all due to you, Ace."

Then she went on to say something else to him.

"I have to tell you, Ace, that I'm real pleased that Holly has come to terms about her father. She was so bitter about the whole situation. She told me that it was her patient, Mr. Harkins, who helped her. He's giving her away, you know."

Ace nodded. "I know, and I think it's wonderful that he means so much to her."

"I think so, too. Anyway, she said he helped her understand why her father acted as he did. She said she realized, too, that she was not the same person now that she was at eighteen. That her life experiences have made changes in her, have made her the woman she is now. And then, Ace, she said something else that really floored me."

"What was that, hon?"

"She said that her father must have been a very special person for me to take on the monumental responsibility of having his child. 'I could never have done that,' she said to me.

"I told her then *that* was the father I wanted her to know, not the confused eighteen-year-old."

Ace offered her another cracker, which she refused by shaking her head no.

She picked up her tea cup, looked at him over the rim as she took a sip. She waited for his response.

He was standing at the foot of their bed, holding the tray. She looked at him, aware of how much this man meant to her. He had come into her life at the very nadir of her life, when she had almost lost the will to go on. His beryl-green eyes looked into her face. Tall, stalwart, gentle, perceptive, she reveled in the certain knowledge of what he had brought her. He had given her all of himself, his support, his tender care, his concern for her well-being, his loyalty, his creativity, his patience, his . . . love.

Ace said nothing at first. Then he placed the tray on top of the dresser. He walked over to the bed, took the tea cup from Elyse, placed it on the nightstand beside the bed and sat beside her. He took her face into his hands.

"Elyse, you are the most amazing woman I have ever met, and I am honored and privileged to have you as my wife, my lover, my life partner. I didn't think it was possible, but I love you more and more each day. I want you to know how much I admire the way you have battled against the odds life put in your path. Girl," his voice softened, "you're some kinda strong momma, and I defy anybody to say anything different."

When he kissed her, Elyse felt tears stinging behind her closed eyelids. Her husband's lips were soft and gentle as they molded and caressed her tender mouth.

He lowered her back onto her pillow.

"Rest, honey, you have a big afternoon ahead of you. I'll come back up and help you when it's time for the wedding. How's that?"

"You're so good to me, Ace."

"Only doing what I'm 'sposed to do, my dear. Now you rest."

"Aye, aye," she said as she touched two fingers of her right hand to her forehead in a military salute.

With a broad smile, he clicked his heels, returning the gesture, and left the room.

Elyse turned over on her left side, tucked her hands under her cheek and sighed deeply. Even the baby seemed to have quieted down. She was happy, everything had come full circle. She drifted off to sleep, content at last.

CHAPTER 35

Ace hired the same trio that were at his wedding to Elyse to play at Holly and Branch's wedding and reception. He also took charge of making their family room into a small chapel. He moved most of the furniture to the garage and arranged white folding chairs facing a small chest of drawers covered with a sparkling gold lamé cloth. On the chest was a gold cross, with two slim white candles in crystal holders on either side.

A profusion of flowers, asters, chrysanthemums, large vases of waxy green leaves with white daisies, spires of blue delphiniums and birds of paradise warmed the room and made it festive and pleasant.

Silver sconces on the walls cast soft, glowing lights that lent a quiet ambiance for the five o'clock ceremony. Large bronze vats of waxy green foliage stood on either side of the door that led into the room.

Guests began arriving at a quarter to five, mainly Elyse's family, close friends of the couple, and Branch's father.

Elyse was escorted to her seat in the front row as stepmother of the bride. Then the ceremony began.

Little Missy, dressed in a pink dress, wearing white Mary Jane's, her dark curls bouncing on her shoulders, entered to the music of the trio. As the flower girl, she smiled broadly as she scattered rose petals from her little basket.

Holly's friend from Prime Care, Leola, was her matron of honor, and Leola's two pre-teen daughters, Pearl and Diamond, served as junior bridesmaids. Both were thrilled to be in the wedding party.

"Now, mind," their mother, Leola, had warned them. "There will be *no* cuttin' the fool, or you'll have to deal with me!"

"Yes, ma'am," both answered in unison.

Branch came in, took his place beside his best man Ace as the musicians began the traditional wedding march.

As Holly entered with Mr. Harkins as her escort, Branch gasped and his eyes filled with tears. Ace touched his shoulder. "Steady man, steady," he said. He, too, was struck by the bride's beauty.

She wore a slim, white sheath of silk moiré that clung to her slender body. From her bare shoulders to her white satin sandals she was stunning. On her head she wore a moiré silk caplet with seed pearls and a chin-length veil that fell around her face.

Her proud escort, Mr. Harkins, nodded to the guests as he accompanied the young bride, He was not using his cane, but held his left hand firmly over her arm.

When they reached Jane Dagleish, who was wearing a black robe and a pearl necklace, she asked, "Who gives this woman in holy matrimony?"

Mr. Harkins announced in a firm, clear voice, "I, Alexander Harkins, am proud and privileged to have the honor of giving this bride to her intended." Then he handed Holly over to Branch. The two men shook hands and the old man took his seat.

The guests chuckled softly, and more amusement came forth when Missy, who was standing near the junior bridesmaids, piped up, "And she's my big sister, too!"

Smiling down on the child, Holly instinctively drew her to her side and the justice of the peace began the ceremony.

From her seat in the front row, Elyse listened to the words being spoken that would unite her dead husband's daughter to her bridegroom. She saw Barry's resemblance in each of his children and in her mind she thought, *Barry, you did keep your promise and you've given me a wonderful family.*

A sudden kick in her abdomen made her gasp. *I know, Ace Junior, you are part of my family, too! Just get here as fast as you can.*

≈∾©

The wedding reception was a warm family affair. Aunt Ginny had prepared golden croissants filled with chicken salad. A lovely crudite platter of vegetables was offered to the guests. She had also prepared a creamy dip in the center of the large platter.

After everyone was seated, Ace rose at the bridal table to make a toast to the bride and groom.

"Relatives and friends, it is my very great pleasure to welcome into our family Holly and Branch. May their days be happy and fruitful, and may their troubles be few and far between. Every happiness to you both. To Holly and Branch!"

"Hear, hear," was the enthusiastic response from the group.

The wedding cake was a chocolate raspberry torte, layers of white cake with robust raspberry preserves between each of three layers.

Later that day Missy asked her mother, "Did I do good, Mommy?"

"Couldn't have done better, sweetheart," Elyse told the child. She hugged her and again her thoughts turned to Barry.

You would love her, I know, Barry, and I am so happy you left me this precious child.

Ace had been watching his wife, hoping that she was not becoming weary. He rose from his seat at the head table, excused himself to the bridal couple, explaining, "Want to check on Elyse," and joined her at the table she shared with her parents, Aunt Ginny and Branch's dad, Arthur Adkins.

He reached over to offer a firm handshake to the groom's father.

"Sir, you have a mighty fine son. You must be very proud of him."

"Indeed, I'm very proud. Couldn't ask for better than my son Branch. Everything he's done, he's done on his own. Offered him money for schooling, but he told me, 'No thanks. Do it on my own.' And he did, too. And that daughter of yours, she's a real treasure, no doubt about that. No sir, no doubt. Truly believe they belong together Just wish Branch's mother had been here to see this."

"We're sorry for your loss," Ace said.

As he looked around for an empty chair, Aunt Ginny noticed, got up from her seat beside Elyse saying, "Here, Ace, sit beside your wife. I must check the kitchen."

"Thanks, Aunt Gin."

He sat down, his arm around his wife's shoulder, whispered in her ear, "Everything okay?"

Elyse whispered back, "Couldn't be better!"

She knew all was well. She had somehow been able to bring Barry and his eldest daughter together, and she was proud that she had been able to do so. Now that that chapter was over, and as her child stirred vigorously beneath her heart, she was happy with her new beginning. She felt her husband's concerned eyes searching her face for any signs of distress or discomfort. She gave him a bright, reassuring smile. He responded with a broad happy grin of his own.

The humid days of August had passed and everyone relished the cooler invigorating days of September, no one more than Elyse. Her due date was finally approaching, and she was ready.

Missy had been registered for all-day sessions at a preschool daycare center, and each day Ace dropped her off in the morning on his way to his art store and picked her up again in the late afternoon.

Emerald had made up her mind that it was not safe for Elyse to be driving into work, considering her advancing pregnancy, so she drove to Elyse's South Shore home to pick her up. They both enjoyed the ride into the city and, as always, had plenty to talk about. Elyse wanted to hear about Emerald's budding relationship with Omar, and Emerald was always anxious to assess her friend's impending confinement.

This crisp September morning she started out by teasing Elyse.

"Didn't need my help this time, eh, my friend? No more needles in your rear end?" she teased.

"Yeah, right, I just know you were tickled pink when you were sticking those old needles into me!"

"Only tried to be helpful," Emerald smirked as she drove through the morning traffic.

"Well," Elyse said, "I really did appreciate your help, but I must tell you, girl, conception this time around was *real, real* nice! Hope you find yourself in the same situation real soon." She laughed.

Emerald made a quick sign of the cross over her chest. "God willing, Omar is coming over for Christmas, you know, and . . . well . . . I'm hoping. Elyse, I really love that man!"

"I know, and both Ace and I want the best for you. We think Omar is just that . . . the best."

"Thanks, Elyse," Emerald said as she pulled the car up in front of their store so that Elyse wouldn't have to walk from the parking area behind the building.

"Could be next year you'll be hauling a fat, pregnant wife like me around! Wouldn't that be a hoot!" she giggled.

"It would be my pleasure, you know it would. See you in a few."

Slowly, Elyse climbed out of the front seat, taking her store key out of her bag. As she entered the store she could hear the phone ringing. She waddled back to her office as quickly as she could.

"Hello?" she breathed, panting from the exertion she needed to reach her desk.

"Honey? It's Ace, are you sitting down? Now I don't want you to worry, but there's been an accident . . ."

"Missy? What's happened to Missy? It *is* Missy, isn't it?"

"Yes, it's Missy, hon, but we think she's going to be fine."

"Tell me! What's wrong with her?"

Emerald came into the office at that moment, took one look at Elyse's stricken face, immediately went into their small kitchen and quickly returned with a glass of water.

"Drink!" she demanded. Then she picked up the phone on her desk and listened as Ace explained.

"Seems that she ran out into the play yard, slid down the slide and landed on her backside. She said she was hurting, so she was taken by ambulance to Children's Hospital. I'm calling from there. Now, don't worry . . ."

"Ace," Emerald interrupted, "we'll be right there. We're on our way."

Emerald drove carefully, but still it took a good twenty-five minutes before they reached the hospital. Ace met them at the front desk, his face wreathed in smiles.

Elyse almost collapsed in his arms.

"How . . . how is she, Ace?"

"She's fine, just a bruised tailbone from where she struck the ground. X-rays are negative and all her vital signs are stable. I think maybe we'll be able to take her home later today. Are *you* all right? Here, have a seat. Don't want you to be a patient, too."

As he helped his wife sit down, he mouthed to Emerald, *Thank you, my friend*, to which she mouthed, *De nada*.

The doctor met them at Missy's bedside and explained that the little girl could be discharged later that day.

"I think she may need to sit on a rubber ring for awhile, but her coccyx is *not* fractured. She just lost her footing at the end of the slide and sat down hard on her bum."

"Is she in a lot of pain?" Elyse asked.

"Some, but I think she's more frightened by what happened. If she can swallow pills, you may give her baby aspirin, or you can crush the pill in applesauce. Every four hours as needed."

"Thank you, thank you," both Ace and Elyse said as Ace shook his hand.

"My privilege," the doctor said. "You have a bright, lovely daughter."

Elyse remained at her daughter's bedside, reading some children's books the hospital's librarian had brought her. She also fed her a lunch of chicken broth, crackers, milk and Missy's favorite, chocolate ice cream.

Noticing Elyse's advancing pregnancy, the head nurse of the unit had a lounge chair brought in so that Elyse could elevate her feet.

"You're very kind," she told the nurse, who smiled and winked at her.

"Been there, done that a few times myself. You are quite welcome. Girl or boy?"

"A boy, and I can hardly wait."

Later that day Ace returned with a small bouquet of flowers for Missy.

To the bravest little girl in the world. Love, Mummy and Daddy, the card read.

Deep in her heart Elyse knew how fortunate she was to have a wonderful man like Ace in her life. He truly loved Missy as his own child, had been present at her birth and was the first person after Dr. Kellogg to hold her. She knew she would never forget the look on his face as he handed her Missy.

"Meet your daughter, Elyse."

It was memories like those that made her love him more each day. She could hardly wait to see him with their son, who moved vigorously to let her know he was just about ready to make his appearance.

Whether it was due to the worry over Missy's accident, Elyse did not know, but that night after she and Ace settled Missy down for the night, her contractions began.

"Call Emerald! No, call Dr. Kellogg first and tell him my labor has started."

"Right away, Elyse. Just try to stay calm."

From their bedside phone he made the calls, his troubled eyes fastened on his wife.

"Are the pains close, honey?"

"Four to five minutes," she panted.

"Em will be here in about fifteen minutes. Think you can hold on? The doctor said if your membranes have ruptured, you should come right in."

"Not yet, Ace. I think we have a little time before . . ." She clutched her abdomen as she breathed deeply to ride out the next pain.

"I'm going to put your bag in the car and bring the car around front. Hang in there, hon, be right back."

As promised, within fifteen minutes Emerald was bounding up the stairs, Ace having left the front door unlocked for her.

"Okay," she bounced into the bedroom, "let's get this show on the road! Ace," she grinned at him, "you're experienced in this birthing business, so I expect you to do a great job!"

Together they helped Elyse down the stairs and into the car.

Emerald kissed Elyse before she closed the car door. "Good luck." Then she told Ace, "Drive carefully."

The grimace she saw on Elyse's face told her that Ace Junior was in a hurry, so she waved them off, watching the twinkling tail lights of Ace's car as it sped off into the night.

After two hours of intense labor, Dr. Kellogg told Ace it was time to suit up and get ready to meet his son.

As he scrubbed up this time and put on the blue scrubs, he recalled Missy's birth. He prayed that this delivery would be easy for his wife. She had been through so much, he couldn't bear to see her suffer.

He breathed a quick prayer as he followed the nurse into the brightly lit delivery room.

Elyse looked up at him with a crooked, tentative smile.

"I'm ready, Ace. Are you?"

"You betcha. Ready, willing and able!"

Within ten minutes after Elyse gave several strong pushes, their nine-pound son was born.

Tears streamed down Ace's face as he held his baby.

"Welcome, son, we've been waiting for you."

"He's here, Elyse. Meet your beautiful son."

"Thanks, Ace."

She kissed the baby's forehead. As she gazed at him, his eyes opened wide open and he stared back at her.

"Thanks, Ace. Thanks for . . . for everything."

"Honey, it's I who owe you. You're wonderful and I love you."

CHAPTER 36

Little Austin, as the baby was called, was a happy, placid baby. He seldom cried and delighted his doting parents with his charming smiles and sweet coos. He truly loved his big sister, and she claimed him as "her baby."

Holly and Branch were taken to him, too. They couldn't wait to hold the chubby, bubbly little boy.

"He's just beautiful," Holly told Elyse.

Elyse thanked her stepdaughter and was inwardly pleased with the couple's reaction to her son. She could tell by their responses to Little Austin that this pair were going to be good and loving parents.

"How is everything going at your place?" she asked Branch.

With his eyes on Holly as she cuddled the baby, he responded, "Everything's coming along nicely. We've furnished the living room, bedroom and kitchen, but that's about it for now. You'll have to come visit soon."

"We will . . . love to see what you've done," Elyse said to him.

At Thanksgiving it was Holly who prepared the Thanksgiving dinner. She asked Aunt Ginny to help her and found the gregarious woman delighted to participate in the food preparation. She gave plenty of advice and encouragement.

"You're taking to this like a duck to water," she told Holly.

"I did watch my gram sometimes, but I can't cook like she did."

"You'll do just fine, I know. It's in your genes. Now, today I'm going to show you how to make sweet rolls."

Holly saw how Aunt Ginny mixed all the ingredients together until she had a mound of soft dough. She placed the dough into a lightly greased large bowl. "Now," she said to Holly, "we cover this with wax paper and a clean towel and let the dough rise. Let's sit down, have a nice cup of tea and some of those ginger cookies I brought."

When the feast day came, it was sunny, but with a brisk wind that blew in from the ocean. The house was warm and cozy, with a lively fire that Branch had going in the living room fireplace. The house smelled great from the roasting turkey and the other goodies that Aunt Ginny had helped Holly prepare.

Besides Ace, Elyse and their children, Holly and Branch had invited Elyse's parents, Aunt Ginny, and, of course, Branch's father. Branch had already gone to Prime Care to fetch Mr. Harkins. There were ten at the table, with the baby in a carry-all seat on a chair near his mother.

Everyone praised Holly for the meal. She accepted the compliments and acknowledged Aunt Ginny's help.

After the meal the men went out to the closed deck that faced the ocean and the women made quick work of the dishes and storing the leftover food, but not before "care packages" were made for each to take home.

"This is much more than Branch and I could ever eat," Holly said.

Mr. Harkins only wanted "a piece of that wonderful sweet potato pie. And," he continued, "I'll chop the hand off anybody who tries to take it from me!"

Kitchen duties completed, the women returned to the living room, but Holly took Elyse to one side.

"I have something I want to show you, upstairs in our bedroom."

She led Elyse into the master bedroom. French doors opened onto a small balcony that faced the Atlantic Ocean. A queen-sized bed with a white bedspread and colorful pillows faced the balcony doors. A bentwood rocker, a tall floor lamp and a double chest of drawers completed the room. To Elyse it seemed serene and peaceful.

Holly went to one of the nightstands and pointed to a photograph. "I wanted you to see this."

"Holly! Your father! Where did you get this?" Elyse gasped.

"Emerald. She gave me the snapshot and asked me if I wanted it."

Elyse held in her hand an enlarged photograph of Barry Marshall wearing military fatigues, grinning at the camera as if he didn't have a care in the world.

Holly's voice was tremulous when she spoke.

"I know for a long time I hated the idea that I had a father who gave me away. When I found out from my granny what he'd done, I felt that he had thrown me away, like garbage. A bit of nothing that no one wanted."

Seeing the tears welling up in Holly's eyes, Elyse moved to sit on the bed beside her. She took the girl's hands in hers.

"Holly, please, please don't think like that. I could never have loved a cruel, heartless man. He was never like that. Perhaps he was scared of the frightening situation he found himself in . . . bringing a new life into the world, not knowing how to cope. His life had not been an easy one, raised by a single mother, struggling all his life to succeed. Maybe he feared a similar life for you and wanted you to have better, Oh, Holly," she begged, "please forgive him."

She put her arm around the trembling girl.

"Because of Barry, I have two beautiful daughters, you and Missy, and I see in each of you the same drive and perseverance that I saw in him. His legacy will live on, and I'm happy about that! Besides, you both look very much like him and that makes me doubly happy. I have a part of the husband I loved and can't ask for more. I love this picture of Barry, and I'm glad that you have it. He would have been so proud of you."

"I hope so. Thanks, Elyse." She stood up. "Guess we'd better get back to the folks."

"I can hear the ladies chatting away. I don't think they've even missed us."

Springtime always comes to New England with a flourish of warm weather, budding trees and a profusion of color as the forsythia bushes burst into bloom, crocuses push through the moist soil and wintering birds return to nest and produce new offspring.

Elyse began to feel a latent surge of activity stirring within her.

Ajay, as little Austin was being called, was crawling around and occasionally tried to pull himself up to stand.

Elyse had been doing some of her store's work on her computer at home. Ordering new books, checking inventory and conferring daily with Emerald could be done easily when the baby was napping in the afternoon. And she was glad to be active.

Emerald had hired an older woman, a retired school teacher, part time to help out at the checkout counter. A teenager helped out after school stacking books and attending to janitorial duties.

"Girl, we're doing just fine!" Emerald told her when Elyse asked about the place.

"I know you are, but, Em, I want to come back soon. I miss the place."

"Talked it over with Ace?"

"Not yet, but I intend to, soon."

"What about Ajay? I know Missy is in daycare."

"At the rate he's going, he might be ready for daycare, too. I know Building Blocks does take infants, and Ajay is almost ready to walk. He's already talking," she added proudly. "Mama, Daddy, and even tries to say Missy. It comes out Mith-mith," she laughed.

That night, after the children were tucked in for the night, Ace and Elyse shared a glass of wine and talked about their respective day's activities.

Ace was telling her about some new African artifacts Omar had sent from Cameroon.

"Very colorful attractive masks, vases and urns, and this time Omar sent a large batch of textiles."

"I can see you're very pleased."

"I am. New material always brings in customers, and that's good for business."

Elyse put her wine glass down on the coffee table in front of the sofa where she sat. From his comfortable leather chair nearby, Ace looked at his wife. His skin prickled and he sensed that Elyse had something on her mind.

"What's up, hon? Something botherin' you?"

"I want to go back to work at the store," she blurted out.

"You do? How long have you been thinking about that?"

She took a sip of wine before answering him.

"I miss the store, Ace, I really do, and . . . so far everything's been going well. But . . ."

"How about Ajay?"

"I was thinking about Building Blocks. They take infants, and Ajay is almost eight months old, crawling, and I think he's going to be walking soon."

"I don't know, Elyse. I'm not sure he's ready for daycare."

"Why? It's a great place for the children. The staff is well qualified, and Missy has always loved it."

"I'm not sure about sending Ajay to daycare just yet. I kinda thought you wanted to be home with him awhile longer. He's only eight months old, Elyse."

"Ace, I know how old he is. I brought him into the world, remember?"

"Of course I know that, but I thought you wanted to be a stay-at-home mother."

"Ace! How could you think that? You know how much the store means to me! I've put my total inheritance in it, and I love it. I really do. I thought you understood."

"I figured that motherhood was what you wanted. You went to many lengths to have Missy, as I remember."

Stunned by the sarcasm in her husband's statement, Elyse's jaw dropped. She had not expected this reaction and realized that they were having their first major disagreement.

Suddenly it became clear to her.

"Ace, you said you loved Missy, but here you are, making a difference."

"I'm *not* making a difference. The difference is evident!" he blurted out. "Ajay is my biological child and Missy is not! It's only natural for me to feel different about each of them. One has my genes and the other . . . well . . ."

"Well what? I'm supposed to give my child away? I had the same pains to deliver your son as I had with my daughter!"

"Elyse, you know how much I adore Missy, I was there when she was born, but . . ."

"You're jealous of Barry. Admit it, Ace!"

"Guess I am. I see his face in his child and I know he must have been a vital part of your life for you to have his child the way you did. Honestly, Elyse, I'm envious of every moment that you shared your life with someone else."

"You needn't be, Ace. That chapter of my life is closed. And now it is up to us to make *our* lives and *our* family's life what we want it to be."

"I know that."

"I do love you, Ace, with all my heart. But my loving you means that you accept all of me. And that means my daughter and my ambition to manage a business. I have an MBA from Harvard that gives me the credibility . . ."

Ace interrupted her, his beryl-green eyes flashing with indignation. "So, you have *more* education than I have, just a degree from art school . . ."

Elyse shook her head.

"Ace, I would never, ever belittle you. You have more artistic ability than most people. You are a truly gifted artist, and I respect that. I'm only trying to tell you that I cannot be a whole person unless I can follow the path that feeds my soul. Could you live without art? Think about it."

She stood up, the half-empty wine glass still on the coffee table.

"I'm going to bed. See you in the morning. Good night."

Ace watched his wife walk out of the living room. He sighed deeply, realizing they had just had their first disagreement. He wondered if he had been wrong resisting her wish to return to work. They had never discussed her return to the Kwanzaa Store. He had assumed total motherhood was what she wanted. How could he have been so mistaken? She seemed so happy in her role as a mother, even including Holly and Branch.

He drained the last of his wine and rose from his chair. He picked up Elyse's half-empty glass and went into the kitchen to wash them, turned them over on the drain to dry. He stood for a few more moments thinking about this impasse. One thing he knew for certain, he wanted Elyse to be happy.

He walked down the hall, went into the living room to turn off the lamps and then checked the doors. As he mounted the stairs to their bedroom, he murmured a prayer. *Please, God, help me make the right decision.*

Before going to bed, Elyse checked on her sleeping children. *Was she wrong in wanting to return to the store, even part time?* she thought as she tucked them in. Missy was a squirmer and, as usual, her bedclothes were askew. She replaced them and wondered about Ace. He had always been a loving father to Missy, the child whose birth he had witnessed. Was his dominant interest in his son's welfare something she should have expected?

She washed her face, brushed her teeth, put on her nightgown and slid into bed.

She could hear Ace going about his nightly checks as he secured their home. She drew a deep breath, exhaled slowly. *Now what?* she thought. She turned over on her right side, closed her eyes as if already asleep.

Ace quietly slid into bed. He put his arm across Elyse's body. She did not move or acknowledge his presence.

"Elyse," he whispered into her ear, "I will not let this problem come between us. I love you and always will. Trust me, I believe in us and I know you do, too."

Although Elyse heard his words, this stumbling block reminded her of her mother and *her* strong, opinionated manner. But now *she* was the mother, and she vowed silently to herself that night to be a mother that not only loved her family but wanted the best for them. But she knew she could never attain that goal unless her own cup of life was fulfilled. She had to be a whole, satisfied human being before she could be anyone's wife or mother. That meant, for her, to increase her activity in The Kwanzaa Book and Gift Shop.

Sighing deeply, she turned to face her husband. In the darkened bedroom she whispered, "Do you love me, Ace?"

"Honey, you know I do, with all my heart."

"Then remember this. If I can't be a truly whole person, I can't be a good wife and mother. Think about that. And, Ace, I love you, too." She kissed him and turned her back to him.

Ace lay wide awake, thinking. He had to remember that his wife was a person with goals and ambitions of her own. He had always admired her strong will and her tenacity in reaching her goals. How many women would have gone through what she had endured to have her dead husband's child?

He remembered, too, the night Missy was born, and Ajay. What courage, what stamina she went through to become a mother, and . . . make him a father. It came to him then. If he expected Elyse to be a total mother, why shouldn't he be a total father?

Before he finally went to sleep that night, he knew what he had to do.

The next morning found them both busy with their morning activities, getting breakfast for themselves, feeding the children, getting Missy ready for daycare.

When Ace kissed Elyse goodbye that morning, he said, "I'll be home for lunch and we'll talk."

True to his word, around noon Ace bounded into the kitchen where Elyse was feeding their son.

"I'm here, Elyse. I brought lobster rolls for our lunch!"

He kissed her, than Ajay. "How are *you*, my man?"

He was rewarded by a crooked grin, a small chin covered with strained applesauce.

"Just let me put him down for his nap, and maybe you'll pour some ginger ale to go with our lobster rolls."

"Will do, no problema," he said.

When she returned, Ace had set up a card table in the family room and Elyse joined him there. "Ajay is already napping," she said.

He had placed attractive placemats on the table, with matching napkins. He placed the lobster rolls, sprigs of parsley and sliced tomatoes on attractive salad plates. Ginger ale sparkled in the tall, slender glasses. A small vase of white daisies rested in the center of the table.

When Elyse came in, Ace was sitting at the table, waiting for her. He sprang up from his chair to seat her. As he did so, he planted a light kiss on the top of her head.

"El," he said quietly, his hands resting on her shoulders. She could hear the deep emotion in his thickened voice. He cleared his throat and started to speak again. She did not miss the gravity in his voice.

He caressed her shoulders, then took his seat, reached for her hands.

"Oh, El, honey, I owe you an apology. I can only say that at times I am the dumbest man on earth! Never, as long as I live, will I ever forget the day you walked into my arms and into my life, a sad, bewildered young woman whose pain asked me to hold her. I love you, girl, always will, and I'm proud to have you as my wife and the mother of our children. And I do want to be a loving father to them. Can you forgive me for my stupid thinking?"

With tears in her eyes, she nodded, swayed by his tense emotion.

Ace continued, "My darling Elyse, I never want to lose you, couldn't live without you. What made me think that because my mother was a stay-at-home mom you would be too? My God, I'm almost thirty-seven years old and why shouldn't a talented, educated woman like you enjoy a career if she wants to?"

"Do you mean that, Ace?"

"I do, and I'm doing some planning. You say two days a week at the store?"

"Right, two days to see how it goes."

"Here's what I'm thinking, hon."

Their lobster rolls were forgotten as Ace explained.

"You know the back room in my shop where I slept? Well, now it's an office-like area. Something like what you have at your store. That's what gave me the idea. So this morning I rented a crib, playpen and swing. Also," he grinned as he saw Elyse's face light up, "also, I've bought a microwave, small hot plate and a small refrigerator that fits under my desk."

"Ace, you . . . you mean?"

"I mean that Ajay can spend two days of the week with me! Why should his mother be the only parent to see him get his first tooth, take his first steps? Aren't dads supposed to see new things, too?"

He started to pick up his lobster, but before he could do so, Elyse bounced out of her seat and began to kiss him frantically.

"Oh, Ace, how wonderful you are! Are you sure you don't mind taking Ajay to the store?"

"It's my pleasure and privilege to do so. Ajay and I have already bonded, but this is the start of a wonderful time for me and my son. And while we're talking about *our* children, I will always thank Barry Marshall for you and Missy."

He pulled her into his lap. As they looked at each other, their intense need compelled them to act. Hand in hand they ran up the stairs to their bedroom. The unmade bed was not a deterrent as they tossed their clothes to the floor.

With a moan of deep hunger, Ace held his wife close, mindful of the chasm that had threatened their happiness. The past turmoil was forgotten as they clung to each other, their bodies aflame with the need for comfort and reassurance that only this loving act could give them.

"My darling, forgive me."

Elyse shushed him. "Just love me, Ace, please."

"My pleasure."

He nuzzled her ear, began to trace his tongue along the soft recesses of her outer ear. His gentle kisses soon became demanding and his lips created tantalizing sensations from her ears to her cheeks and neck, finally reaching her breasts. He marveled at the voluptuous changes in his wife's body since the birth of two children. Elyse had nursed two babies, but today Ace reveled in the knowledge that these glorious orbs were his . . . his alone to enjoy.

As his lips reached the erect nub of her breast, he closed them firmly around it, while with the other hand he caressed its mate.

The mewling sounds from Elyse's throat excited him even more, and she clasped his head to her.

He moved over her and she raised her hips to allow him to join her body with his. She met him, thrust for thrust, their cries of ecstasy mingling as they soared, reaching the pinnacle of wild passion. Neither could speak as they clung together, trembling from the tumultuous experience.

Finally, their breathing returned to a normal rhythm. Elyse was the first to speak.

"Going back to the store?"

He shook his head.

"I'm still the boss and have decided to spend the rest of the afternoon right here with you, my dear wife."

"What a nice idea," she whispered, nuzzling his cheek.

"Glad you like it. But I haven't had enough yet. Come here, sweet lady!"

She did not resist as he began to nibble her ear again. Nor did she protest.

EPILOGUE

It was one of those Norman Rockwell days, a perfect fall day in New England. The sky was a deep cobalt blue, with fluffs of meandering white clouds floating around the edges of the horizon.

There was little or no wind, and the few fall leaves that clung tenaciously to maple and oak trees—the willow trees had long been barren—scarcely moved. The wind seemed somehow to quiet the earth into holding its warmth close to its heart as if to husband it against the approaching winter.

Overhead a flock of Canada geese were vee-shaped into their flight pattern south despite the unexpected warmth of the day. They were not fooled by the alluring, deceptive weather. Winter was coming as it always did, so they did not wait, but flew south as usual.

Ace had enjoyed his daily two-mile run. It had been a perfect day for his workout.

"When a man has a family," he told his wife, "he has a responsibility to take care of himself, so he can take care of them."

Toweling himself off as he walked in the back door into the kitchen, he found his wife standing in front of the sink, drying her hands with a paper towel.

"Good run?" she asked.

"Perfect," he panted, "just perfect. It's a great day out there."

She reached into the refrigerator, handed him a chilled bottle of spring water.

"Thanks." He raised the bottle in a salute to her.

"I really need this. Whew!" he puffed as he opened the bottle and took a deep swallow of the refreshing water.

He cleared his throat with a satisfied exhalation. "A-a-ah, good. How's the cooking doing?" he asked, nodding at the stove where several covered pots and skillets were boiling and bubbling with a mixture of fragrant cooking odors seeping beneath their lids.

"Everything's coming along nicely, we're right on time. The turkey has another half hour to go, and then I'll make the gravy," she reassured him. "Don't worry, my dear, you will not be embarrassed at your first big family dinner in our house."

He shot right back with his response.

"Are you kidding me? Girl, I never worry about *your* abilities! I know you can do anything you put your mind to!"

"Oh, Ace," her words came, solemn and slow, "you have to know that it was the support and confidence that you have always given me that has had so much to do with any little success I've had."

She sat down across the table from him, a serious expression on her face.

Ace reached across the table for her hand.

"Honey, it was the strength you had to follow a dream and see it come to fruition. I knew that I had to measure up or I would lose you, the only woman I have ever loved. That day when you walked into my arms, you walked into my heart. And let me tell you, here and now, no man can live without his heart."

Then he stood, moved to her side of the table. He reached to help her stand. Their lips met, almost as if for the first time in their lives, touching, yearning, seeking and confirming. Not a word was spoken. None was needed. The moment between them said it all.

Elyse smiled to herself as she heard her husband go upstairs to shower, shave and get dressed to meet their dinner guests. The only missing person was Emerald, who was on her way to Cameroon to visit Omar. They were to be married in the spring. Omar had all the necessary documents and Emerald was very happy with the coming change in her life.

She opened the oven door to check on the roasting twenty-pound turkey. There would be ten at the table today, including her parents, her beloved Aunt Ginny, Holly, Branch and other aunts and uncles. She had decided that little Missy was old enough, almost four, to sit at the table near Aunt Ginny, who would supervise her. The baby would be in his high chair, close by his mother.

Armed with the turkey baster, she poured the hot juices over the turkey. Then she turned her attention to the dining room. She had set the table the night before. She was pleased with the white china, the delicate wine goblets and sparkling silverware. The final touch was the centerpiece she had ordered from the florist. It was a glorious autumn arrangement of yellow chrysanthemums, deep purple asters with large, waxy green leaves interspersed with orange-red bayberries.

Looking at the beautiful table, Elyse thought of the changes that had come into her life the past few years. Today she felt triumphant. As steel is tried by fire, she thought, she had come through crisis after crisis and was stronger as a result of those experiences.

She was deeply in love with her wonderful husband, her two children were healthy and happy. Her relationship with Barry's daughter, Holly, was based on solid grounds of respect and friendship. Her bookstore was doing very well, so much so that she'd had to hire more staff. Even her strongly opinionated mother had remarked to her, "I'm proud of you, Elyse, for what you have gone through. You're more woman than I could ever be."

But as she went about her dinner preparations, placing chairs around the table, she began to think.

The fortitude and determination I needed to succeed was within me all along. All I needed was to believe in myself and allow my self-esteem and self-confidence to sustain me.

It had been a hard-fought battle to win over her mother. As she took an apple pie and sweet potato pie from the freezer, placed them on the table to thaw, she thought back to that day of confrontation.

After Barry's death, her parents had insisted that she have occasional Sunday dinners with them. She knew it was their attempt to ease her sorrow. It was on one of those Sundays that she'd told them of her plans to have Barry's child.

She remembered she was twirling her coffee cup around in its saucer. Noticing this, her father had asked, "Something on your mind, Leese?"

Her dad was always the perceptive one, and she had responded, "Yes, Dad, there is. I'm going to have a baby!" she blurted out.

Her mother slammed her hand on the table, sputtered, "What on earth are you talkin' 'bout? What do you mean, you're 'having a baby'?"

So, she had explained the whole situation to them. When she added that she was two months into her pregnancy, her fathers had said, "Good for you, Leese, good for you!"

"My God, Jerome," her mother had cried, "are you *crazy*! This is the dumbest thing I have ever heard! You must be out of your mind! Why on earth . . . ? Don't you know how hard it will be to be a single mother?" Without waiting for an answer, her mother threw her napkin down and ran into the kitchen, but not before Elyse had seen the tears cascading down her mother's cheeks.

Her father indicated to his daughter that she should go and talk to her mother.

"If it's what you want, child, go and help her understand. She *is* your mother."

She found her mother standing beside the open dishwasher, preparing to load it.

Elyse sat at the kitchen table, waited for her mother to face her.

"Mother, I'm sorry if I've upset you. I know how hard it must be to raise children and I thank you for giving me life . . . being my mom. It's the greatest gift anyone . . ."

Her voice began to quaver a bit as her mother, open-mouthed, stared at her child, almost as if not believing what she was hearing.

Elyse saw the look, the anger rising in her mother's widened eyes at this unexpected defiance from her daughter.

"But Mother, that is the bottom line! You gave me life, but how I live it is up to me!" She held up her hand to stay the comments that she knew her mother was forcibly holding back. Elyse could see the cold anger on her mother's face.

She got up from the table and went to the sink to face her mother. She wanted her mother's understanding.

"Momma, *you* never had *your* husband snatched away from you." Her voice broke and tears welled up in her eyes. "Never had to see his body lowered into the ground, thank God. You never had to go through *that*, but I *have* and now I have the chance to do something . . . reach for a dream we both had, to have *our* baby. And," her mother heard the determination in Elyse's voice, "that's what I'm doing. I'd like to have your blessing, but if you can't give me that, so be it."

She felt as if her knees were turning to jelly, and knew she had to sit down quickly. She stared at the obviously shocked woman, who remained speechless and continued to fill the dishwasher.

Frances Joyce, stunned by Elyse's news, finally closed the dishwasher, straightened her back and crossed the kitchen to sit at the table across from her daughter.

"I don't like this idea, Elyse. Not at all. But if you're woman enough to take this on, having a baby, no husband, I'm woman enough to say as long as you know what you're up against . . ." Her voice trailed off as the tears continued to well up in her eyes. With a brusque gesture, she attempted to wipe her eyes.

"I do, Mother. Know it won't be easy, but I'm ready for whatever comes . . ."

"Well, all right then. Like you said, 'It's your life.' "

That had been over five years ago. Elyse was finally the serene, fulfilled woman she had always wanted to be.

It was apparent that this was Thanksgiving Day and she was truly grateful. She removed the turkey from the oven, turned off the heat, placed the pies into the warm oven. Then she heard the sounds of cars coming up the drive. She removed her apron and tossed it onto a chair in the kitchen. She went to the front hall, called upstairs to her husband.

"Ace, they're here."

"Coming," was his response as he bounded down the stairs. Elyse thought he looked so handsome dressed in black slacks and a white silk turtleneck shirt.

She smiled at him. "You look great, husband mine."

"Think I'll pass muster?" he teased.

"Absolutely! You're top ace with me," she quipped, "and you always will be. And all I'll ever need is your love."

He kissed her cheek and linked her arm with his, and together they walked to the front door of their home to greet their guests.

THE END

ABOUT THE AUTHOR

Mildred E. Riley is a native of Connecticut. She is a member of Romance Writers of America and is the author of ten romance novels. A retired nurse, she lives in Massachusetts.

2009 Reprint Mass Market Titles

January

I'm Gonna Make You Love Me
Gwyneth Bolton
ISBN-13: 978-1-58571-294-6
$6.99

Shades of Desire
Monica White
ISBN-13: 978-1-58571-292-2
$6.99

February

A Love of Her Own
Cheris Hodges
ISBN-13: 978-1-58571-293-9
$6.99

Color of Trouble
Dyanne Davis
ISBN-13: 978-1-58571-294-6
$6.99

March

Twist of Fate
Beverly Clark
ISBN-13: 978-1-58571-295-3
$6.99

Chances
Pamela Leigh Starr
ISBN-13: 978-1-58571-296-0
$6.99

April

Sinful Intentions
Crystal Rhodes
ISBN-13: 978-1-585712-297-7
$6.99

Rock Star
Roslyn Hardy Holcomb
ISBN-13: 978-1-58571-298-4
$6.99

May

Paths of Fire
T.T. Henderson
ISBN-13: 978-1-58571-343-1
$6.99

Caught Up in the Rapture
Lisa Riley
ISBN-13: 978-1-58571-344-8
$6.99

June

Reckless Surrender
Rochelle Alers
ISBN-13: 978-1-58571-345-5
$6.99

No Ordinary Love
Angela Weaver
ISBN-13: 978-1-58571-346-2
$6.99

2009 Reprint Mass Market Titles (continued)

July

Intentional Mistakes
Michele Sudler
ISBN-13: 978-1-58571-347-9
$6.99

It's In His Kiss
Reon Carter
ISBN-13: 978-1-58571-348-6
$6.99

August

Unfinished Love Affair
Barbara Keaton
ISBN-13: 978-1-58571-349-3
$6.99

A Perfect Place to Pray
I.L Goodwin
ISBN-13: 978-1-58571-299-1
$6.99

September

Love in High Gear
Charlotte Roy
ISBN-13: 978-1-58571-355-4
$6.99

Ebony Eyes
Kei Swanson
ISBN-13: 978-1-58571-356-1
$6.99

October

Midnight Clear, Part I
Leslie Esdale/Carmen Green
ISBN-13: 978-1-58571-357-8
$6.99

Midnight Clear, Part II
Gwynne Forster/Monica
    Jackson
ISBN-13: 978-1-58571-358-5
$6.99

November

Midnight Peril
Vicki Andrews
ISBN-13: 978-1-58571-359-2
$6.99

One Day At A Time
Bella McFarland
ISBN-13: 978-1-58571-360-8
$6.99

December

Just An Affair
Eugenia O'Neal
ISBN-13: 978-1-58571-361-5
$6.99

Shades of Brown
Denise Becker
ISBN-13: 978-1-58571-362-2
$6.99

2009 New Mass Market Titles

January

Singing A Song…
Crystal Rhodes
ISBN-13: 978-1-58571-283-0
$6.99

Look Both Ways
Joan Early
ISBN-13: 978-1-58571-284-7
$6.99

February

Six O'Clock
Katrina Spencer
ISBN-13: 978-1-58571-285-4
$6.99

Red Sky
Renee Alexis
ISBN-13: 978-1-58571-286-1
$6.99

March

Anything But Love
Celya Bowers
ISBN-13: 978-1-58571-287-8
$6.99

Tempting Faith
Crystal Hubbard
ISBN-13: 978-1-58571-288-5
$6.99

April

If I Were Your Woman
La Connie Taylor-Jones
ISBN-13: 978-1-58571-289-2
$6.99

Best Of Luck Elsewhere
Trisha Haddad
ISBN-13: 978-1-58571-290-8
$6.99

May

All I'll Ever Need
Mildred Riley
ISBN-13: 978-1-58571-335-6
$6.99

A Place Like Home
Alicia Wiggins
ISBN-13: 978-1-58571-336-3
$6.99

June

Best Foot Forward
Michele Sudler
ISBN-13: 978-1-58571-337-0
$6.99

It's In the Rhythm
Sammie Ward
ISBN-13: 978-1-58571-338-7
$6.99

2009 New Mass Market Titles (continued)

July

Checks and Balances
Elaine Sims
ISBN-13: 978-1-58571-339-4
$6.99

Save Me
Africa Fine
ISBN-13: 978-1-58571-340-0
$6.99

August

When Lightening Strikes
Michele Cameron
ISBN-13: 978-1-58571-369-1
$6.99

Blindsided
Tammy Williams
ISBN-13: 978-1-58571-342-4
$6.99

September

2 Good
Celya Bowers
ISBN-13: 978-1-58571-350-9
$6.99

Waiting for Mr. Darcy
Chamein Canton
ISBN-13: 978-1-58571-351-6
$6.99

October

Fireflies
Joan Early
ISBN-13: 978-1-58571-352-3
$6.99

Frost On My Window
Angela Weaver
ISBN-13: 978-1-58571-353-0
$6.99

November

Waiting in the Shadows
Michele Sudler
ISBN-13: 978-1-58571-364-6
$6.99

Fixin' Tyrone
Keith Walker
ISBN-13: 978-1-58571-365-3
$6.99

December

Dream Keeper
Gail McFarland
ISBN-13: 978-1-58571-366-0
$6.99

Another Memory
Pamela Ridley
ISBN-13: 978-1-58571-367-7
$6.99

Other Genesis Press, Inc. Titles

A Dangerous Deception	J.M. Jeffries	$8.95
A Dangerous Love	J.M. Jeffries	$8.95
A Dangerous Obsession	J.M. Jeffries	$8.95
A Drummer's Beat to Mend	Kei Swanson	$9.95
A Happy Life	Charlotte Harris	$9.95
A Heart's Awakening	Veronica Parker	$9.95
A Lark on the Wing	Phyliss Hamilton	$9.95
A Love of Her Own	Cheris F. Hodges	$9.95
A Love to Cherish	Beverly Clark	$8.95
A Risk of Rain	Dar Tomlinson	$8.95
A Taste of Temptation	Reneé Alexis	$9.95
A Twist of Fate	Beverly Clark	$8.95
A Voice Behind Thunder	Carrie Elizabeth Greene	$6.99
A Will to Love	Angie Daniels	$9.95
Acquisitions	Kimberley White	$8.95
Across	Carol Payne	$12.95
After the Vows	Leslie Esdaile	$10.95
(Summer Anthology)	T.T. Henderson	
	Jacqueline Thomas	
Again My Love	Kayla Perrin	$10.95
Against the Wind	Gwynne Forster	$8.95
All I Ask	Barbara Keaton	$8.95
Always You	Crystal Hubbard	$6.99
Ambrosia	T.T. Henderson	$8.95
An Unfinished Love Affair	Barbara Keaton	$8.95
And Then Came You	Dorothy Elizabeth Love	$8.95
Angel's Paradise	Janice Angelique	$9.95
At Last	Lisa G. Riley	$8.95
Best of Friends	Natalie Dunbar	$8.95
Beyond the Rapture	Beverly Clark	$9.95
Blame It On Paradise	Crystal Hubbard	$6.99
Blaze	Barbara Keaton	$9.95
Bliss, Inc.	Chamein Canton	$6.99
Blood Lust	J. M. Jeffries	$9.95
Blood Seduction	J.M. Jeffries	$9.95

Other Genesis Press, Inc. Titles (continued)

Bodyguard	Andrea Jackson	$9.95
Boss of Me	Diana Nyad	$8.95
Bound by Love	Beverly Clark	$8.95
Breeze	Robin Hampton Allen	$10.95
Broken	Dar Tomlinson	$24.95
By Design	Barbara Keaton	$8.95
Cajun Heat	Charlene Berry	$8.95
Careless Whispers	Rochelle Alers	$8.95
Cats & Other Tales	Marilyn Wagner	$8.95
Caught in a Trap	Andre Michelle	$8.95
Caught Up In the Rapture	Lisa G. Riley	$9.95
Cautious Heart	Cheris F Hodges	$8.95
Chances	Pamela Leigh Starr	$8.95
Cherish the Flame	Beverly Clark	$8.95
Choices	Tammy Williams	$6.99
Class Reunion	Irma Jenkins/ John Brown	$12.95
Code Name: Diva	J.M. Jeffries	$9.95
Conquering Dr. Wexler's Heart	Kimberley White	$9.95
Corporate Seduction	A.C. Arthur	$9.95
Crossing Paths, Tempting Memories	Dorothy Elizabeth Love	$9.95
Crush	Crystal Hubbard	$9.95
Cypress Whisperings	Phyllis Hamilton	$8.95
Dark Embrace	Crystal Wilson Harris	$8.95
Dark Storm Rising	Chinelu Moore	$10.95
Daughter of the Wind	Joan Xian	$8.95
Dawn's Harbor	Kymberly Hunt	$6.99
Deadly Sacrifice	Jack Kean	$22.95
Designer Passion	Dar Tomlinson Diana Richeaux	$8.95
Do Over	Celya Bowers	$9.95
Dream Runner	Gail McFarland	$6.99
Dreamtective	Liz Swados	$5.95

Other Genesis Press, Inc. Titles (continued)

Ebony Angel	Deatri King-Bey	$9.95
Ebony Butterfly II	Delilah Dawson	$14.95
Echoes of Yesterday	Beverly Clark	$9.95
Eden's Garden	Elizabeth Rose	$8.95
Eve's Prescription	Edwina Martin Arnold	$8.95
Everlastin' Love	Gay G. Gunn	$8.95
Everlasting Moments	Dorothy Elizabeth Love	$8.95
Everything and More	Sinclair Lebeau	$8.95
Everything but Love	Natalie Dunbar	$8.95
Falling	Natalie Dunbar	$9.95
Fate	Pamela Leigh Starr	$8.95
Finding Isabella	A.J. Garrotto	$8.95
Forbidden Quest	Dar Tomlinson	$10.95
Forever Love	Wanda Y. Thomas	$8.95
From the Ashes	Kathleen Suzanne	$8.95
	Jeanne Sumerix	
Gentle Yearning	Rochelle Alers	$10.95
Glory of Love	Sinclair LeBeau	$10.95
Go Gentle into that Good Night	Malcom Boyd	$12.95
Goldengroove	Mary Beth Craft	$16.95
Groove, Bang, and Jive	Steve Cannon	$8.99
Hand in Glove	Andrea Jackson	$9.95
Hard to Love	Kimberley White	$9.95
Hart & Soul	Angie Daniels	$8.95
Heart of the Phoenix	A.C. Arthur	$9.95
Heartbeat	Stephanie Bedwell-Grime	$8.95
Hearts Remember	M. Loui Quezada	$8.95
Hidden Memories	Robin Allen	$10.95
Higher Ground	Leah Latimer	$19.95
Hitler, the War, and the Pope	Ronald Rychiak	$26.95
How to Write a Romance	Kathryn Falk	$18.95
I Married a Reclining Chair	Lisa M. Fuhs	$8.95
I'll Be Your Shelter	Giselle Carmichael	$8.95
I'll Paint a Sun	A.J. Garrotto	$9.95

Other Genesis Press, Inc. Titles (continued)

Icie	Pamela Leigh Starr	$8.95
Illusions	Pamela Leigh Starr	$8.95
Indigo After Dark Vol. I	Nia Dixon/Angelique	$10.95
Indigo After Dark Vol. II	Dolores Bundy/ Cole Riley	$10.95
Indigo After Dark Vol. III	Montana Blue/ Coco Morena	$10.95
Indigo After Dark Vol. IV	Cassandra Colt/	$14.95
Indigo After Dark Vol. V	Delilah Dawson	$14.95
Indiscretions	Donna Hill	$8.95
Intentional Mistakes	Michele Sudler	$9.95
Interlude	Donna Hill	$8.95
Intimate Intentions	Angie Daniels	$8.95
It's Not Over Yet	J.J. Michael	$9.95
Jolie's Surrender	Edwina Martin-Arnold	$8.95
Kiss or Keep	Debra Phillips	$8.95
Lace	Giselle Carmichael	$9.95
Lady Preacher	K.T. Richey	$6.99
Last Train to Memphis	Elsa Cook	$12.95
Lasting Valor	Ken Olsen	$24.95
Let Us Prey	Hunter Lundy	$25.95
Lies Too Long	Pamela Ridley	$13.95
Life Is Never As It Seems	J.J. Michael	$12.95
Lighter Shade of Brown	Vicki Andrews	$8.95
Looking for Lily	Africa Fine	$6.99
Love Always	Mildred E. Riley	$10.95
Love Doesn't Come Easy	Charlyne Dickerson	$8.95
Love Unveiled	Gloria Greene	$10.95
Love's Deception	Charlene Berry	$10.95
Love's Destiny	M. Loui Quezada	$8.95
Love's Secrets	Yolanda McVey	$6.99
Mae's Promise	Melody Walcott	$8.95
Magnolia Sunset	Giselle Carmichael	$8.95
Many Shades of Gray	Dyanne Davis	$6.99
Matters of Life and Death	Lesego Malepe, Ph.D.	$15.95

Other Genesis Press, Inc. Titles (continued)

Meant to Be	Jeanne Sumerix	$8.95
Midnight Clear (Anthology)	Leslie Esdaile	$10.95
	Gwynne Forster	
	Carmen Green	
	Monica Jackson	
Midnight Magic	Gwynne Forster	$8.95
Midnight Peril	Vicki Andrews	$10.95
Misconceptions	Pamela Leigh Starr	$9.95
Moments of Clarity	Michele Cameron	$6.99
Montgomery's Children	Richard Perry	$14.95
Mr Fix-It	Crystal Hubbard	$6.99
My Buffalo Soldier	Barbara B. K. Reeves	$8.95
Naked Soul	Gwynne Forster	$8.95
Never Say Never	Michele Cameron	$6.99
Next to Last Chance	Louisa Dixon	$24.95
No Apologies	Seressia Glass	$8.95
No Commitment Required	Seressia Glass	$8.95
No Regrets	Mildred E. Riley	$8.95
Not His Type	Chamein Canton	$6.99
Nowhere to Run	Gay G. Gunn	$10.95
O Bed! O Breakfast!	Rob Kuehnle	$14.95
Object of His Desire	A. C. Arthur	$8.95
Office Policy	A. C. Arthur	$9.95
Once in a Blue Moon	Dorianne Cole	$9.95
One Day at a Time	Bella McFarland	$8.95
One in A Million	Barbara Keaton	$6.99
One of These Days	Michele Sudler	$9.95
Outside Chance	Louisa Dixon	$24.95
Passion	T.T. Henderson	$10.95
Passion's Blood	Cherif Fortin	$22.95
Passion's Furies	AlTonya Washington	$6.99
Passion's Journey	Wanda Y. Thomas	$8.95
Past Promises	Jahmel West	$8.95
Path of Fire	T.T. Henderson	$8.95
Path of Thorns	Annetta P. Lee	$9.95

Other Genesis Press, Inc. Titles (continued)

Peace Be Still	Colette Haywood	$12.95
Picture Perfect	Reon Carter	$8.95
Playing for Keeps	Stephanie Salinas	$8.95
Pride & Joi	Gay G. Gunn	$8.95
Promises Made	Bernice Layton	$6.99
Promises to Keep	Alicia Wiggins	$8.95
Quiet Storm	Donna Hill	$10.95
Reckless Surrender	Rochelle Alers	$6.95
Red Polka Dot in a World of Plaid	Varian Johnson	$12.95
Reluctant Captive	Joyce Jackson	$8.95
Rendezvous with Fate	Jeanne Sumerix	$8.95
Revelations	Cheris F. Hodges	$8.95
Rivers of the Soul	Leslie Esdaile	$8.95
Rocky Mountain Romance	Kathleen Suzanne	$8.95
Rooms of the Heart	Donna Hill	$8.95
Rough on Rats and Tough on Cats	Chris Parker	$12.95
Secret Library Vol. 1	Nina Sheridan	$18.95
Secret Library Vol. 2	Cassandra Colt	$8.95
Secret Thunder	Annetta P. Lee	$9.95
Shades of Brown	Denise Becker	$8.95
Shades of Desire	Monica White	$8.95
Shadows in the Moonlight	Jeanne Sumerix	$8.95
Sin	Crystal Rhodes	$8.95
Small Whispers	Annetta P. Lee	$6.99
So Amazing	Sinclair LeBeau	$8.95
Somebody's Someone	Sinclair LeBeau	$8.95
Someone to Love	Alicia Wiggins	$8.95
Song in the Park	Martin Brant	$15.95
Soul Eyes	Wayne L. Wilson	$12.95
Soul to Soul	Donna Hill	$8.95
Southern Comfort	J.M. Jeffries	$8.95
Southern Fried Standards	S.R. Maddox	$6.99
Still the Storm	Sharon Robinson	$8.95

Other Genesis Press, Inc. Titles (continued)

Other Genesis Press, Inc. Titles (continued)

Tiger Woods	Libby Hughes	$5.95
Time is of the Essence	Angie Daniels	$9.95
Timeless Devotion	Bella McFarland	$9.95
Tomorrow's Promise	Leslie Esdaile	$8.95
Truly Inseparable	Wanda Y. Thomas	$8.95
Two Sides to Every Story	Dyanne Davis	$9.95
Unbreak My Heart	Dar Tomlinson	$8.95
Uncommon Prayer	Kenneth Swanson	$9.95
Unconditional Love	Alicia Wiggins	$8.95
Unconditional	A.C. Arthur	$9.95
Undying Love	Renee Alexis	$6.99
Until Death Do Us Part	Susan Paul	$8.95
Vows of Passion	Bella McFarland	$9.95
Wedding Gown	Dyanne Davis	$8.95
What's Under Benjamin's Bed	Sandra Schaffer	$8.95
When A Man Loves A Woman	La Connie Taylor-Jones	$6.99
When Dreams Float	Dorothy Elizabeth Love	$8.95
When I'm With You	LaConnie Taylor-Jones	$6.99
Where I Want To Be	Maryam Diaab	$6.99
Whispers in the Night	Dorothy Elizabeth Love	$8.95
Whispers in the Sand	LaFlorya Gauthier	$10.95
Who's That Lady?	Andrea Jackson	$9.95
Wild Ravens	Altonya Washington	$9.95
Yesterday Is Gone	Beverly Clark	$10.95
Yesterday's Dreams, Tomorrow's Promises	Reon Laudat	$8.95
Your Precious Love	Sinclair LeBeau	$8.95

ESCAPE WITH INDIGO !!!!

Join Indigo Book Club©
It's simple, easy and secure.

Sign up and receive the new releases
every month + Free shipping
and
20% off the cover price.

Go online to www.genesis-press.com and click on Bookclub
or
call 1-888-INDIGO-1

Order Form

Mail to: Genesis Press, Inc.
P.O. Box 101
Columbus, MS 39703

Name _____
Address _____
City/State _____ Zip _____
Telephone _____

Ship to (if different from above)
Name _____
Address _____
City/State _____ Zip _____
Telephone _____

Credit Card Information
Credit Card # _____ ☐ Visa ☐ Mastercard
Expiration Date (mm/yy) _____ ☐ AmEx ☐ Discover

Qty.	Author	Title	Price	Total

Use this order form, or call 1-888-INDIGO-1	Total for books	_____
	Shipping and handling: $5 first two books, $1 each additional book	_____
	Total S & H	
	Total amount enclosed	_____

Mississippi residents add 7% sales tax

WIN A
FREE
GENESIS PRESS BOOK

Please fill out this form with your email
address and send it to us at:

**Genesis Press,
Post Office Box 101,
Columbus, MS 39703**

or email it to
customerservice@genesis-press.com

and we will put your name into a
drawing for a free Genesis Press Book.

WRITE EMAIL ADDRESS HERE

Winners will be chosen on the first of
each month. ONE ENTRY PER CUSTOMER

Dull, Drab, Love Life?

Passion Going Nowhere?

Tired Of Being Alone?

Does Every Direction You Look For Love

Lead You Astray?

Genesis Press presents
The launching of our new website!

RecaptureTheRomance.Com

Ignite
The Flame!